Contains Original Stories by

Ann R. Brown
Mildred Downey Broxon
Esther M. Friesner
Craig Shaw Gardner
Sharon Green
Caralyn Inks
Ardath Mayhar
Shirley Meier
Sandra Miesel
Kathleen O'Malley
Claudia Peck
Carol Severance
Rose Wolf
Timothy Zahn

D1208171

Look for all these Tor books by André Norton

THE CRYSTAL GRYPHON
FORERUNNER
FORERUNNER: THE SECOND VENTURE
GRYPHON'S EYRIE (with A.C. Crispin)
HERE ABIDE MONSTERS
HOUSE OF SHADOWS (with Phyllis Miller)
MAGIC IN ITHKAR (trade edition edited with Robert Adams)
MAGIC IN ITHKAR 2 (trade edition edited with Robert Adams)
MAGIC IN ITHKAR 3 (trade edition edited with Robert Adams)
MAGIC IN ITHKAR 4 (edited with Robert Adams)
MOON CALLED
WHEEL OF STARS

Magic In Ithkar 4

Edited By
André Norton
And
Robert Adams

A TOM DOHERTY ASSOCIATES BOOK

MAGIC IN ITHKAR 4

Copyright © 1987 by Robert Adams and André Norton

First printing: July 1987

A TOR Book

Published by Tom Doherty Associates, Inc.
49 West 24 Street
New York, N.Y. 10010

Cover art by Steve Hickman

ISBN: 0-812-54719-5
CAN. ED.: 0-812-54720-9

Printed in the United States of America

0 9 8 7 6 5 4 3 2 1

CONTENTS

PROLOGUE

Robert Adams

The Three Lordly Ones are said to have descended in their sun-bright Egg and come to rest on a spot near to the bank of the river Ith. The priests of their temple reckon this event to have occurred four hundred, two score, and eight years ago (and who should better know?). Though the Three never made any claim to godhead, they now are adored as such, and for at least four centuries, many pilgrims have come on the anniversary of the day of their coming to render their worship and to importune the Three to return.

The Three are said to have remained on the spot of their descent for almost a generation—twenty-one years and seven months—though they journeyed often in smaller Eggs that, it is told, could move far faster than even a shooting star and so bore them in only a bare day across snowy and impassable mountains, across stormy and monster-infested seas, to lands that most folk know only in fable.

Since not even the learned priests can fine down the exact date of their coming closer than a ten-day, pilgrims came and still come all during this period, and centuries ago, the Ithkar Temple and its denizens lived out the rest of each year on the donations of the pilgrims, the produce of the temple's ploughlands, orchards, and herds, plus whatever edible fish they could catch in the Ith.

But wheresoever numbers of folk do gather for almost any purpose, other folk will come to sell them necessaries and luxuries. Pilgrimage Ten-day at Ithkar Temple was no different. Each year succeeding, more and more peddlers and hawkers gathered around the temple, the more astute arriving before the start of Holy Ten-day, so as to be well set up for business upon the influx of even the first-day pilgrims. Of course, other sellers, noting that these merchants always appropriated the best locations, began to plan their arrivals even earlier to claim these spots for their own. Within a few more years, most of the merchants were in place a full ten-day before the beginning of Holy Ten-day and many of the pilgrims then began to come earlier, in search of the bargains and rare merchandise often to be found at Ithkar Fair, as it was coming to be called far and wide.

Now, in modern times, the Fair at Ithkar has lengthened to three full ten-days in duration and still is extending in time even as it increases in size.

Nearly seventeen score years ago, the then high priest of Ithkar Temple, one Yuub, realized that the priests and priestesses of the shrine were mostly missing out on a marvelous source of easy, laborless income. He it was who first sacrificed the nearer gardens—betwixt the temple enclave and the river-lake—and made of them three (later, four) campgrounds for the merchants and tradesmen, so that they no longer surround the temple on all sides as in the past. He it was, also, who first hired on temporary fairwards—local bullies and old soldiers—to maintain order with their bronze-shod staves, enforce the will of the priests, and collect the monies due for the marked-off shop-spaces during the fair.

As the Temple at Ithkar waxed richer, successors to old Yuub continued to improve the temple and its environs. A guest house was built onto the northwestern corner of the temple's main building in order to house the wealthier and nobler pilgrims in a greater degree of comfort (for which, of course, they were charged a more substantial figure than those who bode in tents, pavilions, or wagons or who simply rolled in a blanket on a bit of ground under the stars). A guest stable followed shortly, then a partially roofed pen for draft oxen. The next project was a canal to bypass the terrible rapids that lay between the East River's confluence with the river Ith and the Harbor of Ithkar.

Two centuries ago, a high priest arranged to have huge logs of a very hard, dense, long-lasting wood rafted down from the northern mountains, then paid the hire of workmen to sink them as footings for the three long docks below the lower fair precincts, these to replace the old floating-docks which had for long received water-borne pilgrims, fairgoers, traders, merchants, and the like. Now these docking facilities are utilized year-round by users of the main trade road that winds from the steppes up the northern slopes of the mountains, through demon-haunted Galzar Pass, then down the south slopes and the foothills and the plain to the Valley of the Ith. Southbound users of the main trade road had, before the building of the docks and the digging of the canal, been obliged to either ford the East River well to the northeast, prior to its being joined by tributaries and thus widened, then to follow a road that led down to a ford not far above the Ith, or to raft down the East River, then portage around the rapids and falls.

With the great success of the temple or eastern canal there clear for all to see, the great noble whose lands lay just to the west of the lands of the temple in the Ith Valley had dug a longer, somewhat wider canal connecting Bear River to the harbor and its fine docks, charging fees for the use of his canal and, through arrangement, sharing in the commerce-taxes that the temple derived from year-round use of its docks by the transmontane traders, hunters, trappers, and steppe nomads who tended to use the Bear River route rather than the main trade road.

Before Bear River was rendered navigable by an earthquake that eliminated the worst of its rapids, the folk who used it had come down into Ith Valley via the longer, harder western road rather than the eastern through well-founded fear of wide-ranging denizens of the Death Swamp.

Many long centuries before the blessed arrival of the Three, it is related, a huge and prosperous city lay on the banks of the Ith somewhere within what now is deadly swamp but then were pleasant, fertile lands and pastures, vineyards, and orchards. But the people of this city were not content with the richness of the life they enjoyed, so they and other cities made war upon another coalition of lands and cities, using not only swords and spears and iron maces and bows, but terrible weapons that bore death from afar—death not only for warriors, but for entire cities and lands and all of their people and beasts. It was one such weapon as these that destroyed the city, rendered all living things within it dead in one terrible day and night, left all of the wrecked homes and empty buildings not destroyed outright clustered about a new lake created by the weapon, a long and wide and shallow lake with a bottom composed of green glass.

In those long-ago days it was that lands surrounding the destroyed and lifeless city earned the name of Death Swamp, for many of the most fertile of the former city's lands had lain well below the usual level of the river Ith and had been protected from riverine encroachments by miles of earthen levees, but with no care or maintenance of those levees, spring floods first weakened them, then breached them and inundated field and farm, pasture and vineyard and orchard. Within a very short time, reeds waved high over expanses that once had produced grain-crops, while monstrous, sinuous shapes wriggled through the muck that had so lately been verdant pasturelands filled with sleek kine.

Monstrous beasts, kin of the mountain dragons, dwelt in many swamplands and in as many near swamp wastes—this was a fact known to all—but the denizens of Death Swamp were not as these more normal beasts, it was said, being deformed in sundry ways, larger ofttimes, and more deadly. It also was said that the Death Swamp monsters were of preternatural sentience.

Descriptions of the Death Swamp monsters were almost all ancient ones, for precious few ever deliberately penetrated the dim, overgrown, terrible place that even the Three had warned should be avoided, adding that there were other places akin to it in lurking deadliness hither and yon in the world, sites rendered by the forgotten weapons of that long-ago war inimical to all forms of natural life.

Of the few who do brave the Death Swamp, fewer still come out at all, and many of those are mad or have changed drastically in manners of thinking, acting, and speech, and seldom for the better. The sole reason that any still venture within the lands and waters surrounding that blasted city is the extraordinarily high prices that wizards will pay for artifacts of that ancient place, many of which have proven to be of great and abiding power. And magic is as much a part of this world as the air and the water, the fire and the very earth itself.

The fair precincts are surrounded by palings of peeled logs sunk into the earth some foot or so apart, and those entering the gates must surrender all weapons other than eating-knives. Be they merchants or traders, they and the wares they would purvey must undergo questioning, weighing, and scrutiny by the fair-wards and the wizard-of-the-gate, lest spells be used to enhance the appearance of shoddy goods. Some magic is allowed, but it must be clearly advertised as such in advance and it must be magic of only the right-hand path.

Those apprehended within fair or temple precincts practicing unauthorized magic, harmful magic, or black magic can be haled before the fair-court. The high priest or those from the temple he appoints then hears the case and decides punishment, which punishment can range from a mere fine or warning up to and including being stripped of all possessions, declared outlaw (and thus fair game for any cheated customer or other enemy), and whipped from out the precincts, naked and unarmed.

The Ithkar Fair is divided into three main sections, each of which is laid out around a nucleus of permanent shops and booths; however, the vast majority of stalls are erected afresh each year, then demolished after the fair. Most distant from the temple précincts lies the section wherein operate dealers in live animals and in animal products—horses and other beasts of burden, hounds and coursing-cats, hawks, cormorants and other trained or trainable birds, domestic beasts, and wild rarities, many of these last captured afar and brought for sale to the wealthier for their private menageries.

In this fourth section, too, are sold such mundane things as bales of wool, hides, rich furs, supplies for the hunter and the trapper. Here, also, are places wherein performing animals can be shown and put through their paces, offered for sale or for hire to entertain private gatherings and parties of the well born or the well to do. Of recent years, quite a number of all-human performing acts have taken to auditioning here for prospective patrons:

The westernmost section of the main three houses craftsmen and dealers in base metals—armor, tools, and smaller hardware of all sorts and descriptions. Once the folk dealing in the sundries of wizardry were to be found here as well, but no more. Farrier/horseleeches are here, as are wheelwrights, saddlers, yoke-makers, and the like.

The middle section of the main three holds dealers in foods, clothing, and footwear. Here are weavers, tailors, embroiderers, bottiers, felters, spinners of thread, dealers in needles and pins, booths that sell feathers and plumes, metalcasters' booths with brooches, torques, and arm- or finger- or ear-rings of red copper or bronze or brass or iron. Cookshops abound here, some of them with tasting-booths from which tidbits can be bought, some of them offering cooks and servers for hire to cater private parties or feasts. Also to be found here are the dealers in beers, ales, wines, meads, and certain more potent decoctions, with the result that there are almost always more fair-wards—proud in their tooled-leathern buffcoats and etched, crested brazen helmets, all bearing their lead-filled, bronze-shod quarter-staves—in evidence about the middlemost section.

The easternmost of the three main sections houses the workers in wood and stone—cabinetmakers, woodcarvers, master carpenters; statuette-carvers to master masons. Dealers in glassware are here to be found, candlemakers, purveyors of medicinal herbs, decoctions, scented oils, incense, and perfumeries, potters of every description and class, and lampmakers as well.

In this section one may purchase an alabaster chess set and, a little distance farther along, an inlaid table to accommodate it. Here to be seen and examined are miniature models of the works of the master masons and carpenters, with whom contracts for future work may be arranged; likewise, custom furniture may be ordered from the cabinetmakers.

Within the outskirts of the temple complex itself is a newer, much smaller subsection, centered around the temple's main gate. Here, where the ever-greedy priests' agents can keep close watch on them and on their customers, are the money-changers, dealers in letters of credit, public scribes, artisans in fine metals and jewelry, image-makers, a few who deal in old manuscripts, pictures, small art treasures, and oddities found or dug out of strange ruins or distant places. Here, also, are those who deal in items enhanced by magic.

There are a few scattered priests, priestesses, mendicants, and cultists from overseas or far distant lands who worship other gods and are allowed to beg in the streets of the fair. They are, however, strictly forbidden to proselytize and are kept always under strictest surveillance by the men and women of the temple. One such alien god is called Thotharn, and about him and his rites of worship some rather odd and sinister stories have been bruited over the years: a committee of the priests of the Three is conducting secret studies of this god and his servants, while considering banning them from the fair.

Since all who legally enter the fair or the temple must surrender their weapons at the gates and swear themselves and their servants or employees to be bound by fair-law and fair-court for the duration of their stay, the well-trained, disciplined, and often quick-tempered fair-wards, armed with their weighted staves, seldom experience trouble in maintaining order.

The bulk of their work takes them to the middle section, with its array of pot-shops, or to the outer fringes of the enclave, where gather the inevitable collection of rogues, sturdy begggars, bravos, petty wizards, potion-makers and witches, would-be entertainers, snake-charmers, whores, and, it is rumored, more than a few assassins-for-hire.

And now, to all who have paid their gate-offering, welcome to the Fair at Ithkar.

THE CLOCKWORK WOMAN

Ann R. Brown

Ugtred's stubby fingers moved delicately, burnishing flakes of gold leaf on the wings of a clockwork finch. From his high stool in the back workroom of the booth, the dwarf could see through the curtain to the stage, where, in his black-and-silver robe, his tall partner Kavdah was entrancing the crowd of yokels and peasants who had come to spend their coppers at Ithkar Fair.

In a liquid voice the man in black continued his pitch. "The wonder of the ages, a miracle of the gods. She does not speak, eat, nag, spend silver, or demand attention. She is all that is graceful, beautiful, and sensuous. My friends, the perfect woman. Anima."

Ugtred sat up straight and laid down his burnisher. He caught a glimpse of a blue gown as the murmurs of the crowd rose.

From his voluminous robe, Kavdah drew a small silver flute. Notes like water trickled forth as the clockwork woman glided rather stiffly across the rough stage and curtsied slowly, her silken skirts spreading like the foam of a wave.

Kavdah reached a black glove from his black sleeve and grasped the fingers of the clockwork woman, raising her arm. She twirled slowly, as in a dream, and Ugtred saw the

9

wondrous pink enamel face come into view and then turn away, appear and turn away, as she pivoted.

Anima accepted a rose from Kavdah's hand, lifted it to her cloisonné lips, and tossed it to the crowd. A prosperous merchant in a cape of weasel fur called out hoarsely:

"How much, goldsmith?"

Kavdah replied smoothly, "Who can find a virtuous woman? Her price is above rubies."

"How much?" cried the merchant. His coarse face shone with enthusiasm.

Anima raised her slender hands to her lips and swept off the stage to the sound of Kavdah's oratory and the whistles and cheers of the Ithkar rustics.

Ugtred turned on his three-legged stool as Anima entered and turned her back to him, lifting with her hands the mane of yellow spun-glass hair. His skillful fingers unlaced the hooks of the blue silken gown and released the long curved grille in the marionette's back.

Ugtred held the metal body steady on its legs as his partner Mere released her arms and hands from the pulleys and wires inside the torso and unhooked her short legs from the stilts.

"Did you like the rose? It's a new idea," asked Mere, crawling down with the aid of Ugtred's hand. She smoothed her homespun skirt and wiped sweat from her forehead with a kerchief.

Ugtred smiled, and his smile was good to see. It showed him to be still a young man, despite the sprinkle of gray in his short rough hair.

"Yes, it's good," observed Ugtred critically, "but the action of the right arm is still uneven. I'll adjust the gears tonight."

The woman fluffed back her mop of butter-colored curls. Her face, like the other dwarf's, was flat and wide, but she had beautiful hair and clear green eyes.

She helped Ugtred lay the empty body of Anima down on a bench.

"How long until Adamo is ready?" wondered Mere. "I can't understand why you don't want to work him yourself. It's lovely being tall and beautiful!"

Affection shone in Ugtred's brown eyes. "You're more beautiful than Anima. She's only a puppet."

Mere pushed her stool next to Ugtred's, and both hopped up on their perches as the curtain was swept aside and their partner entered, pushing back the black hood of his robe to reveal a smooth, dark, languorous face. His eyes moved across the two artisans absently and fixed on the mechanical bird perched on Ugtred's finger.

The actor touched the wing of the bird thoughtfully, saying, "I sold two silver jumping fleas and took an order for a white mouse with red garnet eyes. Are you putting this bird on a stalk of asparagus, as the buyer instructed?"

"Finches make their nests in hawthorns," observed Ugtred, picking up a fragile scrap of gold leaf with tweezers.

"The farmer raises asparagus, and he gets what he pays for," stated Kavdah with a fluid shrug. "Let's have a look at Adamo."

Without waiting for the two artisans, Kavdah pushed aside the curtain of an alcove and gazed down at the bronze figure of a man, strong-chested, with legs like pillars and the shoulders of a wrestler. The head had been riveted to the neck but gaped open like a bowl. Ugtred had not yet attached the face. Gears, wheels, and wires lay on the earthen floor.

Ugtred watched Mere for a moment while he debated what he meant to say. Intently she leaned over the worktable, a quill pen in her short fingers. The design of a monarch butterfly came to life beneath her pen: segmented silver body and tissue wings, dainty as a breath.

Firmly Ugtred declared, "If I'm going to finish the white mouse and the finch, you'll have to find another small man to sit inside Adamo. I'm your partner, not your slave, and it offends me to be what I'm not."

Kavdah's classical face didn't change. He stretched his

long legs languidly and poured himself a cup of wine from a flagon on the table.

"Life is artifice, my clever friend. You make the toys, and I sell them. I've had an offer of nine hundred silver pieces for Anima."

Mere's hand jerked, and a blob of black ink smeared the butterfly. "You can't—she's mine!"

Ugtred said through his teeth, "Since Mere doesn't go with the mannequin, the buyer would only demand his money back. Unless he wants to spend nine hundred silver pieces for a lifeless doll."

Kavdah said amiably, "I don't intend to cheat the yokel and have my hand cut off for fraud. I also don't care what he does with the thing afterward. But I'll split the proceeds with you, three ways, and you can make another Anima when you've finished the mouse and the asparagus. Have Adamo completed by next week, and Mere can sit inside him. Put a sword in his hand. I think a duel between myself and a mechanical opponent will draw crowds."

The actor strolled away toward the stage, jingling coins in his pockets. "By the way, Mere, someone saw you at the baker's booth. Don't go out before dark, or the rustics will guess how the magical clockwork woman is animated."

He wandered out toward the vintner's, humming to himself.

Mere dropped her head into her hands, sobbing wretchedly. "I can't behave like a man. The only happiness I have is in being lovely for a few minutes a day."

Ugtred's square face was grim. "Kavdah has always treated us as fair partners. He's too lazy to cheat us very much. I'm sure he thinks the offer is a decent one. But come with me for a moment, Mere."

The two of them walked back to the long bench whereon lay the faceless bronze automaton. Kneeling, Ugtred reached into a hidden box beneath the bench and drew forth a hammered mask. He placed it across the empty head.

The features were strong, manly, resolute, with a look of intent thought in the frowning brow.

Mere exclaimed in wonder and touched the wide cheek-bones. "Ugtred—Adamo looks like you!"

The dwarf nodded curtly. "Haven't you ever noticed that Anima was made to resemble you?"

Mere's green eyes filled with tears, and her voice faltered. "Do I look like that to you?"

Ugtred turned a wrench over and over between his hands. "I hate this," he said harshly. "I especially hate your feeling more beautiful when you're not yourself. I object to it with all the force of my soul."

Ugtred paused and drew a harsh breath. His hands were trembling. "But I'll finish Adamo, and put a sword in his hand, and run Kavdah through, if you want to keep Anima as much as that."

He swallowed once or twice.

Mere stared at him, her green eyes wide. She twisted the hem of Anima's blue gown between her hands. Her lips quivered with suppressed emotion.

She whispered, "How long would it take for you to finish Adamo?"

Ugtred went white. Already he seemed to feel the hairy touch of the hangman's noose around his neck. But he only said calmly, "Midnight."

Said Mere unsteadily, "I'll be back then. I have to think."

When she pushed open the side flap of the tent and vanished into the twilight, Ugtred caught a glimpse of the other booths, bright with red and yellow canopies. He stood still for a moment, listening to the growls of the wrestling bear on the nearby green and the shrill whoops of the acrobats. He was alone with the two puppets.

He worked steadily by the light of an oil lamp, riveting the forehead to the metal skull and bending down locks of wire hair to conceal the joint.

The bronze face did resemble Ugtred's, in an idealized way. If fate had been kinder, he might have grown to be just such a tall, sturdy fellow. But Ugtred had long ago accepted his destiny. He was what he was: a craftsman, a world traveler, and the true lover of a true woman. Inches could not make him more a man.

Hour after long hour passed before Mere returned. He recognized her quick footsteps long before she reentered the workroom.

She handed him a fried meat pie folded into a semicircle, and another flagon of wine, since Kavdah had polished off the last of their bottle.

She looked down at the completed body, and then at Ugtred, who was calmly eating his pastry and replacing his pliers and files in their slots in the wooden toolbox.

"There's something I have to know," she said at last. "Something I want you to do for me."

Ugtred wiped his hands on his leather apron and waited for her request.

"Will you work him, while I work Anima? I want to walk around the fair with you, and around the town like ordinary people."

Without speaking, Ugtred pulled from beneath the bench a bundle of clothes Mere had sewn. Together they dressed the automaton, pulling on its tight-fitting yellow hose, its woolen hooded tunic and boots. Then Ugtred pulled the bronze man into a seated position, opened the door in its back, and clambered awkwardly into the cavernous body. It was stifling inside, despite the slits in the door. Ugtred fit his legs into the stirrups of the stilts and forced his hands into the tangle of wires and pulleys that moved the arms and head.

Mere was ready long before Ugtred. The movements of the female marionette were smooth and practiced as she took a seat beside Adamo.

She spread out her billowing skirts flirtatiously and tilted the head slightly. Through the spyholes near the collarbones of the mannequin, Mere could see clearly the strong metallic form next to hers.

She tried to imagine herself as Anima in truth, tall and

lovely, as so often before on stage she had dreamed. And the handsome fellow sitting beside her was Ugtred as fate had meant him to be.

She placed the pink hand of Anima over the golden-brown hand of Adamo. "I'm holding your hand, Ugtred—can you tell?" Her voice was rather hollow.

His voice echoed roughly. "No."

"Can you see me?" Mere asked. "You look so handsome."

"No, I can't see you," replied Ugtred's voice. "You're inside the doll."

Mere tried again. "Let me get a mirror. You practice walking, if you will, so we can stroll around Ithkar. It's a wonderful town, with a splendid temple. I walked down by the river and fed the ducks."

She rose smoothly and glided into her sleeping quarters, returning with a small hand mirror. She held it out at arm's length, so both of them could be seen.

But Ugtred was concentrating on working the levers and weights that controlled the legs. He spread the feet apart, then jerkily rose from the bench, balancing warily. It was difficult for him to judge distances through the spyholes, and his head was jammed into the figure's neck. He lifted one leg slightly and nearly toppled the automaton but caught his balance by bending forward. Sweat was pouring down his face, and he couldn't free his hands to wipe his forehead.

"How do you feel?" Mere pleaded.

"Give me a minute," he grunted, and waggled the hollow bronze arms.

Grief muffled her voice. "You hate this, don't you."

"It doesn't matter," he said firmly. "Reach me a sword, so I can practice for the duel. If I'm going to stick Kavdah, I ought to try and make it look like an accident."

Mere wished she could see his face. The metal mask was expressionless.

"You'd do that for me?" she queried.

"For you, yes. I wouldn't do it for Anima."

He heard the echo of her sigh. "I thought we could love

each other better this way. But I can't see you or touch you or even hear you clearly. This isn't working out the way I hoped."

Ugtred heard the rattle of ball bearings and the scraping of metal against metal as Mere released Anima's door and climbed out, then opened the door in Adamo's torso and helped him clamber out.

Ugtred wiped his brow with his sleeve. His wide face was grim, but steadfast. "I'll do this every night of my life, if you like it," he stated.

Mere's face was downcast. "I don't like it very much at all," she replied.

Ugtred reached out and took her warm, living hand between both his own. "I'm touching you, Mere . . . can you tell?"

She smiled faintly. "Yes."

"Can you see me?" he queried.

She nodded and lifted up the hand mirror. She saw his square, honest face and hers. Their gazes met in the looking glass.

"Shall we walk down to the river, and feed the ducks?" he asked. "They must be hungry again by now."

Mere hesitated, then said softly, "Ithkar seems a pretty town. I'd like to see the river by daylight."

Ugtred lifted her hand to his lips and breathed for a moment on her ink-stained fingers. "I have a suggestion," he began. "Let Kavdah sell both the mannequins and give us our two-thirds. I'm weary of wandering from town to town. We'll open our own goldsmith's booth here in Ithkar."

She withdrew her hand from his clasp and turned back to the worktable, where the metal finch lay on its side. Ugtred thrust his fists deeply into the pockets of his leather breeches. He was surprised at how roughly his heart was beating as he waited for her answer.

It was a long moment before she replied. "Then you wouldn't have to put any more finches on stalks of asparagus."

Ugtred slipped his arm around her shoulders, and she kissed him lightly as he silently thanked the gods.

At last he said in a rather uneven voice, "Listen—can you hear the minstrels on the green? This fair never closes. Let's enjoy ourselves. I'll even stake you to a few coppers to bet on the wrestling bear."

She laughed, and they walked arm in arm from the stuffy tent into the rollicking sprawl of Ithkar Fair.

FIRST DO NO HARM

Mildred Downey Broxon

A bitter wind blew Lithras from the north through Galzar Pass. She had little but the dress on her whip-scarred back and her knife, brown with her captor's blood. The murder had been needful, but never would she wash that stain from her mother's steel.

There was a blessing in the snow that came early in the mountains: her feet, thin shod, were so cold that the pain had stopped. This blizzard would cover her tracks. Her pursuers were probably long since back in camp, warm with mulled wine. She wasn't worth much trouble. No one knew of her bloodstained knife; no more had any been suspicious after the sudden deaths of each of her previous owners, ever since she was woman tall. *When I began to bleed, my mother would have initiated me. I would have taken vows as a healer. Then* they *came. And slavery.*

"Could I do magic, I might have made things warmer." This, mumbled through lips grown thick. She must speak aloud to fight the cold. She fell to her knees and crawled behind a boulder. Ice lay crisp on sodden autumn leaves. "If I perish here, or if I reach Ithkar, it scarcely matters. I am broken and useless."

She curled into a ball and burrowed beneath the snow.

The leaves prickled. Once safe, she drew out her amulet. It was a small blackstone carving of a sekh, cat-bodied and winged. This was her lifegift. The wing had snapped on the night when soldiers slew her mother. She cradled the image in her hands and somehow felt warmed. She would live, or not, however it happened. Little did she care.

Above her the wind whimpered and howled.

The cold, unseasonable wind hit Ithkar, too.

Anvadlim stood in a death room and twisted a length of metal cable in his hands, something brought by the Three Lordly Ones. As he twisted, it snapped. Colored wiring burst forth like guts. *Useless!* He kicked it across the floor.

Other metal devices clustered around the bed where Father Silva lay at rest under a black pall. In the temple cellars, Anvadlim had found equipment left by the Sky Lords; it still worked, or so he thought. In the first flush of excitement he had thought the machinery might heal the old priest. Instead they had pinned him to a life of thinness and pain. They held no true magic.

The useless machines were stilled, and the surfaces had begun to gather new dust. Silva's chamber would be sealed. Centuries would sift down before anything was disturbed.

Anvadlim blew his nose. ''By the swollen sinuses of Synkalos, I grow morbid. So, the Three Lordly Ones aren't the fount of all knowledge. Why should anyone be?''

He had already done his grieving at the wane of life. No need to watch a shell decay. He closed the door and left the place of silence.

The way was long and the stairs steep to his small workshop. He had not been there for days. Dust filmed his crystal vials, lay gray on his workbench, and scummed the water jars. He dropped a packet of instruments on the table and set water to boil. His tools were contaminated. Time to renew the stasis spell.

The wavery window glass admitted dying light. Anvadlim opened to the crisp scent of cookfires and pine. *Another*

season, and the fair comes again. Only last year he, with
Silva's help, had closed it for fear of plague, though this
had made the other priests wild. Silva had been a man of
science.

Behind him the door creaked. He knew who stood there
even before the other spoke. "You'll be leaving us," Glykso
wheezed. Anvadlim did not turn but stood looking at the
crowds. "I hope you're satisfied," Glykso continued. "Now
that you and your heathen ways have managed to kill the
old—"

Anvadlim wheeled. Glykso pressed his fat bulk against
the workbench. Vials trembled. "The old *what*?" the physician demanded almost pleasantly. "Was it *fool* you were
about to say? How inappropriate, if so." For once Glykso
stood speechless. "And as for killing, death comes to all
men. Even the most religious." Anvadlim gestured toward
the door. "My task here is done. Father Silva no longer
requires aught I might do. Enjoy your chants and rituals.
Well may they serve."

The priest left, and Anvadlim turned back to the pageant
beneath his window. There, a lord's household fluttered in
with pink-and-silver banners, shoving aside a small drab
figure in a cloak. *Young Krimar has come. May his new
rank have sobered him, and may his father rest.*

The small drab figure had paused at the gate—Krimar's
household was bowed through—and when it threw back its
hood Anvadlim saw the dark braided hair of a northern
woman. He caught his breath. But no, this waif was far too
young. Since the war, all northern lore was ground into
dust.

Anvadlim finished packing his small wooden chest, stowed
his few belongings in a knapsack, and closed the door on
his workroom. It too would be a place of silence, for
centuries. The living man wanted drink, and loud voices.

Glykso himself greeted Krimar's party. He paused to
survey their splendor. All seemed well, save for the young

lord himself, who seemed peaked. This was not too strange. It was only last year— "Welcome in the name of the temple, Lord Krimar."

The youth huddled deeper into his pink-and-silver cloak. The heraldic colors clashed with his sallow skin. "There is a draft." He waved one thin hand toward the open casement. A servant hastened to seal it, and another proffered a werthorn-inlaid box and opened the lid. The young noble rummaged amid carved crystal bottles, selected one, and quaffed a dose. He grimaced and coughed. "I must take care. It was within this very guest house—"

"Your father's death was a tragedy." Glykso preferred not to dwell on the subject. Plague, at the fair! No matter what that charlatan Anvadlim said, the matter should have stayed secret. Money had been lost. "We all regretted his untimely passing. He was a great patron of the temple." Perhaps that would plant a suggestion.

The young noble was not attending. He gazed around at the stone walls and shivered. "According to your custom, Glykso, I have come without any sorcerer, defenseless, to the fair. I require a bodykeeper skilled in the healing arts, one who can guard this frail vessel of life. I wish to engage one here at the fair. I must rest now. See it done."

This whelp dares to order me! Aloud, Glykso spoke only to Krimar's steward. "You have my permission to see to it. If you require assistance, one of the novices will gladly advise you." The steward raised his right hand in salute. The palm was marked with a triangle and crescent moon. Glykso nodded to Lord Krimar and swept from the room.

At Ithkar's gate Lithras could barely find coins to meet the entrance fee. She could have bartered, but she owned only her sekh amulet, her knife, and a few packets of herbs. As she rummaged in her pack a noble's retinue thrust her aside. They were ushered through without paying. A fat temple priest hurried toward them.

When Lithras finally produced a few coppers, the novice

on guard clanked them in his fingers, unimpressed. "What is your trade?" Behind him, a huge fair-ward shifted from one foot to the other.

I cannot say healer. Lithras drew back her hood. The novice raised his eyebrows.

"A woman of convenience?" He sounded incredulous. Her appearance was, she knew, scarcely seductive: she was skinny, her black hair was pulled back and tightly braided, and her homespun dress was an unbecoming brown. "That way." He pointed.

The guard gestured with his pike. "You want the dark sector."

Lithras covered her head again and stepped into the fairgrounds. Here all trades mingled; life and commerce brawled about her. An acrobat made a blue-furred beast leap through a hoop of living serpents. Something that looked like a sekh cringed between wagon shafts, its wings clipped. A woolseller walked past, his wares bulky bundles on his back. A slim, quick youth jostled a gemseller, who yelled; the thief was immediately seized by two huge fair-wards. After the silence of the open spaces, the din, movement, and color were dizzying.

Lithras drew her cloak closer. Near night it was, and she with nowhere to sleep. Here she dared not curl up in the open as one did in the woods. She had an idea of what the dark sector might be and had no wish to go there. She decided to wander. Fate had protected her thus far.

Krimar's heralds cried the news, and for the few literate fairgoers, servants posted notices. Lithras saw a sign and puzzled out the writing. Two of the languages she knew from her mother's books, but this spelling was odd. A "bodykeeper"? She might qualify. Here at Ithkar Fair, where magic was controlled, she could show as well in a contest as any anointed healer. It would be pleasant to live in a noble's house, fed and warm. She'd had her fill of cold

and hunger. She stroked her sekh amulet. Unless she took to
the streets again, she had nowhere else to go.

This early in the fair, the Bibulous Bullock still had
drinkable beer. Its wine could use another week to age.
Mim's customers were not fastidious folk: the smell of
greasy cooking scarcely masked that of unwashed bodies
and dung-covered boots. However, the Bibulous Bullock
was cheap, warm, lively, and relatively safe: Mim had years
of experience in spotting trouble.

The tavern was a huge tent, set up on semipermanent
wooden foundations. Mim had run it every fair for many
years, first with her husband and now alone. Support poles
and trestle tables marked it into areas, and each area had its
own denizens. A party of trappers, skin clad and wild from
the woods, worked at getting drunk. They made no sound
until one tall fellow surged to his feet and swore to kill any
man in the house. A wench embraced the would-be warrior,
loosed his money pouch, and tossed it to Mim. The leather
smelled of woodsmoke.

"I'll give it back tomorrow," Mim promised, "if you
live." The fellow quieted.

Near the door, where the rushes were cleaner, Elki the
pony trainer beckoned a serving wench, who set down her
pitcher and sidled close. Elki was young and well formed.
His red leather suit concealed little of this fact. He drew the
girl onto his knee, then noticed Mim's disapproving gaze.
The tavern-keeper folded her brawny arms. Elki grinned,
cocked his head toward the door, and swaggered out. Mim
had rules: any private business the wenches did was on their
own time, off premises.

In the cleanest section, where lanterns clustered and a
brick oven fought the chill, Anvadlim leaned on the counter.
His hands thawed around a mug of mulled beer. "So there I
am, no roof but sky, a few coppers to my name and winter's
coming early. But Synkalos must love me after all. I see
this notice: some noble's hiring a physician for the south,

where it's warm." He sipped his beer and shivered. "Fruit on the trees. Sunshine. Flowers. I'd forgotten how I missed it."

"You're from Tsobbet yourself, aren't you?" Mim wiped the counter with a rag.

"They are all dead. Plague." Anvadlim sat silent. He'd seen enough plague to last him. Then he cheered. "Anyhow, this was a hiring contest, for what they call a bodykeeper. Started today. All sorts turned out: barbers, horseleeches, wortcunners. Well, how many real physicians can there be in Ithkar?" He drained his tankard and waved aside a refill. "Got to be fresh for the morning. Today was ordinary stuff: boils, sprains, head colds. See 'em all the time."

"As does every barber or wortcunner."

Anvadlim turned to face the speaker, who had slipped onto a nearby stool. She could be no more than a girl, surely, so short and slight. Though there was something in the darkness round her eyes—well, hunger and hardship might do that even to the young. She was northern dark, clad in a rough brown dress. Probably one of the war refugees, come to Ithkar to seek employment. She was so plain-featured as to fade into the background. Something about her, though, stuck in his memory. "Didn't I see you hanging about the hiring?"

"As well you might have done, I being entered in the contest myself." The girl fingered something on a thong about her neck.

Anvadlim began, then stifled, a laugh. Any practitioner of northern herbal arts must be older than this child—old enough to be her mother, at least. Since the conquest, the old ways were no longer taught.

Her smile showed teeth. "It's considered sporting to wish luck, I'm told. Even in civilized lands, among gentles. Or was I misinformed?"

"Oh, no, of course not . . . er, milady. Naturally I wish you all good fortune, you and your . . . er, skills."

"Whatever those poor skills may be, you mean?" She motioned for a tankard, tasted its contents, and winced. "The name is Lithras. Tell me, in the test today, did you lance that boil or apply fomentation?"

"What boil?" Then Anvadlim realized that all contestants must see similar cases, or it would be no test at all. "I lanced it, of course."

Lithras curled her lip. "Oh, you're a *cutter*. Well enough, it will probably fester. By rights the knife holds little place in healing." Her hand strayed to her belt. Then, as if burned, it jerked back into sight. "A hot herbal poultice, however—"

"Indeed? Of which herbs?"

She smiled. "Which herbs? That would be telling. And it wasn't the dung and marble dust I saw one idiot use. Might as well kill the patient and have done, spells or no spells." She set down her almost untouched tankard and stood to leave. "Well, see you in the morrow. If you're called back, that is."

"I might say the same, *my lady*." Anvadlim watched her thread toward the door. No, he had nothing to fear from such a child, come though she might from northern witch stock. The stories were old and exaggerated. Wortcunning indeed! Time to turn in. He must be fresh for the morning.

On the contest's second day, the number of aspirants had dwindled to three, and Krimar's household set up individual booths. Lithras and Anvadlim eyed each other with suspicion. From the third tent emerged an imposing figure, tall, broad, and glittering

"Ah, my distinguished colleagues!" There was something about his speech, not so much an accent as a slurring. Under the black-furred hood his face was pallid. Vague eyes struggled to focus. "I am Doctor Peldras, from the medical school at Sossini."

"Sossini, eh? That old place still in business?" Anvadlim was deliberately rude.

Lithras tried to show better manners. "Ah, yes, Sossini. Ancient, and full of knowledge." Her mother's library had kept one of its books as a lesson in ludicrous anatomical error, but she forbore to mention that.

"Good to meet you both," Peldras said, unaware that he had not been given names. "May the greatest skill prevail." He muffled his hands in furred sleeves, beamed, and weaved toward his tent.

Lithras found the facilities reasonably complete: a raised cot, a worktable, jars of fresh water, and a lantern. A servant stood by for orders. Lithras gestured toward quill, ink, and parchment.

"Those, *milady*, should serve for your records. If you cannot write, a scribe will be provided. Within reason, we shall also supply any other materials you request."

She pondered. "Clean soft rags, a beeswax candle, and a sharp knife." The one in its sheath concealed by her belt was unclean for healing. When the candle was brought she untied the thong from her neck and set out her amulet: a blackstone carving of a winged cat. She touched its broken left wing. *Not much of an altar,* she told the sekh, *but the best I can provide.* Only after she lit the taper did she take out her packets of herbs.

Anvadlim set down his bundles of instruments. He could hear his first patient wheezing before the man shuffled in and stood, clutching the tent's center pole. Anvadlim bade him sit.

His garments hung here, strained there, as if his frame had changed. His hands were aged and scarred from work, but the honest calluses had split on fingers swollen at the tips. The old man sucked in breath with a wet sound, like sea caves.

Anvadlim waited until the soughing eased. "Is your problem mostly in breathing?"

"Naw, in the livin' mostly, these days." The patient tapped his chest, then pointed at his swollen ankles.

Anvadlim switched to dialect. "How makes it, then, thy living?"

The man's breath bubbled. "I lives on the sea. Islanders, my peopling, always. Took out the small boats ownself, when younger; now me sons brings back the fish, I salts them and we takes silvers to the fair." He paused to cough. "It's the alltimes way, me kin. Me da went samelike, sea got him at last. She creeps in our lungs, she do, an' drownded we is ashore."

Anvadlim pressed one finger to the man's swollen ankle. A mark remained, white and deep. He sighed. *I've seen this before. Indeed, the sea does call the old ones back at last. She owns some families.* There was nothing he could do to cure, and little that might even help. He rummaged among his medicine bottles. "A pinch of this thrice daily may dilute the curse. Best not to anger the sea further; eat no more salt fish."

The patient peered at him and chuckled. "An' what else be island-born eatin', three-fourths of the year? Well for you to say, mainland man. Sea gave me a livin', has her rights to give me dyin'. I'll no fling yer herbs to her face, youngster." He shuffled from the tent.

Anvadlim rested his head on his hands, closed his eyes a moment, then picked up a pen. What, really, could medicine do for a life held in thrall by the sea?

Into Lithras's tent a woman led her child. It was short and sickly pale, its eyes dull under swollen lids. The slack mouth drooled, and coarse hair tufted from its scalp. Lithras could not even determine the creature's age or sex: it waddled on stubby legs, swathed in a toddler's gown.

The woman herself looked tired and ill. Her skin was gray, and despite the cold the neck of her dress gaped open—probably to accommodate the swelling at her throat. She slumped at the edge of the cot. Her bright wool garments marked her as a dweller of the heights. Lithras's people, in the Kelcann uplands, rarely encountered snowfolk. Rumors went they were dwarves, and unchancy.

This woman, though, might have been of Lithras's own tribe. When she did not speak, Lithras hazarded a query in her own language: "What would be the aging on your child?"

That called forth a tear. "Man old, but never man tall. A stunted weedling."

Indeed, the child barely reached the middle of Lithras's breast, and she was a short woman. He sat lumpish on the floor, uninterested in his surroundings. Perhaps he was a dwarf's changeling child. But how? She asked his mother, "Whence came you to the fair?"

Again the woman sighed. "I am myself Kelcannish of birth. I was a grown maiden at the time of the Great Scattering. The soldier band which took me pursued nobles to the high country. There was much killing. I stole away from camp and made my way deep into the hills, in hope to find some of my own people, but those I found lay dead. At last the mountain folk took me in, and I have lived these years in the valley behind White Peak." She began to cry. "Always I was told ill luck followed those who went with the mountain men. So it is. My child is a changeling, and I am ill. I fled home to Kelcann when my husband died, but all had changed. Conquerors have razed my village and built new." She held out work-reddened hands. "I wash their rags, and for that they took me with them to the fair."

The woman's fingers were icy, as were the face and whole body of the child: chill as snow on the mountain peaks. The skin of both was dry and thick, but whether from a curse or only cold and wind, Lithras did not know. She shivered and touched her sekh, but it held no warmth. The broken wing scratched her finger. Her mother would have known the proper ritual to appease the peak gods and the outraged spirits of both tribes, but her mother was dead. Lithras had no magic. All she had was her scant knowledge of herbs, and nothing that grew was effective against such curses.

At least she might ease sorrow. Among her herb packets she kept merrywort. She handed over her whole supply.

When the mother and child left, she sat long with a piece of parchment blank before her.

After the day's testing, the Bibulous Bullock glowed with warmth and cheer. Lithras and Anvadlim sat at Mim's counter. Lithras sipped beer and made a face. The brew had begun to sour.

Anvadlim shrugged. "Happens every year. Won't keep without spells." He set down his tankard and called for wine. "After such a day, I prescribe drink. In great quantity."

Lithras held out her goblet. "My cases were depressing. There was no help for most of them."

"Well I know." Anvadlim swallowed. "At least things grew more lively after midday. I treated a truly hideous burn. I know the woman; she owns that fryshop one street hence. She'd spattered hot grease over her breast, half her right arm, and part of her face."

"You as well? That's odd. The man I treated," Lithras said, "was a scribe, and mute. He, too, had been burned on arm, breast, and face. Binding it was difficult. I know not how it may go. But with the virtue of egg white—" She stopped. Best not to reveal trade secrets. "With the usual treatment, I trust he may not take fever. He must have overset his oil lamp. I made offerings for him to the god of the clumsy. I hope he may not be punished; I think he was slave to a noble."

A wench, red-eyed, came sniffling to stand before Lithras. "Pardon, my lady, but how fares Elki?"

"Elki?" Lithras turned to Anvadlim. "Should I know him?"

"The pony trainer," he told her. Then, to the wench, "What ails him?"

The wench sniffled again and wiped her nose on her

apron. "During his midday show, it was. One of the ponies trod his foot. Oh, the blood and hurt!"

"Ah, so that's who the fellow was," Lithras said. "He should recover. He'll be limping for some months, but a pony trainer must expect hooves." With a watery smile, the wench thanked her and went about her work. "Crushed foot," Lithras explained. "An accident; it can't have been part of the contest."

"That's odd," Anvadlim said. "Late this afternoon I myself dressed a crushed foot."

"Another hapless pony trainer?"

Anvadlim shook his head. "My patient was a young woman. She never spoke, but I can guess her trade. She was beautiful, her hands had never worked, and she wore flimsy silks. Come to think of it, she may not have plied a trade at all; she may have been property. On her thigh I saw a skin tattoo: a triangle and a crescent moon."

"A *what*?" Lithras spilled her drink. Before she could speak further, cold wind made her turn her head. The tent door stood open, and torchlight shone on two men, warmly cloaked. Lithras and Anvadlim held silent as the newcomers sought the darkest, most disreputable corner.

Those who drank there bought mixed wine—cheaply— from the slop bowls. If they were quiet, Mim tolerated them. The Bibulous Bullock had few pretensions. Odd, to see a prosperous pair choose such company. When they removed their cloaks, light shone off pink and silver.

Shortly, one of the shabby drinkers slumped over, and the two carried him out. Lithras set down her goblet, unfinished. "I shall turn in early," she said. "Goddess alone knows what the morrow will bring." Outside, she kept to the shadows. Ahead, on the darkened street, she saw a flash of silver. She followed it.

Even a plain woman as soberly dressed as Lithras entered this part of the fair at her own peril. In the dark sector it was assumed that a lone female would be selling the use of her

person. Here strolled no glamorous courtesans. Few fair-
wards walked these streets. The selling of flesh, drink, and
drugs was merely another commercial activity. Those who
entered the dark sector knew what they sought. Here sprawled
the cheaper drinking places and foodshops, along with other
unmarked establishments. Strange scents wafted from some,
and those who emerged wandered dazed.

Lithras caught a flash of silver by the lone torch near a
dreamhouse. She waited a moment, pulled the leather curtain aside, and peered into the blue haze. A customer,
stumbling out, grabbed her by the waist.

"Jus' what I wanned. How much?"

She shook her head. "Not selling." No anger; she knew
the customs of this place. At times, in her cold and lonely
past—with luck she would never have to sink that low
again.

He grabbed higher and held on. "What mean, not selling?
Giving?" His spittle sprayed her cheek.

She pressed one finger to his throat, in the way she'd
learned. He stepped back, unable to speak. Again she shook
her head. "Not selling." He shrugged, coughed, and vanished into the night.

She peered back inside, into dimness, and saw the noble's servants hand the landlord a clinking purse. Soon they
dragged a limp redheaded figure out the door.

She made as if to follow, then hesitated and fingered the
amulet around her neck. Its broken wing felt sharp. She was
hungry and cold, but even worse, she was afraid. *I am no
healer. I took no sacred vows. I can work no spells.* She
was not convinced. She crept toward the lean-to where she
spent her nights.

Dreams scratched at Lithras's sleep. A small sekh followed her, dragging its crippled wing. As it crawled it
whimpered.

When sunlight struck the canvas of her shelter she relaxed
into true sleep, only waking when the food vendors' cries
grew too strident to ignore. She groaned, pulled on her

coarse brown dress, and stumbled forth. Late! She hurried to the contest area. On its cord, the sekh amulet scraped her breast and drew blood.

She saw her first case and shivered. He lay on a pallet, unconscious. His breath reeked sweet. Drugged, of course. She knew the stink of dreamweed, had known it last night. But since she'd seen this man carried from the dreamhouse he had been assaulted. A huge lump bulged beneath his red hair. After a brief examination she stepped out in search of the nearest fair-ward.

The guard looked at the patient and frowned. "No, milady, he warn't thrashed in no brawl last night, nor any time yestiddy, either. I'd of heard. We tells each other, an' the chief writes it all down an' reads it forth to everyone." He paused. "So's we know the trouble places, that is. Or the troublemakers. No matter where we's posted, we hears of the nasties." He straightened, proud. "An' never mind the dreamweed, it ain't unlawful in the dark sector." Lithras stood, defeated. "If that's all, milady, unless you'd be wanting to make a complaint? I has me duties." The guard shuffled out of the tent.

Anvadlim's first patient was borne in by two servants. Faces impassive, they lowered the litter to the floor and left. *Slow, stertorous breathing. Obtunded or comatose.* The man's face was crusted with vomit and dirt. When Anvadlim brushed the thick black hair, lice scuttled. The injury was obvious: a blue throbbing lump told of a sharp blow to the skull. *Broken, perhaps.* He leaned closer and winced at the man's sour breath. He pulled down the blanket: rough clothing, but well made. It still smelled of woodsmoke. The fellow could not be a longtime derelict.

He pulled back the eyelids and held a candle close. *Bad.* It meant ill when the windows of the soul gaped wide.

"Head injury, yes," he mused, "and little I can do about that. But there's something else. How came he so ne-

glected?'' He pulled the blanket all the way down. Leather
boots, worn at the heels—well soled, though, and the up-
pers made of fine warm fur. The leather trews were stiff
with dirt and urine, but once they had been double sewn
with sinew. He opened the laced shirt: good muscle, not yet
wasted to thinness. He frowned. Something was familiar—

With a wet cloth he wiped the face. The skin was tanned
by wind and weather. Anvadlim rocked back on his heels.
He knew this man. He'd been drinking at the Bibulous
Bullock, only last night. Too drunk to stand, perhaps, but
not injured. Mim never tolerated brawls.

Hadn't he seen this man carried out? Something strange
about that, too: it was by a servant in pink and silver. Why
would Krimar's household bother with a drunken trapper?
With shaking hands Anvadlim penned his notes: *Serious
head injury. Nothing to be done save rest and pray.* Then he
stumbled from the tent. Fortunately, a fair-ward stood just
outside.

Anvadlim hailed him. "I'd like you to look at something
for me.'' He shoved the man into his tent and pointed to his
patient.

"Not you, too,'' the guard protested. "Never saw this
man. Never heard no report. Want to file a complaint? As
it's their contest, it would go to House Krimar, I'd be
supposing.'' Anvadlim shook his head, and the guard left.

"So that's how it is!'' Anvadlim started to slam his
belongings into his small wooden chest. Behind him, the
patient's breath slowed. "May Krimar rot alive!''

A contest indeed! Lithras's hands shook with fury as she
scooped up her sekh amulet. *I'd sooner sell myself on
the street—it's honest work and less harm to it.* True, the
position of "bodykeeper'' would have been an easy living,
in a noble's house. But her mother had been a healer.
Lithras was not, but some things are sacrilege, even to the
unsanctified.

Her eyes were so clouded with tears that she stumbled

into Anvadlim without recognizing him. He seized her by the shoulders. "Just a moment. Where are you going?"

"What does it matter to you? You and Peldras are welcome to your pus-filled contest. I give you joy of it." She sniffed, wiped her eyes on her sleeve, and looked up. Why was Anvadlim carrying his wooden chest? And a leather knapsack? "So you're already packed to move in with Lord Krimar? I'm sure he'll keep you entertained. You can practice cutting. You'll have plenty of subjects any time you wish." She struggled to get away. "Let me go!"

The flap of Peldras's tent opened, and the old physician came blinking into sunlight. "I say, it's hard to do my work with all this noise." Then he recognized his fellow contestants. "Is something amiss?"

"Pestilential right there is!" Anvadlim roared. Then, more quietly, "What sort of case are you treating at present?"

"I'm not certain I should—" Peldras began.

"Tell me, then, is it a head injury? A bad one?" Both waited for his answer.

"Well, yes, as a matter of fact . . ." The fellow bumbled into silence.

Lithras and Anvadlim reached the tent as one and pulled aside the flap. On a cot lay a comatose form: a woman whose long hair was matted with blood. Lithras staggered back. The woman wore bright upland clothing, and her hands were work rough. Lithras had seen her only the day before and given her the entire supply of merrywort. She felt as if she might vomit. "How was she hurt?"

Peldras shrugged. "That does not concern me. She was brought in as one of the test cases. I have made my diagnosis, and determined there is nothing to do. I await my next assignment. Interesting, is it not?"

Glykso's voice boomed out, and all three jumped. "Consultations are forbidden. Do you wish to be disqualified?"

Perhaps a holy man could help, Lithras thought. "There is something wrong. Surely you, a priest of the Three Lordly Ones, would wish to know."

Glykso's lips curved in what might have been a smile. "There is little of which I am ignorant, child."

"Reverend Father, it is about House Krimar's hiring trials. For bodykeepers. You must know that it was set up as a test of skill, to determine the most qualified contestants."

"House Krimar is accustomed to seek the best." Glykso's voice held no inflection.

Anvadlim broke in. "What my young colleague means to say—and what I mean to say, as well—is that some of the cases were no accident. We have seen identical injuries: burns, crushed feet, and head wounds. I fear willful harm is being done. Two of yesterday's patients were slaves of House Krimar."

"And theirs to deal with as they wished," Glykso said. "I gave leave for the testing. I do not concern myself with trifles. Slaves are mere property."

Lithras's hand flew to the killing knife hidden at her belt. She herself had been a slave. Anvadlim held her arm.

"What, then," the physician roared, "of free citizens—supposedly under protection of Ithkar law? One lies dying in my tent."

"I fail to see the problem," Peldras interjected. "We were in a trial of skill, were we not? And thus we were given interesting cases." He gestured vaguely and backed toward his tent.

"Precisely," said Glykso. "House Krimar has long held a special place with the temple. You, Anvadlim, should appreciate their patronage of . . . science." The physician dropped Lithras's arm and took one step forward. Glykso scurried behind the guard. "Arrest them for causing a disturbance." The fair-ward hefted his pike but made no move.

"Please," Peldras said, "can we not be civilized?"

Anvadlim ignored him. "I'd curse you, Glykso, but my spells never work. And of course sorcery is unlawful at Ithkar."

Lithras spat at the priest's feet. "My mother would have wished you this: May you receive always what you deserve." She turned toward Peldras. "You, it seems, have earned the same."

Glykso pounded at the fair-ward's back. "Seize them!" The guard still did not move. "Seize them, I say." He raised his arm again, then clutched at his chest. His face purpled.

Anvadlim smiled. "Warden," he said, "there exists an emergency. You should summon a physician. Only the best will do: the future bodykeeper-in-residence to Lord Krimar." Peldras nodded and smiled. "Your first patient," Anvadlim told him, "is even more illustrious than Lord Krimar and his household." Glykso now had sunk to his knees. Peldar stumbled toward him. His hands wavered in mystic passes. They left him to it.

A cold wind harried Lithras and Anvadlim toward the gate. Lithras strode angrily. Despite his greater height, Anvadlim had to hurry to keep up. "Stay a moment!" he gasped. "A healer must never stop learning. I've always wanted to study the herbal secrets of the north, though none would initiate me."

"Nor me either," Lithras said. "My mother was to do so, but she died in the war." She shrugged off the intervening years of misery and shame. "What I know, I have picked up myself, here and there. I've taken a notion to study cutting, of late." She must be honest. "I warn you, I can work no magic. This is not only at Ithkar, under the ban. I am no anointed healer, but a maimed thing, unfinished."

Going out through the gate, they struggled against an incoming tide of fairgoers. At last they reached the banks of the river Ith. Boats bobbed at moorage; one could carry them anywhere. The river bank was trampled by thousands of feet, rutted by hundreds of cargo wagons. Heedless of her shoes, Lithras stepped to the water's edge.

The knife at her belt had stuck in its sheath. She drew it for the first time since it had been soiled. Her captor's blood was only brown dirt. Cold currents rinsed it away.

As she resheathed the blade she felt a scrabbling at her breast. Curious, she pulled out her amulet. The blackstone carving gleamed in the thin sunlight. Both the sekh's wings were whole. She smiled. *Well, it might be some minor magic happens, from time to time.*

The year was running to autumn. From Galzar Pass down to the river Ith, the wind swept cold, sharp as a clean knife. Lithras filled her lungs, tucked the amulet inside her dress, and walked beside Anvadlim toward a southbound boat.

HONEYCOMB

Esther M. Friesner

Rain at Ithkar Fair: an inconvenience, surely, and a rare occurrence, but nothing that had not happened before. The nobles lodged in the temple guest house stood by the windows in the common room and watched the gray skies tip out their load of rain. Some went so far as to write bad poetry, which was meant to evoke the day's morose quality in the hearer, but which somehow succeeded in its aim for all the wrong reasons. The lovely young lady Demaris produced a sonnet that was pregnant with world weariness and heartfelt sighing after Higher Things. Lord Yevri paid her an embarrassment of compliments on her flawless way with morbidity, and soon the pair of them were closeted in his room, finding better ways to pass a rainy day than poetry.

Rain at Ithkar Fair: The less fortunate attendees prayed to the Three Lordly Ones to call back the waters, at least until fair's end. They cursed the muck that puddled under their blankets as they struggled to keep dry. Strangers became close comrades, writhing together under the wagon-beds, trying to avoid the gusty showers. When curses and prayers did nothing, they tucked their heads deeper into the folds of

39

their sodden blankets and imitated the winter-deep slumber of bears, waiting in oblivion for things to improve.

Rain at Ithkar Fair, like rain anywhere, must end. And many new things sprout to life after a good rain. Scarron crawled out of his soaked woolen cocoon and wiped dripping strands of brown hair out of his eyes, blinking at a clear sky and what had come to Ithkar under cover of the rain.

"Malfora, look there." He prodded the dun-colored lump huddled into the small of his back. "We've got a new neighbor."

The lump grunted and produced a sleepy-eyed face framed by damp yellow curls. "Where?" She scrubbed her eyes and hauled herself on top of her companion for a better view.

"Over there, to the right. Get down, you're too high up to see. One stall over from the fat man's magic dishes."

It was so. Malfora squirmed farther out of her blankets and bobbed her head down, as her brother instructed. None of the stalls in their vicinity had true walls. Most had cloth partitions that stopped two spans above the ground. From her cat's-eye vantage, Malfora spied a pair of slim white feet going busily back and forth inside the stall that had been vacant only the other day. They were bare feet—a lady's feet with the toenails tinted dusty rose—and very pale, yet somehow they passed through the ubiquitous fairground mud without stain. The grimy pair under the ramshackle wagon exchanged a knowing look.

"Magic," said Malfora.

Her brother nodded. For those two there had always been something sorcerous about ordinary cleanliness, but the dainty, disembodied feet two stalls over were a miracle walking on mud. Scarron slid from under his little sister's bedroll, sending her tumbling into the muck with a squall of outrage. He hauled himself up by the nearest cartwheel and tugged the hem of his green tunic down sharply.

"What do you think you're doing?" snarled Malfora,

wriggling out of her blankets. A bucket hung from the side of the wagon, more than halfway filled with water. The girl watched as her brother washed the morning's dirt from hands and face, disturbing several more ancient layers of soil at the same time.

"We're going to pay a visit," Scarron mumbled through cupped hands. "Can't pay a visit looking filthy."

"You're not *that* filthy."

"No, but you are." And before Malfora could escape, he had her by the scruff of the neck and was scouring her down to the skin. A few minutes later, the children presented themselves at the curtained front of the nearby stall.

Like their own place, it was a rickety thing, a mere formality of canework overspread with a thin cloth roof to keep off the sun. Some of the better stalls fronting the path boasted a narrow counter at the front, but for the most part the tradesmen backed their wagons into the stalls and used either the footboard or a "found" plank balanced across the wagon-bed to serve the purpose.

A knowledgeable visitor paying a call at one of these stalls before it was opened for business could not knock to announce his presence. One good rap on the cane struts might topple the whole structure, especially after a hard rain had softened the ground to goo. A better way would be to shout the stall-keeper's name. But . . . if you did not know that person's name?

"Well, go on! What are you waiting for?" Malfora gave her brother a jab in the ribs that sent him stumbling forward, limping slightly. (Malfora had not accepted her enforced cleansing without a good fight.) Recovering his balance, Scarron cleared his throat a few times, uttered several anonymous hailing cries, and finally clapped his hands imperiously at the dangling green baize curtain.

At first his summons drew no reply. Malfora began to curse his ineptness so fluently that a passing bravo did a double take and added several new expressions to his own scurrilous vocabulary from the ten-year-old's supply. Malfora had run out of words for her brother and was going on to excoriate the unseen stall-woman when a hand as white and slim as the feet glimpsed earlier pulled back the curtain.

"Yes, child? May I help you?"

Scarron gulped. There was some mistake. There had to be. A lady with a face so fair, slanted eyes the color of amber, hair a floss of snow, did not belong so far from the temple guest house. No, even that wasn't fit to house her. She belonged in the temple itself—not as servant, nor guest, nor even priestess, but as mistress. In that first moment, Scarron was convinced that someone had miscounted; there had been more than three Lordly Ones, and this was the unreckoned fourth come home at last.

Malfora was still too young for religion to be more than a hasty charm mumbled to keep off the night grims. She shoved her brother aside and said, "I'm Malfora. This is my brother, Scarron. We sell carved bowls, two stalls down from you. What do you sell? When did you get here? Where did you come from? Did you come in the rain? Wasn't it awful? I hate the rain. What's your name?"

The lady threw back her head and laughed, a liquid, rippling sound. She extended her hands to the little girl, and Malfora took them. Seven silver rings glinted in the new-washed sunlight.

"I am very pleased to meet you, Malfora. I am Siluia, and I am a candlemaker."

The child nodded solemnly. "Good. You can stay."

"*Malfora!*" His sister's unthinkable rudeness to the visiting goddess shocked Scarron out of his daze. He jerked her back by the shoulder and gave her a shake. "You say you're sorry!"

Malfora set her lips in a way that declared she'd sooner die. In the five years since death had made him her parents as well as her brother, Scarron had come to recognize that look. It meant business.

"My lady, forgive her. My sister hasn't any more manners than a piglet. In fact, I've seen some pigs that—*ouch!*"

The piglet in question kicked like a mule. Rubbing his assaulted shin, Scarron threatened every facet of Malfora's life while his sister danced out of range, giggling.

"Please, I take no offense," Siluia said. She laid her ringed hand on Scarron's arm. He felt blood flush his face at her touch, cool and tingling even through his thick tunic. "You were certainly here before I, and first-comers ought to have some say in who becomes their neighbor."

"Last year we had another carver set up *right next* to us." Malfora crossed her arms, frowning. "His bowls weren't nearly as nice as ours, but he sold them cheaper. And he polished them with fish oil. *Stinky* fish oil!" Her short nose crinkled at the reeking memory.

"Well, I promise that my business will not compete with yours, little one." The pale lady beckoned, and Malfora ventured back to have her curls stroked and smoothed. Scarron glowered, caught in the snare of unreasoning envy. "My candles are sweetly scented, made only of the finest, freshest beeswax. I use no tallow, which smokes and stinks. What's more, it may happen that those who buy my candles will afterward buy your bowls, to set them in for burning." Her golden eyes sparkled with merriment. "I will suggest it."

"My lady, you needn't—"

"Don't call me that!" All warmth vanished from Siluia's voice. Her back stiffened, small breasts pressing against the smooth azure cloth of her dress. "I am Siluia; nothing more!" She spun on her heel and ducked back behind the green curtain.

"What did you *say* to her?" Malfora demanded, pounding her brother's arm. "You stupid ox, she's *nice*! She said she'd *help* us! What did you say to insult her like that?"

Scarron stood there, staring at the wavering sheet of baize, his mouth moving without sound. At last he said, "I don't know . . . I don't know . . ."

Malfora spat on his sandals, totally disgusted. She had never seen any person—any *thing*—to compare with the strange stall-woman for beauty. She tucked her icy paws into her armpits to warm them and flounced off to prepare for the day's business. She left her stone-struck brother to follow her or take root, whichever.

Scarron shook off his stupor and was soon helping Malfora arrange their stock of bowls for sale. A treasured plank, wide enough to display two score and ten bowls to best advantage, was laid across the tail end of their wagon. The bowls came in all sizes, an assortment of shapes, and a rich variety of woods.

As the elder by fully four years, Scarron had charge of the family purse. Now he hauled it up from its hiding place inside his tunic and flicked the coins into separate piles, by denomination. He nodded once, content that there were enough of each to provide change for the day's customers without his having to send Malfora sprinting to the changers' booths. Somehow his half-wild little sister always managed to "lose" a handful of the smaller coins en route back from the changers—a loss accompanied by the scent of burnt sugar on her breath.

The sun was climbing the sky. It would be a good day, a day made better by yesterday's rain. The more pious among the pilgrim throng would have no complaints, since rain could not affect the course of services inside the great temple. But the majority of pilgrims came as much for the fair as for the holy observances, and if yesterday's weather had forced them into piety, they would make up for it today. Already the grounds were bustling, the gawkers and strollers and jingle-purses coming to look and admire and buy.

Scarron arranged his change in a specially carved sectioned bowl, one of his best labors. In form it aped the nautilus's honeycombed shell, even to having that creature's weirdly filamented face for stem and foot, each chamber holding a different kind of coin.

"How fine."

Scarron's head jerked up. Siluia's golden eyes were on

him, alight with amusement, her delicate lips parted to show a double row of small, peculiarly sharp teeth. She traced the curve of the nautilus's shell with one snowy finger. "You have him to the life. If you'd put him in water, he'd fill his chamber and shoot away over the waves. Although . . . No, I see you've weighed him down with coins. How wise you are, Scarron. Nothing holds tighter than a golden snare."

Her words washed over the boy like songs in a foreign tongue. All that remained with him was the music. He raised the bowl to her as he'd seen the temple acolytes do with the thank-offerings the departing merchants made to the Sky Lords.

"If you like it . . . it's yours."

Siluia laughed. The sun painted streaks of gold on her frothy hair. "I come to give you an apology, and you try to give me a present. Why weren't you the one—?" She made a little rasping sound in her throat, and a frown flickered over her face. Whatever had troubled her, she dismissed it quickly and was soon smiling again.

"Well . . . I want to ask your pardon for my brusqueness earlier, but— Dear me, I see that I must soon open my stall if I want to accomplish anything today. A proper apology can't be a quick one, though. Ah, I know!" Her right hand darted down to pluck one of the seven silver rings she wore. She pressed it into Scarron's hand. "My pledge. If I don't redeem it with an apology by sundown, you may redeem it for a kiss before sunrise. A bargain?" She did not wait for his answer but flew past the fat man's stall and disappeared into her own.

"What cracked your skull? Wake up!" Malfora's strident baby voice scraped on Scarron's nerves after Siluia's purling music. "Come on, help me polish the rest of these. We're behind! Fatty's got a crowd all to himself already."

It was so. Scarron slipped Siluia's ring over his smallest finger as the fat man's sales cry boomed in his ears: "Step near, see clear, my lords and my fine ladies! A minor magic, and yet a mighty one! Who would not yearn for strawberries while snow covers the ground? Who has not hungered for delicacies out of season? But place your chosen dainty in one of my bowls, position the lid—so!—and press down . . .''

One of the ladies nearest the fat man's counter gasped at the violent hiss that issued from the covered bowl. The merchant beamed paternally.

"How perceptive, my dear. That hiss you hear is the captive spriteling bound to serve the mistress of the bowl. One bowl, one spriteling, not one without the other, and all the enchantment these delightful creatures can do is to suspend time within the tiny compass of their prisons. Time, and whatever else you put into the bowl! Come now, who'll be first to buy? . . .''

"Fine bowls! Pretty bowls! All kinds! All woods!''

Malfora had an astonishingly robust set of lungs for such a stringy child. Usually her cries were augmented by Scarron's, but today all he was good for was sitting next to the change bowl and looking at one of his hands.

The fair was well and truly under way. One voice the less, one merchant not shouting his wares at the top of his lungs, would make little difference. Every stall-keeper was wrapped up in his own affairs, paying no mind to his neighbors' doings. No one noticed when the green baize curtain came down.

Lady Demaris was the first to discover the new stall. She and her old nurse were part of the throng at the fat man's booth when her nose began to twitch. Of course, being a poet, her senses were far more refined and responsive than those of the commonalty. It was only a thin wisp of fragrance, but it drew her as surely as the goldcup blossom drew bees.

A thin white candle burned on a silver disk, its perfume too heavy to issue from such a slender taper. Other candles lined flimsy shelves tacked up between the stalls' cane struts, none of them lit. One was enough for the lure.

"Mind the coins, Malfora." Scarron vaulted down from

the wagon, no more able than the lady Demaris to resist the candle's call. Others came, too, their eyes holding a glow too deep to come from a single flame. The shabby stall held darkness in broad day to back the burning candle, a wedge of trapped nighttime that defied explanation. Thin cloth spread over cane frames could not keep out the sun so thoroughly.

Siluia's face hovered above the flame, a lozenge of ivory and gold. Her white hair spilled down over her breast and wove itself into smoke.

"Come to me, come, my lords, my ladies. My scents are sweet, my candles buds of light that flower at a touch. I capture sun and honey, flowers and the golden sheen of summer on a bee's wing. Come and buy, come and buy . . ."

The fat man stopped his shouted spiel of spritelings trapped in magic dishes. The horn-handed carver of children's toys who held the stall across the way was also silent. Malfora still cried her wares, but Siluia's softer call hushed the edge from the child's voice and made it almost musical. The crowds ebbed from every stall but hers, and many of the vendors did the same.

"What is that scent?" The lady Demaris croaked her question.

"A flower essence; a single one, my lady. Do you like it? I have other shapes and sizes and fragrances for sale if you'd prefer." The spell's surface cracked. Siluia sounded like any other stall-woman, mouthing her stock for the clients. The darkness behind her leaked away through that sudden flaw in her glamour, letting light steal in through cloth walls grown gradually translucent again.

The lady threw off the scraps of spell with a shiver, recovering herself nicely. "Yes, my good woman, I would like something a trifle—gayer than white, with perhaps a musky perfume. And this candle is too thin by half to fit the sockets in my dining hall. Would you have something about *so* big around?" Her thumb and forefinger described the desired ring size.

The white-haired woman nodded and tripped toward the back of her stall, where a second baize curtain cut off two-thirds of the rear area from view. She vanished behind it for a moment and returned with a candle colored like the rain-bright sky.

"Take this with you today, my lady, and kindle it in your room, with your own hands. See how you like to live with its light. If it pleases you, I can promise you more. If not . . . well, bring it back to me tomorrow."

It was a queer way of offering the customer a test of the wares, but Ithkar brimmed with queer ways. The lady Demaris was more than pleased when the strange stall-woman required no pledge from her to guarantee the return of the candle. She and her nurse departed to see more of the great fair.

Other clients came, not all so highborn or particular as the lady Demaris. Siluia did brisk trade, and as she'd promised, she sent many of her buyers over to Scarron's stall.

"A candle of that type burns best if cradled in a bowl about this height, good sir. I'm sorry, I don't sell what you'd need, but I believe I saw a very handsome example at a booth not far from— Why, *there* it is, two down. Thank you, sir. You won't regret it."

As that memorable day went on, the chambers of the carved nautilus began to overflow. Scarron cursed as he tried to keep the coins in their proper places; no use. They spilled over, and some even fell out of the bowl altogether, sending Malfora to grub for them in the dirt under the wagon.

"Better trade up." Scarron clenched his teeth, laboriously counting out most of the smaller coins. He poured them into his pouch and passed it to his sister. "Here. Go to the money-changers and have that turned to five gels and three ryvers."

"There's the change fee—"

"I put in enough to cover that. *Evenly,* so don't get any ideas. Scoot!"

Malfora took off in a flash of dirty heels. Scarron sat back on his haunches and sighed, looking over his stock. In one day he'd sold as many bowls as would go in a ten-day under ordinary circumstances. He had additional stock tucked away in a chest slung under the wagon-bed, but of the bowls he'd put on display that morning, only seven were left.

Seven bowls unlike any others: they were carved of a rich black wood supposed to come from a single island in the Western Sea; a wood so hard that the skilled carver could turn the burnished grain to frozen lace with his blade. Last year Scarron had used nearly half of the fair profits to buy himself a block of that wondrous wood. Perhaps it was foolish—Malfora surely said it was—but he felt himself ready to try his skill on it. The seven bowls were the result, seven cobweb flowers, seven blackfrost stars. Their price was high—it had to be—and nothing short of starvation would convince Scarron to lower it. No haggling for dreams.

The day was waning, the crowd wandering off to where the flaming cressets of the food-sellers beckoned. Scarron's mouth watered at the thought of the fair's delicacies. The fat man was closing up his booth for the dinner hour, locking his magic bowls into a sturdy chest and waving down a passing fair-ward for advice on procuring a trustworthy guard for his wares until he came back.

Over at Siluia's booth the green baize curtain was up again.

Now the sun was down. Vagrant threads of light still sent their questing brightness down the rows of stalls. One fell on Scarron's hand as he held up one of the precious black bowls, admiring his own handiwork. Silver winked, a star in the lattice of night; her ring. Her pledge, and unredeemed before the sun set.

Scarron felt his heart begin to beat faster. There was a hard aching in his chest that he could not name. Golden eyes slanted up at him from the black wood netting.

He stowed the few coins left in the secret chamber of his nautilus and locked it away in a chest similar to the one the fat man used. Six black bowls went into the chest as well, each shrouded in soft leather. The seventh remained in his hand, a gift to give her when she honored her promise.

A kiss; a kiss that doubting souls would say he was too young to value. Siluia's phantom beauty had enchanted many men that day, but she had turned aside their whispered suggestions with cool grace. She had not turned him away; a ring, a pledge, a kiss. A promised kiss, and he was old enough to imagine its taste on his lips, sweet and cold as summer wine.

A quick bit of negotiation with the guard at the fat man's stall got Scarron his services for a fraction of the price—two adjoining stalls were as easy to mind as one. All secure, he presented himself at Siluia's stall.

"Siluia! Siluia!"

No answer. Scarron shifted from foot to foot, wondering whether she had shut up shop and gone off while he was readying the coins for Malfora. The silver ring on his finger burned cold, or maybe it was only the evening chill coming up from the river.

"Call louder, lad. She's in, but might be doesn't hear you." It was the toymaker from across the way. He too was going to find a meal, tossing off his words as he passed. The boy called her name again, and again had no reply.

Later he might blame his actions elsewhere. At the moment, he thought it was his own idea to softly pull aside the green curtain and slip into her stall. The candles stood in their perfect rows like ranks of ghostly soldiers. For a woman who had done so much business, her stocks seemed not at all depleted. Not one candle was missing from the shelves.

A line of glow seeped across the muddy floor to lap at Scarron's sandals. The second curtain rippled, showing strands of silver woven through the green. Beyond the curtain, Scarron heard voices: Siluia and a man.

"—won't warn you again."

Laughter. "That robe makes you brave, but still you slink

in to see me by the back way. Do you fear me even now, half of what I was?''

''Siluia, I don't have time for your games. Will you give it to me or not?''

''You think I still have it?'' Her voice was arch, taunting. ''You flatter yourself.''

The man's voice grew harsh, with a deep undernote that made Scarron's legs tremble. ''What else would you do with it? Destroy it, and you destroy yourself along with me.''

''And you think I wouldn't have the courage for that? Maybe I've lived long enough. You certainly have.''

A pause, then all the mirth gone out of her words. ''No, Evro; you're too good a liar not to recognize another's lie. I have it, but you never shall. I've come to Ithkar to stay—forever! You ran from me, but I'll be faithful to you. A chance to enter the temple at your age, at such a rank—Well, many of your earthbound race would break a score of lovers' vows for the chance to fly so high. The wealth, the power, the knowledge . . .''

The slap was loud as wood cracking in the fire.

''You *dare* . . .''

''I'll strike you again, Siluia; harder, if I like. I'll have you driven out of Ithkar tomorrow, or worse, if you don't give it back to me. Take off that brave face. All of your kind are cowardly at heart, except when lechery makes you bold. Lord Father Demetrios has songs that can rival your own for power. He'll know how to deal with you if I tell him what you truly are.''

Her words came as a hiss. ''And how will he deal with my most faithful lover?''

Evro chuckled. ''Once he learns that I've picked up most of your pretty tricks, he'll forgive me, if only to learn them himself. I'm only sorry that you never taught me the spells of binding that you lay on your handworks. That would cast light on more than the temple pilgrims bargain for, these days!''

"I gave you what I did because I loved you. Love made me a fool, but not a total idiot. Some good sense told me not to give you every secret I had."

Scarron heard her laugh again, a laugh that twisted off into a sudden cry of pain. "Let me *go!*"

"Where is it, damn you? I'll tear this cursed stall to pieces and you with it! Give it back to me while you've got two unbroken hands, you witch!"

She was crying, struggling, and every breath she took spat out in hatred. "Never! Never!" Scarron's soul leaped out to her. The silver-shot curtain tore away, slashed in two by the woodcarver's knife he always wore. Beyond the curtain were blurs of white and blue and flame: Siluia fighting to be free of a temple priest's cruel hold, Evro's grim face melting to angry surprise, then splitting to a howl of outrage as Scarron's knife scored his cheek.

Scarron gave a wordless shout, a hoarse, exultant cry. The priest crossed his hands before his face to ward off further blows, stumbling backward, toppling racks where strips of emptied honeycomb waited for the candlemaker's caldron. He cursed loudly as the hem of his robe came inches from the fire lit beneath the black iron pot.

The boy felt battle hunger for the first time, more potent than any promised kiss. He would have driven Evro into the fire, but white hands held him back. Siluia seized his tunic from behind and would not let it go. Evro saw what she was doing and took courage to rush past them, out of the back of the stall.

Scarron was panting as if the fight had lasted ten times as long. "Why—why did you do that, Siluia? Why did you let him go?"

"Because you would have killed him." She touched his carver's blade. "And that would have been your death."

"Who is he? What does he want from you?"

Her eyes were warmer, mirrors of the flames beneath her caldron. She raised his chin with a touch and smiled. "Little busy-ears, what would you understand of lovers? No, don't scowl. There is no sin in lingering innocence, child.''

"I'm no child!" Scarron jerked his head away. "I'm grown enough to protect you from him. I won't let him hurt you—not him or anyone!''

"Ahhh." Her glance strayed to the bubbling kettle. "So you would serve me? Make a vow never to betray my trust? So did Evro, and I believed him then. I believed him so much, loved him so well, that I took his word alone . . . but gave him more. Our lives are bound, sweet Scarron. I made the proof of it with my own hands, and sank half my magic into it. Half! So that without him near me, I am diminished.''

"Magic? He called you a witch. Are you—?"

Her hands stole up to cradle his face. Waves of sweet coolness stole across his senses, and the world wavered like a candle flame. "Will that change what you feel for me? Will you not do what I think to ask? Will you be strong enough to part with a proof of love to equal mine?" Her lips brushed his, and all ties broke except the cord that tightened between those two. "Does what I am matter?"

"Where have you been? Thought you got killed." Malfora sounded pretty cheerful about it. She'd passed a warm night wrapped in both Scarron's blanket and her own. "When I came back, I had to pay off the guard you hired, so you better give me more pocket coin today. What a waste of money! He said he didn't see or hear a thing." She stretched the ground kinks out of her bones. By the dawn light she saw her brother leaning his back against a wagon wheel, staring at something in his lap. "What you got there?"

"Carving." He mumbled the word so badly that she made him repeat. "Open the stall yourself today; you know how." He took out his knife and breathed a prayer over the blade.

Malfora stole peeks at his work while she set up their wares. "That's not wood," she said. "What is it?" She got no answer. "Want something to catch the chips? Maybe I can sell them later—"

"There won't be any chips."

"You're loony. There's always chips from carving, even when you bought that piss-dear black wood for . . . Say, there's only six of those fancy bowls here. We sell one yesterday after I went to change?"

If Scarron intended to reply, he never got the chance. The early-rising merchants who shared that part of the fair heard a rumor of commotion issue from the temple guest house, rumble through the paths, and burst like a spring freshet before the candlemaker's stall. It was a party of twelve nobles, the lady Demaris and her nurse among them. The lady wept and groaned, her nurse only wept. The others in the party—lords and ladies both—took turns shouting for Siluia and telling the weepers to shut up.

"Yes? May I help you?" Siluia emerged and spied Demaris, still holding yesterday's candle, still lit. Two flames burned from one wick: great, small. The candlemaker nodded.

"What's all this witchery you've sold my daughter?" Lady Demaris's mother got right to the point, thrusting the men of her house aside. "She came home from her fairing, went to her chamber, and came shrieking out a moment later with *this*." She flicked her hand at the candle. "Why's it got her in hysterics, eh? And why in the names of the Three can't anyone *extinguish* the cursed thing?"

The formidable matron puffed at the double glow several times, then wet her fingers with spit and pinched it to drive home the point. The candle burned on, even when a dipperful of water was emptied over it. The gathering crowd muttered, eyeing the soft-spoken candlemaker.

"My lady, that will be for your daughter to say."

"None of your sauce. We've got laws at Ithkar Fair against evil sorceries, but if you'll make amends, we'll mention no more about it."

Siluia lowered her lashes. "My lady, I sold your daughter nothing, as witnesses will tell you. No coins changed hands.

That double flame was of her own kindling, and she must live with its light. But you see, a candle hates the darkness, and lies hate light. Bring truth to light and the candle may be extinguished.''

"Truth! What truth?''

"Your daughter . . .''

"Oh, Mama, forgive me!'' Demaris tore herself away from her dithering nurse and hurtled into her mother's arms, pouring out a story whose juicier bits involved a certain maidenly error committed two months past. Her partner in misstep had been one of a troupe of wandering players. True to type, he had wandered farther off, but no sense in criticizing a young girl's fancy after the fact. Demaris knew soon enough that she'd need more than regret; a husband might be nice, for the child's sake. A husband, but one worthy of her station, and since Lord Yevri fancied her . . . and fancied himself an honorable man. . . . At least her player-lover had taught Demaris some rudiments of acting before he vanished.

As she ended her story, a tear fell on the telltale candle. The double flame winked out. Lady Demaris sobbed wildly and hid her face in her mother's bosom.

The hoots and merriment of the mob rose in proportion to the discomfiture of Demaris's relatives. Feeling murderous, unable to turn her wrath on her own miserable child, the lady's mother lashed out elsewhere. "Lies! Sorcery! Summon the fair-wards! You'll pay for this insult, my girl!''

"Scarron! Scarron! Why are you hiding under there? Come out! They're calling for the wards! They're going to do something terrible to Siluia! *Scarron!*'' Malfora was jumping up and down on the wagon, making the wheels creak. Her brother only grunted and moved away, so that the jouncing wouldn't jar his arm.

The fair-wards were coming. One might assume they came in answer to the summons of Demaris's mother, but too many of the brass helmets gleamed together for that to be so, and a temple priest led them.

(In his place under the wagon, a skilled carver made a few final touches. Sleeplessness made him incautious, and he touched the knife itself. He cried in pain, cursed, sucked his fingers before finishing his masterwork. He had only touched the smooth flat of the blade, not the cutting edge. He cried out from burning, not cutting, pain.)

"My lord priest, this sorceress has worked a magic of slander—" Demaris's mother tried to make herself heard above her daughter's wails, to say nothing of the loud guffaws and crude remarks coming from the crowd.

"Enough." Evro held up his hand. "She'll come with us. Lord Father Demetrios has some questions to put to her before judgment. Take her."

The fair-wards moved forward to obey. They sought to herd her out of her stall between their lines, using their bronze-bound rods for that rough shepherding. The candle-maker fixed her eyes on the ground.

"You will not take me, Evro. As you would not take me for your lady and your bride, you will not take me for your prisoner."

(A youth in a green tunic crawled out from under a wagon, unnoticed. Shouldering his lanky body through the crowd, he soon stood in the foremost rank. There was a silver ring on his finger. He had given all the magic that would ever be his to weave a binding on that ring. That much she had taught him. In his arms he cradled something shaped like an elfin babe, shrouded in cloth of green and silver.)

The wards balked. The woman was one, and weak, but her voice held them away. Evro made an impatient sound in his throat. "Will you take her!"

"No," said Scarron. The ring was in one hand, the veiled thing in the other. A cold wind stabbed into the heart of the crowd and whipped away the shrouding so that afterward no one could recall that the boy had spoken, only that he held a work of perfection.

It was a bear, a monstrous white bear out of the north,

captured to the life in wax. Gently, swiftly, while the
people still stared and the unchipped wax was yet soft
enough, Scarron thrust the silver ring into the nostrils of the
beast.

He heard his sister's scream first, but she was too far
back in the crowd to have witnessed the change. Bronze-
bound rods scattered, merchants fled into the dubious shelter of their stalls, and idlers ran away shouting for protection.
But who would protect the protectors? The fair-wards were
the first to run yowling for help against the silver bear of
flesh and fur that reared up in Evro's place and bawled its
terror and confusion.

Light as a dancing flame, Siluia leaped to drag the beast
down by the silver nose ring. She swung up onto its back
and dug in her heels, drumming the bear to a gallop that
scattered every sensible soul from their path. The fair-wards
gaped, then remembered their duty. True, they remembered
it only after the bear had a healthy head start, but tardy
pursuit was better than none.

It was the wildest hue and cry Ithkar Fair had seen in
years. People of all callings spilled away from the charging
bear and his jubilant rider only to swarm back into the
swelling mob that followed the fair-wards. At the western
boundary palings the bear leaped over and cleared them
sweet as any stallion, but the wary hunters had to give up or
go around to the gates. Half the fair-wards called it quits
there, as did most of the civilians, but there were enough
diehards left to continue the chase.

Alas, these determined few dwindled, one by one falling
breathless by the way. By the time a mounted troop of
reinforcements cantered along the canal to the Western Road,
all they met was a scarlet-faced fair-ward and a grimy little
girl who had stopped to get a sharp pebble out from between
her toes.

"Don't bother." The fair-ward shed his brass helmet and
mopped his brow. "Long gone. That way." Going the way
he pointed, the leader of the mounted men soon reached the

river bank. Sweeping the terrain with his eyes, it took him several passes before he spotted the lad crouched on the brink. Green tunic, brown hair, the earth colors, and his perfect stillness hid him.

"Boy! A witch and a huge bear, did you see 'em? Did they cross over?"

Scarron watched the rushing waters. "They didn't make it across." His voice was hollow.

"Not surprised. In my old town, they said running water washes out most evils. Thanks, boy." He turned his steed's head and trotted away just as Malfora found her brother.

"No witch." When he spoke, he gave no sign that he knew his sister. He would have told the same tale to the first soul with ears to hear. "I threw the candle in after them, ring and all. He's hers again, and all her old powers with him."

Malfora began to cry. "She was so nice, and now she's drowned!"

"Drowned?" Still he watched the waves. "She can never drown, nor anyone in her keeping. The shape of magic she chose for him was her own idea. A bear, a fitting shape; after all, this is her river. But I had to work the shape's change in the wax that held them. She loved him, so she gave half her powers into the candle, binding them to one another. I had to carve without cutting, melt and mold the wax gently with a knife that burned. It was her life she gave me to reshape. If my hand had slipped . . ."

He shuddered, casting off a dream.

"We'd better get back. No one's watching our stall." He stood up and offered Malfora his hand. She took it reluctantly, leery of the strange emptiness she saw in his eyes. "Maybe the fat man's keeping a neighborly eye on our things." He tried to sound jovial, but a child's instinct was sharp as any knife to cut away a mask. The old Scarron was gone.

As they started east, Malfora glanced a last time at the swiftly flowing Bear River. Abruptly she pulled from

Scarron's clasp to point and cry: "Look there!" She danced on the grass in her excitement.

Something glowed on the bosom of the river. It bobbed and floated across the current's pull to beach itself in the grass at the foot of the river bank. He saw the light, burning with a truer flame than any marshbane torch, calling him. He slid down the bank and took it from the shallows. The waters of the Bear stroked his hand as he retrieved their offering: a bowl of cobwebbed night; a strand of pearls to trickle through Malfora's fingers; a single candle kindled to a star; a silver ring. A gift.

He slipped the ring back onto his finger. He had filled it with all the love he had to offer her, all the magic that would ever be his, and used that force to work the spell to save her. Love. He had poured all his heart's love willingly into her ring: love and all its changing power. He had emptied himself gladly, a beeswax comb drained dry of sweetness to be melted down and molded to the candlemaker's will. For her sake he had done it, but now she was whole again, needing the strength of no other. Her elemental sendings swirled incandescent out of the ring and flowed back into him. The world glowed more brightly than any candle.

Silently Scarron exulted in the miracle filling him. He scooped up his little sister and swung her around, the pearls trailing, Malfora shrieking with delight.

"They're worth a fortune," gasped the girl once he set her down again. She couldn't take her eyes from them. "Oh, Scarron, we're rich!"

"Rich enough for you to start acting like less of a fair-shrike when we get home? Come, Malfora. Not all the pearls in the river bed can keep off what those clouds are bringing."

A line of purple and gray came rolling up from the west. Brother and sister ran, but the storm was faster. The first pattering drops quenched the burning candle left behind on

the river bank and caught up with them just when they had
gained the safety of the palings.

Malfora gave a small mew of distress when the storm
broke, and all the merchants cursed the contrary weather
that drove off pilgrim buyers. But over the sound of curses
came joyful laughter. Scarron stood rooted in the rain, head
flung back, arms wide, letting it wash over him gladly.
People stared to see such a young witling, unable to know
that for him, every drop of water was a kiss, every line of
rain a thousand sweet caresses from the white hands of his
first, his best beloved.

Rain at Ithkar Fair.

DEMON LUCK

Craig Shaw Gardner

Gosha was truly the luckiest man in all the world. To be going to the Fair at Ithkar, ah, that was the sort of pleasure only found in dreams. And with what he had to sell, the finest fruits and vegetables in the entire Zoe Valley, could he leave the fair any less than a rich man?

The late summer sun beat down on his shoulders, warming them under his rough shirt. Small clouds of dust rose about the hooves of the horse that drew the wagon, and motes danced beneath Gosha's feet. The fields to either side of the road were full of butterflies, all yellow and orange, and every tree seemed to hold a bird that called to them as the merchant's wagon passed. Today the world smiled on Gosha, and Gosha smiled in return. What could be better?

"I agree entirely," said a voice close by Gosha's ear.

The merchant started and spun about. A small man, about four feet tall, sat next to him in the wagon. He was fairly well dressed, with quite a dazzling smile, made all the more so by the fact that both the man's clothing and skin were matching shades of blue.

"Close your mouth, please," the blue man said. "Gosha, this is your lucky day. And I am your good-luck demon."

Gosha turned away and looked at the road. The same

gray mare still pulled the wagon. The same yellow fields lined either side, filled with the same brilliant butterflies.

He looked to his right again. The blue man smiled.

"Good-luck demon?" Gosha asked.

The blue man nodded.

Now Gosha considered himself a pragmatic man. One had to be able to assess a situation and act quickly upon it if one was to be successful in the mercantile arts. Therefore, should one find oneself engaged in conversation with a small blue man, whether one believed this was really happening or not, one should attempt to get all the information one could. Therefore, Gosha said: "I thought demons generally brought bad luck."

The demon nodded gravely. "A popularly held misconception."

Gosha persisted: "But wouldn't I have heard of good-luck demons? In this hard world, a magical creature who brings good luck is almost too much to be believed."

"Exactly!" The demon grabbed Gosha's hand and pumped it vigorously. "Not only are you a lucky merchant, Gosha, but an extremely canny one as well. Lucky demons are one of the best-kept secrets in the realm. Let me phrase it thusly: If you were fortunate enough to have something like me to give you an edge over your fellow merchants, would you spread it around?"

Gosha shook his head slowly.

"But I'm being rude!" The demon grabbed Gosha's hand once again. "The name's Hotpoint. Pleased to make your acquaintance."

Hotpoint? Gosha supposed it was a fair name for a demon. That is, if he supposed anything at all. In a few short moments, he had gone from feeling one with the world into a state of total confusion. Gosha studied the short blue fellow at his side. What was the proper response to meeting a demon? The most proper one he could think of was to jump from the wagon and run screaming into the fields. But then what would happen to his fruit? And what about his son, fast asleep in the back of the wagon?

He hadn't given a thought to Lum since the demon's arrival. Nor had Lum taken any notice of what was happening. Not surprising; once the boy slept, it would take a hundred demons to rouse him. Perhaps, when the boy came round, he and Gosha could subdue Hotpoint. But what if the demon were truly what he said he was?

Hotpoint continued to talk as Gosha mulled over the problem. The demon commented on the beauty of the day, which he could appreciate despite the fact that, in his homeland, the standards were somewhat different. Hotpoint went on to praise Gosha's fruit at some length: the beautiful color, the absence of worms and bruises, the wonderful shapes, so round and succulent. Gosha began to worry about the size of the demon's appetite.

"Dear Gosha," the demon remarked, "instead of looking at me, you might do well to watch the road."

Gosha looked about to see a horse-drawn cart coming full gallop toward the wagon. The merchant reined in his own horse at once. "Whoa! Whoa!" cried the other driver. There was a substantial crash.

"Blight and war!" Gosha cursed as he jumped from his wagon. The collision had pushed the two right wheels into the ditch at the side of the road. The cart that had collided with the wagon sat next to it, minus both one wheel and its driver, who sat dazed in the ditch mud, surrounded by Gosha's fruit.

"What have you done?" Gosha cried. "Your carelessness has ruined half my goods! What will I sell in Ithkar?"

The other man groaned. He was short and stout, and, though he was dressed entirely in gray, Gosha could tell, from the cut of the clothes and the fine gold stitching, that the man's wardrobe had been produced by the finest tailors in Ithkar. The nerve of someone of his station being careless on the road!

The stout man looked up at Gosha. His eyes seemed to

have gotten crossed in the fall. There was something in his gaze, though, that made the merchant hesitate.

"Are you all right, sir?" Gosha said in a somewhat softer voice.

"Hm?" The other man uncrossed his eyes. "Yes, yes, never felt better." He rubbed at the mud covering his face. He succeeded more in distributing it rather than removing it. "K'shew's the name. I was hoping to be at Ithkar Fair myself this year until . . ." He paused and coughed. "Until something came up."

Gosha reached out a hand and helped the other man to his feet. "Something came up?" he prompted.

"Yes." K'shew smiled, then grimaced as he tried to walk. "I found I must perform an errand"—he paused again and looked up the road in the direction he had come—"of the utmost urgency!"

"But you've hurt yourself and your wagon. Surely you can rest a bit."

"No, no!" The stout fellow shook his head so violently that his hat fell off. He grabbed it in midair and jammed it across his bald pate. "Most urgent! Most urgent!"

K'shew turned to survey the damage to his cart. He cleared his throat, made three quick passes in the air, and said an extremely long word so rapidly that Gosha couldn't quite catch it. There was a flash of golden light. When Gosha opened his eyes, he saw that K'shew's cart was whole again.

Gosha took a step back. A magician! He should have realized that anyone with an apostrophe in his name had to be important. Now this was an entirely different matter. It was one thing to feel sorry for an addled old man who'd fallen in the mud, but magicians who have accidents should be fully prepared to pay for their mistakes. Gosha pointed to the produce on the ground.

"The fruit," he intoned.

"Yes, a pity." K'shew frowned. "If I hadn't been in such a tizzy . . . well, let's see. I could magically make it whole again. No, no, they don't like that sort of thing in Ithkar, do they? Wouldn't want to get you in bad with the temple people. I guess there's no helping it.''

Lum chose that moment to climb from the back of the wagon. He stretched his long legs and arms and jumped to the ground. With his skinny body and the yellow hair always in his eyes, he reminded his father of nothing so much as a rather untidy broom.

He yawned as he approached. "Has something happened?"

That was it. Gosha's wife might have badgered him into taking his youngest son along, but he would not suffer the adolescent gladly. "Something happen?" he screamed. "I've only been run into by a cart, spilling fruit all over the road! And that's besides gaining a so-called good-luck demon—'' His voice died in his throat. Should he have even mentioned Hotpoint? The magician stared at the wagon seat where Hotpoint sat.

"I don't necessarily know if the 'good luck' part is true," Gosha added rapidly. "We only have the demon's word.''

"I have no idea what you're talking about," the mage replied disdainfully. "Good-luck demons? The fall must have shaken you more severely than you realized.''

"Demons?" Lum pulled his hair from his eyes so he could look around. "Where? What do they look like? I don't see anything.''

"What do you mean?" Gosha sputtered. They had both looked right at Hotpoint. Unless—

Unless only he could see the demon!

The merchant groaned. "Oh, the fall was worse than I thought! My head is spinning! My produce is smashed to the ground, my livelihood destroyed.''

K'shew frowned. "Oh, come, come. I was about to give you something.'' He laughed and slapped his knee. "I have the very thing.'' He ran to his cart, suddenly spry. "This will take but a second, merchant. Then I must hurry, hurry off!''

He rummaged through the things piled high above the

cart for a moment, then gave a cry of discovery. "The very thing!" he repeated as he grunted and pulled and brought forth a bushel basket filled with apples. Nice-looking fruit, Gosha thought, good shape, good size, except that every apple was silver.

"I had intended to sell these at Ithkar Fair myself," K'shew said. "Now I don't know if I'll have the chance." He held the bushel out to Gosha. "A fair exchange, I think, for your damaged merchandise. I might also be able to arrange a prime location for you to set up your wagon, right next to the temple, for a small fee, of course." K'shew glanced back up the road. "Then again, I think it might be time I moved along."

Gosha was astonished. Before he could think of anything to say, the magician hopped back in his cart and spurred his horse to a gallop. Soon Gosha could see nothing but a dust cloud receding down the road.

He looked at the apples. They shone in the sunlight as if they had a light of their own. He inhaled their subtle fragrance, sweet yet tart. It made his mouth water. He wanted to hold one in his hand, to lift it to his mouth, to sink his teeth through that shining skin, to taste—

Gosha closed his eyes and turned away from the bushel. These apples weren't for eating, at least not by him. He was quite sure that, for every apple he consumed, an equal or greater amount of gold should never reach his pockets.

"Lum!" he called. "Salvage what you can from the ground, and find a place for these!"

He passed the bushel to his son. Lum struggled under the weight but finally managed to load the apples into the back of the wagon. Gosha smiled. Today even his misfortunes had happy conclusions. He may have exaggerated a bit when he had yelled at the magician; at most, perhaps, one-tenth of his produce was ruined. And how much more would he make by selling the silver apples? Truly, he was the luckiest man in all the world!

"Exactly as I predicted!" Hotpoint smiled at him. "With a good-luck demon at your side, how can you fail?"

Gosha frowned. Maybe the demon was right after all. It was hard to feel warmth for a creature whose clothes and skin were a matching blue, but Gosha at least climbed back into the seat next to him.

"Ah, those apples," Hotpoint said softly. "Each apple like a separate silver star. No one else in all Ithkar Fair will have their like. Now, friend Gosha, you have not only the finest produce from the Zoe Valley, but the most precious fruit in all the world. With goods like that, you hardly need luck at all."

Gosha allowed himself to smile at last. Maybe the demon was lucky after all. Perhaps he had entered a realm of good fortune so magnificent that it allowed the creature to appear. Perhaps he would be lucky from this day forward, the luckiest man in history.

It was then he saw the rider.

Hotpoint excused himself and hopped back into the wagon.

The horse and rider approached them from the direction the magician had come, moving twice as fast as the mage. The horse was jet black, a huge beast that, as fast as it was approaching, seemed to be moving more at a canter than a gallop. And if the beast was twice a horse, the man atop seemed double-sized as well. He wore robes as dark as the horse or darker, the color of a storm at night. But his face was the palest white, almost as if his skin were transparent and the color of the bone shone through. There seemed to be no noise but the horse's hooves, the sound of thunder rolling toward Gosha and his wagon.

The dark rider reined in his horse as he came abreast of the wagon, and then there was no noise at all. The rider stared at Gosha for a moment through the silence.

"Merchant!" the rider called, in a voice oddly slow and high, as if the large man seldom found a use for it. "Have you passed anyone else on this road?" The rider's eyes looked straight into Gosha's. The rider's eyes were the color of blood. Gosha's tongue felt dry in his mouth. He wanted to speak, but his lips would not part.

Lum jumped from the wagon's rear. "Yes, sir!" he cried. "A chubby gray fellow."

The rider smiled a death's-head grin. "Indeed. Did he say anything as he passed?"

Lum laughed. "He ran his cart right into our wagon."

"You must tell me more." The dark rider dismounted.

Gosha was horrified. He should have spoken up, insisted that no one had passed, and sent the rider on his way. But his idiot son had to feel talkative and prompt the rider to stay. Somehow, Gosha thought, the longer the rider stayed, the worse it would be for Lum and himself.

And where, perchance, was Hotpoint the good-luck demon? Gosha heard rustling noises from within the wagon at his back.

The dark rider approached. "Men call me N't'g'r'x."

Gosha's mouth dropped open again. Never had he heard a name with so many apostrophes. If K'shew, with only one apostrophe, had been a magician of some importance, what station must this dark rider hold? He shivered and cursed the day he learned spelling so that he might worry about such a thing.

"There is a demon here," N't'g'r'x whispered.

Gosha found his voice at last. He wasn't going to let anybody, even if he were to look like death itself, take his demon away. "Demons here?" He tried to laugh, but there was no conviction in it. "I am but a simple fruit merchant."

"So is the man who collided with your wagon," N't'g'r'x replied. "Or so he would like the fair-wards of Ithkar to believe."

K'shew a fruit merchant? Gosha shook his head in disbelief. Still, that would explain why he carried apples in his cart, even though the appples were silver. And he'd given the fruit to a competitor, with hardly any argument at all! Gosha wondered if all the merchants at Ithkar Fair were as just.

N't'g'r'x still watched him. Gosha marveled at just how much the dark rider did look like death itself. He cleared his throat. "K'shew said he was a magician."

N't'g'r'x waved the idea aside with one of his bony hands. "He brags about his demon line, but 'tis a minor piece of work. K'shew says many things. Did he give you anything?"

Gosha's heart sank. He would lose not only his good-luck demon, but his silver fruit as well. Perhaps he could deny receiving the apples from the mage, if only his son would stay quiet. Gosha shot a stern look in Lum's direction.

Lum saw Gosha's cautionary glare and nodded happily. "Yes, good sir," he said to N't'g'r'x. "For damaging our stock, the mage gave us a basket of silver apples."

"Silver apples?" The dark rider laughed, the sound of bones shaken in a coffin. "K'shew always was a rogue."

Gosha's heart fell lower still. Soon it should lodge in his foot. Why didn't his son just take the silver apples and give them to this rider?

"Wait a second," Lum said. "I'll get them for you."

Gosha cried out and fell back into the wagon. Perhaps his heart would pass from his body entirely, to fall among the apples and pears.

With his head atop the fruit, the merchant could hear the rustling sound again. Except, in the quiet of the wagon, it no longer sounded like rustling. It sounded like chewing.

"Hotpoint!" Gosha sat bolt upright. He dug furiously into the produce.

"Don't bother me when I've got my mouth full!" came the muffled reply from somewhere down at the end of the cart. A chill shook the length of Gosha's body. It was the end that held the silver apples.

And the apples drew the merchant's eye. They glowed, even here, away from the daylight. They shone so, he had to touch them and feel the smoothness of their skins. What would it be like to bite into one of them? Would the juice be warm and sweet, heated by the apple's glow?

Gosha could bear it no longer. A demon was destroying his goods, while outside a stranger who looked like death was engaged in animated conversation with his dullard son. What more did he have to live for? He would eat those silver apples, every one! Gosha hurled himself across the wagon, his mouth open to accept the fruit.

The fruit, however, seemed to be otherwise inclined. As Gosha skidded across the top of the produce mound, apples shifted, grapes squeezed, pears bounced, dates rolled. The wagon lurched as fruit pushed toward the rear with such force that Gosha heard the tearing of wood along the wagon's backboard. The board gave way, and he found himself lost in an avalanche.

He pushed himself free and found he was facing Hotpoint. The demon looked somewhat heavier than before. Hotpoint belched.

"I thought you were a good-luck demon!" Gosha cried.

"Ah," said Hotpoint happily. "But I did not mention good luck for whom!"

A dark shadow fell across both demon and merchant. Gosha turned to see N't'g'r'x. The dark man made four passes in the air, adding three noises that might have been words had they been spoken by anybody else.

Hotpoint disappeared.

Gosha yelped.

A skeletal hand appeared before his face.

"Let me help you up," N't'g'r'x intoned.

"Surely," replied Gosha. The man's grip was like ice.

"K'shew was a fruit merchant," N't'g'r'x answered the question in Gosha's eyes. "I am a wizard."

Gosha swallowed and instructed his son to pick up what fruit could be saved. He thought to ask another question. All he could manage was, "But why?"

"K'shew was not just a simple fruit-seller. For years, he has been the largest fruit merchant at Ithkar Fair, with twenty times the produce of other peddlers. Such a large discrepancy between businesses brought him to the attention of certain officials. We are very careful that everything remain honest at the fair. And K'shew's dealings seemed honest enough. But outside the fair''—the dark rider laughed—''you have seen a different story.''

"So he tried to cheat me?" Gosha asked.

"More than that. When you crossed the sorcerous line K'shew had managed to draw over almost every road leading to Ithkar, a demon appeared in your wagon, intent upon destroying your goods. But could K'shew stop there? No, he had to give you magic apples, and those silver apples smell of sorcery even from this distance. If you had shown up at the gate with either demons or apples, they would have turned you away for illegal sorcery, and you would never have been allowed to participate in the fair again."

N't'g'r'x intertwined his bony fingers. "K'shew is a compulsive thief. His type often is. They don't know when to stop, and end up giving themselves away. I'm surprised he did not rent you a prime spot in the marketplace, right next to the temple. And you'd find the spot all right, under several feet of water, in the middle of the river Ith." N't'g'r'x laughed long and hard. It was not a pleasant sound.

An even more horrible noise erupted behind them. Lum stood, staring with horror at the silver apple in his hand. There was a bite out of it.

"This is vile!" he cried. "It tastes like a cross between vinegar and spoiled meat!"

"In an hour," the rider said as he remounted his horse, "your son shall have a stomachache as well." He reached within the folds of his dark cloak and threw something at Gosha's feet. When it hit the ground, the merchant heard the chink of metal.

"For your information on K'shew," N't'g'r'x called. "I go to catch the villain." And off he rode, like a dark leaf blown by the wind.

Lum got the remaining fruit loaded and climbed into the wagon front next to Gosha. The merchant took his son's complaints with a paternal stoicism. Horse and wagon climbed a hill, and at its summit they saw a great city in the distance, full of colored banners and gray-green spires.

"Ithkar," Gosha proclaimed.

Other roads joined theirs as they went down the hill to the city, and they soon fell into a procession of other carts and wagons, all on their way to the fair. The one behind them clanked with metal goods; cooking smells came from the one before. Gosha breathed them deeply, once again relaxed. He would have to send Lum back to the valley somewhat sooner than he had planned to bring more goods, but what he had should still sell quickly, and the money the dark rider had given him would surely more than make up the difference.

It had been a long and rather eventful day. Gosha sighed as the sun dipped below the horizon, and the towers of the city became dark silhouettes framed by violet clouds. Truly, he thought, I am the luckiest man in the world.

A QUIET DAY AT THE FAIR

Sharon Green

Massan was bored. He leaned one wide shoulder against
a tent-post in the noonday sun, looked around without seeing
anything worth looking at, and folded his arms against even
greater boredom. There were certainly enough people visiting Ithkar Fair that year, as many as had been coming for
the past few years, if not more, but being halfway through
the second ten-day period seemed to have calmed them all.
Most of them had been there since the very beginning of the
fair, which meant they no longer rushed from booth to tent
to wagon to stand, to gulp the sight of what was being
offered. They now knew what was being offered and strolled
around taking longer second or third or tenth looks at whatever interested them. They also knew they had as much time
ahead of them as had already passed, so the burning need to
get their last looks in hadn't come yet, either. Even the
usual troublemakers seemed to have taken time off—or
were staying out of Massan's way. If it were the latter, it
proved the wisdom in hiring him that fair, but Massan had
no interest just then in wisdom. With bronze-circled wrists
hidden beneath folded arms, he looked slowly around at
boredom and yawned.

"Hai, Massan, how goes it?" came a rough voice, an-

73

nouncing the approach of Trig through the easy crowd. The
fair-ward was large and as rough as his voice, his brass
helmet and bronze-bound quarterstaff adding to the imposing sight, yet he made no attempt to clap hand to the other
man's shoulder. Massan didn't care for overfamiliarity and
wasn't one to oppose even though he stood supposedly
unarmed. Thank the Three Lordly Ones he had been made a
ward captain this fair!

"It goes slowly, Trig," Massan returned, his gray eyes
continuing their movement, his deep voice as easy as the
crowd—and as potentially dangerous. "P'raps next year I'll
return to merely visiting."

"Naw, Massan, it'll grow brisk again, you'll see," Trig
comforted, the sudden sweat on him having little to do with
the warmth of the sun. For four years Massan had taken to
appearing at the fair to either sell his sword or raise a
company, and that was the first fair there wasn't trouble
because of it. Every fighter on the continent seemed to have
heard of Massan, and too many of them were damned fools
who thought they could face him down without the great,
sleek sword he surrendered at the gates without argument. If
they came at him one at a time they ended no more than
beaten to a pulp, but if they tried ganging—

"Say, Massan, you heard the latest?" Trig said with
sudden brightening, his ugly face grinning as it looked up to
the still moving gray eyes. "There's a reward been offered,
and even fair-wards can claim it. How 'bout *that*?"

"A reward for what?" asked Massan, chuckling inwardly
at Trig's eagerness to distract him. The fair-ward was rough
and almost completely unlettered—but he wasn't a fool.

"This lordling's daughter run off," returned Trig, sharing the news with a guffaw. "Don't want to do his bidding,
she don't, so she up and run off. She's about the fair
somewhere, they say, 'cause the gate wizards say she ain't
passed through. Man who brings her back gets to claim the
reward."

"Even if he's a fair-ward?" Massan asked, finally bringing those eyes to rest on Trig. "How dangerous is she supposed to be?"

"Dunno, but I don't much care," said Trig, his grin still strong as he raised his bronze-bound quarterstaff. "Got this to beat her off with, and somethin' else case I don't care to beat her off. Maybe she was just lonely and come out lookin' for company. A man keeps his eyes open, maybe he gets two rewards."

"She's probably fat and ugly with the temper of a faxit," Massan said with a grin for the other man's overoptimism. "Like as not we'll have to charge her with attacking *you*. If I hear you screaming, I'll come as fast as I can."

"If it ain't me doin' the screaming, just wander around a little first," Trig guffawed, his hopes refusing to be dashed. "See you later."

Massan nodded as the other man turned away to move slowly off into the crowd, watching Trig look the throng over. He hadn't asked how they were supposed to recognize the runaway, as it was highly unlikely that they would find her unless she brought herself to their attention—assuming the story was true. Something about it didn't sound quite right, something Massan couldn't put his finger on—

And then he straightened away from the post he had been leaning on, unfolding his arms as his eyes narrowed. Trig, watching the people all about rather than where he was going, had had a small collision. The incident was unusual enough to make the fair-ward surprised rather than angry; no one jostled fair-wards on purpose, and rarely even by accident.

"Steady, boy," Trig said to the medium-sized youth who had blundered into him, one wide hand on a thinly muscled arm to steady the boy who had almost fallen at the unexpected contact. "You go around attacking fair-wards like that, you'll end taken up and outlawed."

"No, sir, sorry, sir, din't mean t' bump you, sir," said the youth in a high, thin, frightened voice, bowing furi-

ously. "First day at the fair, sir, an' I din't know which
way to look first. Din't mean t'—"

"Calm down, boy, no harm done," Trig interrupted the
flow of words, already beginning to look around again.
"Just take your time an' you'll see it all, without runnin'
folk down."

"Yes, sir, I'll sure do that, sir," the boy babbled, already
backing away from the big man he'd collided with, still
bobbing and bowing. "Din't mean t' break the law, sir. . . ."

But the fair-ward wasn't listening any longer, nor was he
still there. He was moving off through the respectfully
parting crowd and was quickly swallowed up by them. The
youth tugged his loose, ill-fitting coat straight, brushed once
at dark trousers that had seen much better days, then turned
to move off in the direction opposite to that taken by the
fair-ward, his long, stringy black hair hanging down almost
into his eyes. Massan let the youth start to move past him,
then reached out and hauled the thin figure back by the
scruff.

"Oh!" exclaimed the figure in outrage, no longer sounding frightened, immediately beginning to struggle. "Take
your hands off me, you—"

"Ward captain," Massan supplied, looking down with
amusement into eyes as gray as his own—but considerably
wider. "Couldn't you find silver wherever you stole those
clothes from?"

"I don't know what you're talking about," his captive
insisted, trying to swallow annoyed anger, still pulling against
the wide fist holding coat and shirt collars. "These clothes
are mine. Let me go or I'll report you to the fair-court!"

"When you make the report, don't forget to mention
Trig's purse," Massan returned with a grin, enjoying the
audacity of his prisoner. "I doubt it has much more than a
few coppers in it, but it's easier taking a fair-ward's purse
than someone else's, isn't it? No one has the nerve to do
that to a fair-ward, so there's no suspicion even after it's

done. You should have thought to take a few pieces of silver before running away from your father.''

The wide gray eyes looking up at him so belligerently suddenly turned furious and desperate, and the knee came out of nowhere, slamming into him with more strength than he had been expecting. He'd been a fighter long enough to be braced and somewhat turned away against exactly that kind of attack, so it was surprise more than anything else that loosened his grip as he grunted at the jarring blow. His prisoner immediately tore free and turned to run, but the even more immediate kick he launched into the seat of those old black trousers sent her stumbling and sprawling into the nearly dry mud. The nearest fair visitors exclaimed in surprise over the brief scuffle, looked from Massan to the sprawled figure on the ground, then shook their heads as they continued on about their business. One had to be either a fool or a villain to challenge a ward captain who looked like that one, and they had no sympathy for whichever of the two the sprawled figure was.

Massan took his time walking to where the girl lay on the ground, knowing she'd hit hard enough to keep her from running anywhere for a while. It never failed to amuse him when people mistook female for male—or when female tried to pretend to be male. A fighter learned to watch and anticipate the movements of his opponents, and anyone who thought men and women didn't move differently had never faced them both over a sword. Massan had, and had learned from the doing, and knew that difference even when a sword wasn't involved. He reached down and pulled the girl back to her feet by the same collars she'd managed to free for so short a time, and she looked up at him in disgust.

"All right, what will you take to let me go?" she demanded, wincing slightly as she rubbed at the trouser seat his boot had caught. "Since you already know I'm somewhat short of funds, there's no sense in being unreasonable. If you want a cut of whatever else I pick up this afternoon, it's yours."

"Have you always been able to buy whatever you want?" Massan asked, even more amused than he had been. The girl's face and hands were dirty, her raggedy clothes were mud-stained and rumpled, and he could see she still felt where the ground had slammed into her; despite all that she wasn't beaten and wasn't even avoiding his eyes. He'd faced talented fighters who didn't have her heart and was glad he hadn't missed coming across her.

"I've usually been able to buy what I want," she agreed with an unashamed nod. "Not always, but usually. Is it a deal?"

"No," he answered with a grin, tightening his grip as she immediately began struggling again. "There's a reward out for your return, and even if there weren't, I'd do it anyway. Someone's got to protect the fair-wards from you."

"A reward!" she hissed, still trying to fight the grip on her collar. "I should have known he'd do something like that! You can't take me back!"

"Can and will," he corrected, looking around to see exactly where they were among the food-selling tents and stalls. "And if you don't get greeted with a good whipping, I'll see the fair-court takes care of it. It's time you learned you can't help yourself to whatever you like, even if you are willing to take risks most others aren't. Is your father in the guest house, or has he a pavilion?"

"Don't be a bigger fool than you are!" she snapped, now beating at his chest with two small fists that nevertheless made themselves felt. "You know nothing about this, and if you're wise, you'll keep it that way! Let me go, and I won't ever tell anyone you stopped me."

"I find it increasingly more difficult to refuse your unparalleled offers," Massan said with the chuckle he was feeling. "I think I'd better get you back to your father before the temptation overwhelms me."

"No, wait!" she said, and this time the desperation in her voice took his attention. He looked down at her to see those wide gray eyes staring at him with smoldering anger, an anger that was being thrust aside by the desperation. "All right, if I haven't offered enough to suit you, there's only one thing left. Find us a quiet corner, and you'll get your reward without taking me anywhere else."

This time the wide gray eyes seemed to want to avoid his, but the girl refused to allow that. She stared at Massan almost in challenge, and for a moment he was tempted to teach her a good lesson. Taking the ride she offered wouldn't mean he couldn't return her to her father afterward, an obvious point she was naively overlooking. If he hadn't sworn himself to uphold the fair-laws that year, he would have done exactly that; but he *had* sworn, which meant someone else would have to teach his overbold prisoner the ways of the real world.

"I'm afraid you've formed some rather strange opinions about rewards," he told her at last, his tone going very dry. "My tastes don't run to boys. We'll go this way."

She squawked wordlessly as he hauled her along with him by the scruff, but the noise sounded more like deep indignation to Massan than fear. He swallowed another grin as he wondered what could be awaiting her that she was trying so hard to avoid, and he hoped it *was* a whipping. Some lordlings held their daughters with a very tight rein, but somehow he didn't think this girl had been held that way. She needed some small amount of taming to make it safe for a man to turn his back on her, and then she'd be exactly right. If Massan didn't go on to think about right for what, that was only because he was a practical man, and practical men didn't picture fighters paired with lordlings' daughters.

The walk to the temple outskirts didn't take very long, even with the girl fighting every step of the way. People turned from booths and stalls to stare at them as they passed, most amused at the stream of invective the girl screamed at him. Her insults and imprecations were pointed without being foul-mouthed or obscene, and if Massan hadn't been who and what he was, there would have been a good deal of laughter at his expense. She was clever all right, Massan admitted, more than a little amused himself. She'd even tried appealing to a foursome of smiths just about to enter a grog shop, shouting to them that the lout holding her intended taking her somewhere deserted to rape her. The four were just about to come to her rescue when they saw the bronze wristbands Massan wore, a less obvious sign of office than the brass helmets and bronze-banded quarter-staves carried by fair-wards, but one they recognized just in time. Massan had been a breath short of turning the girl loose in order to defend himself from the four, and if he had, he would have then had to chase her through the crowds. The girl was lucky she hadn't caused him that, Massan thought as he steered her toward a temple official. His amusement would have been a good deal less under those circumstances, and she wouldn't have had to wait to be returned to her father before she got that whipping.

The temple official knew all about the runaway girl and the reward offered for her, and he directed Massan to her father's pavilion. The pavilion was very large and shone golden in the sunlight, and once Massan had the girl through the front entrance, her struggles ceased abruptly. She was hot and sweaty and tired from trying to fight against a man his size, but the gray eyes that came to him had lost none of their fire.

"The only good part about this is that you'll surely regret being such a fool," she said, her voice showing her disgust. "If you'd had the good sense to accept one of my offers, or even to ask me why he wanted me back here—"

"Well, well, sir, I see you've found her," interrupted another voice, and Massan looked up to see a tall man in richly jeweled robes smiling at him, a servant standing quietly behind. "I certainly hope she hasn't caused you undue difficulty."

"No difficulty," Massan said, trying to decide if the man were showing a smile of relief or a grin of amusement. "This hellcat is yours, then."

"She certainly is," said the man, and this time there was no doubt about it being a grin. "You have my thanks, sir, and soon will have my reward. Will you join me first in a cup of wine?"

"I could use one," Massan said with a nod, then pulled forward the girl he hadn't yet released. "There are one or two things to be discussed about this one, and she may yet have to be taken before the fair-court."

"For shame, Indelee, have you behaved so badly, then?" the tall man said to the girl, definite amusement behind the scolding. "To be in danger of being brought before the fair-court! And yet, the ward captain seems a reasonable man. Perhaps he'll be good enough to suggest something to keep that from happening."

"You're scarcely as amusing as you think you are, Rothaz," the girl answered, her voice even despite the slight flush to her cheeks. "I tried and I failed, and now I'd like a bath."

"Certainly, my dear." The man called Rothaz chuckled, gesturing to the servant behind him. "By all means make yourself more presentable while the ward captain and I talk."

The servant stepped away from the tall man and reached to pull open a golden curtain before he looked at Massan's prisoner; the girl herself merely stepped away from the hold she hadn't been able to escape till then and walked through the opening in the curtain without a backward look. Massan had found a good deal more reluctance for releasing her than he had expected, and he stood staring at the curtain even after the servant disappeared through it behind her.

"It's quite safe to leave her now, I assure you." Rothaz's voice distracted Massan, drawing the ward captain's eyes. "She won't find it possible to run again, and will rejoin us in a few moments. Will you come this way?"

With a gesture Rothaz led off to the left, through a silver-threaded curtain, one of three along the golden curtains of the pavilion entrance. The man had dark hair streaked somewhat with gray, but his face was unlined, and he moved as a much younger man might. Massan followed him into a comfortably furnished room of couches and cushions, tables and trays, candles and cups. Again silver and gold were the predominating colors, and when Massan was handed a gold-bound glass goblet containing light, silvery wine, he was scarcely surprised.

"Please sit down," Rothaz said with a pleasant smile, gesturing to a silver-silked couch behind Massan. Massan glanced at the couch and then sat, unworried over what his leathers would do to the delicate silk fabric. His boots had already left marks on the priceless carpeting that was untouched by Rothaz's soft slippers, but that didn't bother him, either. If people wanted to surround themselves with flimsies a man must hesitate to breathe on, that was their business.

"I'm pleased you haven't attempted to refuse my reward," Rothaz said as he took a seat of his own on a golden couch. "Indelee is quite a handful, but she *is* all I've got, and I'm most gratified to have her back. You *will* accept the reward?"

Massan smiled faintly as he tasted his silver wine, finding it much more full-bodied than he had expected. This new talk of reward made him think how much of a fool he'd been to refuse the last one offered him, but that was long-gone water under the bridge.

"As it's not against fair-law, I'll be glad to accept your reward," he said to Rothaz, seeing the immediate delight on the other man's face. "I'm curious as to what the girl was running from. An unwanted marriage, perhaps?"

"Oh, the wedding won't take place till midwinter at the earliest, when her suitors bring me the bride-price," Rothaz said with a negligent wave of his hand. "She has refused the lot of them, of course, but that makes no nevermind. No, this time she was trying to avoid a stroll through the fair."

"Why would she run away to avoid a stroll through the

fair?'' Massan began with a frown, but he was interrupted
by the appearance of a newcomer. A young woman stepped
through the curtains, one who was medium tall and held
herself with the relaxed but burning strength of a chained
fighter. Her silver gown clung to the lush curves of her
body, whispering a promise to show them more clearly,
then laughingly breaking the promise. Her long black hair
was brushed full and gleaming, surrounding a high-cheek-
boned face of unadorned beauty, and wide gray eyes smol-
dered in that face. Massan found himself on his feet without
remembering how he got there, realizing at last that this was
Indelee, the dirty, scruffy, smudged, runaway girl he had
just returned. The sight of her took him so hard, it never
came to him that the short amount of time that had passed
should not have been enough to have wrought such a change.

"Indelee, my dear, how good of you to join us," Rothaz
exclaimed in new delight, also rising from his couch. "You
will drink with us, of course."

"I have no interest in drinking with you," the girl answered immediately, showing Massan that not everything
about her had changed. "Just get on with it."

"Always in such a hurry," Rothaz sighed with a shake of
his head, the grin firmly back on his face. "As Captain
Massan will accompany you, why don't you join him on his
couch?"

"So he accepted," the girl said with disgust, giving
Massan a matching look as she began moving toward him.
"I knew he was a fool."

"I've had about enough of that from you," Massan said
with a growl, his annoyance helping him to throw off what
the look of her did to him. He moved his eyes to Rothaz. "I
think you'd better start explaining what's going on here.
How did you know my name?"

"Your fame has spread wider than you realize, Captain,"
Rothaz said with a gesture of his goblet. "And also the
reason for your having been made ward captain this fair.
What else were they to do with a man who cannot be

disarmed? Bar him from the fair? Not when so many of his former employers are so wealthy and also attending the fair. Convict him for doing violence? Not when that violence is done only in self-defense, with all witnesses willing to swear to that. Bind him magically? How, when not one mage at the fair is able to reach the dagger that always comes to him in his need? Where that dagger rests when not in his hand is an unanswered question, most especially as it has been known to appear even when he has been stripped naked and thoroughly searched. The most potent spell used has not been able to keep it from him, and the fair officials were at their wits' end; therefore was he made a ward captain, to discourage attacks on him during the fair. That . . . talent of yours should come in handy, Captain.''

"For what?" Massan growled, even more annoyed than he had been. "If you're thinking of hiring me, I'm not interested.''

"But you've already accepted, my dear Captain." Rothaz laughed, really amused. "The reward you accepted was the honor to strive on my behalf, and that you will do. You will accompany Indelee on a stroll through the fair, and then you will return here. Should you find any—eye-catching mementos—on the way, you will bring them back with you. Stay alert, Captain, for Indelee's sake if not your own.''

Massan, his annoyance having strengthened to anger, parted his lips to call Rothaz mad—but the words never came. One of the tall man's hands raised to a golden square on his robe, only one jeweled decoration among many Massan had thought, and another rose before him to gesture in a way Massan had seen before. The big ward captain had time to note that Rothaz still held his goblet in what seemed to be a third hand, and then the pavilion and all within it melted away.

"Well, what are you waiting for?" a voice demanded, coming somewhere from his right. "Since we have no choice about doing this, let's get on with it."

Massan heard her, but he was too busy staring around at the open, empty plain they stood on to answer immediately. It seemed as though he could see for miles, but there was nothing in those miles to see.

"I thought we were going for a stroll through the fair," he remarked after a long moment, still looking around. "Are we supposed to wait until it's built?"

"We *are* in the middle of the fair," the girl answered with impatience. "Here, I'll show you."

A small hand touched his arm with no hesitation in the grip, and suddenly they *were* in the middle of the fair! To be more accurate, they were still inside the temple gate, not far from the pavilion Massan had been directed to. He could even see the temple official who had given him those directions, refusing to listen to someone begging his attention. The woman put her hands out in supplication, her voice rising in a piteous sob—and then she and everyone and everything were gone, nothing but the plain to be seen. The hand was gone from his arm as well, but the girl was still there.

"We'll have to keep moving if we expect to reach camp before dark," she said, and Massan finally looked down at her to see that she stared off into the distance, in the direction they were both facing. "It isn't an easy trek, but you can make it if you pretend you're dragging me along by the collar. The last time you just about ran."

She started off without waiting for an answer, but Massan had had more than enough. He reached out with the speed that had kept him alive so long, took a split second to realize there was no longer a collar to hold to, then settled for the long, soft black hair. The girl yelped as she was dragged back, and then stood glaring up at him with a look he was beginning to find too familiar.

"What in the name of the Three Lordly Ones is going on?" he demanded, his anger putting a growl into his voice. "Who are you, and what is this place? How can the fair be here one minute and gone the next? Who is Rothaz, and what does he want? And why should it take almost until dark before we reach a place to camp?''

"If I answer all those questions now, we won't get to the camp until after dark," the girl maintained, ignoring the fist in her hair. "After sundown it rains here, and the temperature drops lower than a snake spell. I had to find that out the hard way, and if you want to do the same, be my guest. Just don't expect me to let you forget the choice was yours."

Massan stared down at her for a long moment, then felt the grin trying to crease his face. No, she wasn't one to forget things, especially if they made her wet and cold. Women had never given him exactly that sort of a warning before; it was the sort of thing they gave a man without warning.

"All right, I'll wait until we get to camp," he agreed, letting her hair go. "But not a minute longer."

"I knew I could count on your self-control," she answered, shaking her head to rid herself of the lingering feel of his fist in her hair. "For the second time."

The wide gray eyes barely glanced at him as she took herself off again, and this time Massan didn't try to stop her. He simply followed along across the plains, grinning his grin at her moving back.

They walked for hours through nothing but tall grass waving at an empty sky, the lowering sun and their mounting weariness the only indications that time was passing. Massan was glad his boots were well broken in and only then noticed that the girl was also wearing boots, but silver ones. Somehow they went well with her silver gown, and thoughts about the contents of that gown occupied him for the next few miles. He was diverted from those thoughts when a pile of something indistinguishable appeared in the grass far ahead, which eventually proved to be a small silver silk tent folded atop tent-posts and a small number of well-stuffed leather pouches. Massan put the tent up while the girl looked through the pouches, then watched while she carried three of them into the tent. The sky was darkening with more than the approach of evening by then, a cold wind blowing away the last warmth of the day. Massan followed her inside just as the first raindrops began spattering, and the girl shivered as she left the pouches to close the tent-flap, then went to light a small lantern that hung at the side of the tent.

"That's all there is that's fit to eat right now," she said, turning from the lantern to gesture toward the largest of the three pouches. "The rest is raw, and cooking after dark becomes impractical here. If it isn't enough, you can console yourself with that wine."

Her second gesture was directed at one of the smaller pouches lying to the right of the biggest, and Massan went over to crouch near it. Picking it up proved it to be a wineskin, so he settled himself on the tent floor, opened it, and took a long pull. That it was that full-bodied silver wine didn't surprise him, and when he lowered the skin he looked at the girl.

"I think it's safe to say we're in camp," he observed, watching her pull a sauced oblong of barbecued meat from the largest pouch before sitting back on the tent floor. "Do you need those questions repeated, or do you remember them?"

"I remember them," she said around a mouthful of meat, pausing briefly to lick two of her fingers. "I'm Indelee, I have no real idea what this place is or how we can be moving through here and the fair both at the same time, Rothaz is my stepfather and a wizard, and what he wants is beyond my knowledge. I'll know it when we come across it, though, in the same way I can see this place and the fair, both at the same time. Why it took so long to get here is something else I don't know, but I do know the same amount of ground wasn't covered at the fair. We're barely beyond the temple perimeter right now, just past the money-changers and artisans and a short way into the wineshops and food stalls. If we weren't, we wouldn't be eating and drinking this."

"I can understand now why you didn't want to take all that time explaining things when I first asked," Massan said, his tone a good deal drier than the now rain-drenched ground outside the tent. "You had to save your breath for the walk."

"That walk calmed you down," the girl said, paying more attention to the meat in her hands than to Massan. "If I'd said the same thing back when you first asked, you never would have accepted it. I was supposed to make this walk alone, but Rothaz is punishing me for running away from him. He was hoping you'd get angry enough to beat me."

"It could still happen," Massan answered, his annoyance rising over the fact that she apparently couldn't even be bothered with looking at him. "If that's the only reason I'm here, let's get to it so I can go back."

"That was *one* of the reasons you're here," she answered, still not looking at him but this time likely because of the faint flush in her cheeks. "The other one is that Rothaz has heard of you, and is trying to get you committed to searching for him. If you survive this walk, he expects to have you netted."

"Does he," Massan said, leaning back slightly where he sat. "Why should surviving a walk be so difficult, and what would I be searching for?"

"Tomorrow's walk won't be like today's," the girl said, spilling some water out of the skin at her knee onto her hands before wiping her fingers on a silken cloth. "What you would be searching for would be more of those—things— Rothaz wants so badly, ones whose locations haven't already been found by previous searchers. All we have to do with the one we're after is retrieve it."

She rose gracefully to her feet then and turned completely away from him, something that pushed Massan over the edge. There was something she wasn't saying, something that still didn't make sense. Without thinking about it, he was up nearly as fast as she was, and then his big hand was closing on a slender, silver-gowned arm.

"And why would risking my neck commit me to Rothaz?" he demanded, trying to ignore what touching that warm, slender arm was beginning to make him feel. "Why would he think something like that would net me for him?"

"He—expects you to come to want *me*," she answered with vast reluctance, staring at the faintly illuminated tent wall, her hands held in front of her. "That's what he used to get the others, to make them willing searchers. He's promised to choose among them by midwinter, but I don't care if he does. The next time I get away from him, I'll stay free no matter what I have to do. So now that you know the truth, you'll be able to show him you're not as great a fool as he thinks you are. As soon as we get back you'll turn around and walk away, instead of enslaving yourself to a wizard for nothing."

"For nothing," he muttered, reluctantly opening his fingers. As soon as the girl was free she went to the tent wall she'd been staring at and lay down, obviously preparing herself for sleep. Massan stood in complete silence for a minute, staring at her unmoving form, then turned and went back to the wineskin he'd left. Later he would eat something, but right then he wanted that wineskin.

The night was a long one for Massan, and by the time dawn came he was more than ready to get up. He and the girl shared what was left of the food and water, then they continued on in the same direction they'd been going the day before. The girl said not a single word to him, and he decided not to press the point.

The ground remained damp until midday, but that and sore feet were the worst they risked—until the girl suddenly gasped. Immediately thereafter there was a beast in their path, a kind of beast Massan had never before seen. All fur and claws and glaring red eyes it was, and it seemed to be in the midst of attacking even as it materialized. Massan pushed the girl out of its path and the next instant found the beast's front paws locked around him, ravening fangs intent on tearing off his face. His big hands went to the thing's throat almost as fast, and the cords stood out in his arms and shoulders and neck as he fought to keep those slavering jaws away from his face. He breathed in the reek of the thing's breath, a mixture of long-dead meat and freshly spilled blood, and then the thing's hug was crushing him, forcing the air out of his lungs and replacing it with pain. He grunted with that pain even as he braced his left arm to hold that thick, furry neck and head at bay, intent on doing it just long enough to free his right hand for an instant. He strained and shifted, refusing to feel the pain, and then the hand he had freed was no longer empty. A great silver-and-ruby dagger shimmered to life in his fist, and the next minute it was under the thing's throat and flashing upward, to rise through the thing's mouth and slash its way into whatever brain lurked behind the maddened red eyes. Blood spurted, and the thing screamed, the first sound Massan had heard it make, and then it was gone as abruptly as it had appeared, taking the wash of its blood and the stench of its breath with it. Massan staggered with the abrupt release and was down on one knee before he could catch himself.

"Are you all right?" the girl demanded, hurrying over to put a hand on his shoulder. "Did it hurt you?"

Massan let his head hang as he drew fresh air into his lungs, left hand to right ribs where they felt crushed, not yet up to answering. The pain in his chest eased with every breath he took, showing him that none of his ribs really had been cracked. Sweat rolled down his forehead into his eyes, making them sting, forcing him to bring his right forearm up to wipe at the stream. The silver-and-ruby dagger was gone again, returned to its sheath until he needed it the next time, and only after he had made sure of that did he look up at the girl.

"What in the name of Thotharn's deepest hell was *that*?" he asked with all the strength he could muster, this time taking over the job of glaring. "And if your vast storehouse of knowledge can handle it, I'd also like to know where it came from."

"I don't know what it was," the girl admitted with a flush to her cheeks, her wide gray eyes showing embarrassment. "Where it came from is something else I don't know, but it was caused to be here by the presence of an animal trainer walking one of his animals around the fair. I saw the two of them just before the thing attacked; I knew what would happen, but there wasn't time enough to warn you."

"All morning wasn't time enough?" Massan demanded, pushing himself to his feet. "Or are you simply that fond of giving people surprises? And how were you supposed to survive making this—stroll—alone?"

"I couldn't tell you about it," she answered as she looked up at him, a bitterness now in those eyes. "Just the way I couldn't tell you why you were a fool to take me back to Rothaz and claim his reward. I may have found a way to run from him, but there are certain of his spells I can't get around. If you still don't like the idea, why don't you try giving me that beating Rothaz expects me to get? Go ahead, just try it!"

She stood glaring up at Massan with her fists on her hips, her eyes and expression daring him to try. In spite of himself Massan felt that grin come back, but all he did was move his hand to his ribs again.

"I'll have to owe it to you," he said, wincing at the soreness his hand found. "You still haven't told me how you were supposed to get through this alone."

"When I'm alone I can—fade back—toward the fair if anything materializes," she said, slightly mollified but still proddish. "The appearing beast can't reach me if I move fast enough. Do you want me to look at those ribs?"

Yes, Massan wanted to say, but all he did was shake his head. I'm not a fool, he thought as they continued on their way again, but after a while he wasn't quite as sure.

There were two more beast attacks that day, both smaller

than the first one and easier to dispatch. The girl was able to give him warning each of those times, which also helped him to survive. That night they shared a tent half the size of the one they'd had the night before, and the temperature dropped a good deal lower. Massan awoke in the darkness to the sound of dripping rain, only to find that the girl had moved in her sleep to press herself against him, likely to share his warmth. He put his arm around the small, shivering form and thought, Indelee, her name is Indelee. Other thoughts tried to push themselves into his mind as well, but he wasn't fool enough to let them.

The next day the girl changed their line of march, and barely halfway through the morning they came to a place where the air shimmered above a small circular section of the grassy plain. When she touched his arm Massan could see corrals and barns and tents and wagons, the section of the fair where animals and animal acts were housed. The girl was just about to speak when the flying things and hopping things attacked, and he was quickly caught up in defending the two of them. The fetid green flying things attacked with beaks and talons, scoring Massan every time his flashing silver dagger was elsewhere, the bone-white hopping things jumping in every time the flying things retreated. He could feel the blood rolling down his face and hands and legs even as he swung wildly back and forth to clear the air above him, not knowing how long he could stand against that double attack. He stood for what seemed like hours, his strength seeping out along with his blood, and then suddenly they were gone from all around him, letting him fall to the ground in exhaustion.

"It's all right now, I've got it," came the girl's voice, and a moment later her hands were on his arm, trying to turn him over. "Nothing else will attack us now that we've got—whatever it is."

"Glad to hear that," Massan gasped, trying to fight off the dizziness spinning him around. "Don't think—I have enough—blood left—'' His words ended abruptly as he passed out.

When he came to he knew immediately where he was and felt not the least desire to move. The girl sat near him with his head in her lap, patting gently at his face with a corner of that silver gown. Indelee, he thought without opening his eyes, Indelee. Then he sat up abruptly and struggled to his feet, only to find that the scoring and bites he'd taken and the bleeding he'd done were no longer in evidence. Nothing lasts in this place, he thought as he looked down at her, seeing the hurt in those wide gray eyes before she turned away from him. Nothing, most likely, but death and foolheadedness. He wanted to say something to her to make things better instead of worse, but he couldn't think of anything. All he could do was follow her across the grass of the plains in an entirely new direction, his silence a match to hers.

By the time the sun was low in the sky, Massan had made up his mind. When they reached that night's camp, he would take her in his arms and say her name, then tell her exactly what he was. If she was in the least interested after that, he'd— He didn't know *what* he would do about their lives, but they could work that out later on. The very *first* thing he would do was—

''Well, well, what a lovely memento of your stroll,'' came Rothaz's voice, jerking Massan's head up from the grass he'd been staring at for so long. The tall, robed man stood about five feet in front of him, the silent servant to Rothaz's left, and behind, between them, an even more silent girl— ''Truly lovely,'' Rothaz crooned, peering into a small leather pouch above which the air shimmered. ''How good of you to bring it to me.''

''Rothaz,'' Massan began, taking a step forward. ''Rothaz, wait . . .''

''Do visit my modest little holding, Captain, if you ever find yourself nearby,'' Rothaz purred, raising one hand to a square, golden decoration on his robe, another into the air. "It lies to the east."

Massan tried to launch himself against the wizard even as Rothaz gestured, but that was far too late. Images began sliding about in front of his eyes, images of Rothaz laughing, of the servant holding the girl back by twisting her arm, of the girl screaming in pain even as she tried to escape—

"Indelee!" Massan roared, falling through black space with nothing and no one in it. "Indelee!"

"Are you all right, ward captain?" asked a solicitous voice, and Massan looked around wildly to see the temple gates where nothing but grass had been, the temple official where *they* had been. He had been returned to the fair, and the height of the sun said no more than an hour had passed—if it was the same day.

Without answering the official, Massan ran to the pavilion he'd visited earlier, finding, as he had more than half expected, nothing but silent, unfurnished, unoccupied emptiness. They were gone, all of them—if they had ever existed. The temple official looked at Massan as if he were crazy as the ward captain headed back to the fairgrounds, and maybe that was it exactly. Maybe he'd been so bored he had fallen asleep on his feet and had dreamed the whole thing. Massan ran a big hand through his hair and tried to make himself believe that, but it had seemed so real, and the girl—

By the time the big ward captain was back among the food stalls and the wineshops, he almost had himself believing it had all been a dream. The trekking and fighting hadn't been much to think about, but to believe there was a girl like that, with eyes as gray as his own, a girl who would have made any man take notice— Massan snorted his scorn at himself, to daydream about a female like a boy just into his manhood. Didn't he have better things to do with his time?

"Hai, Massan, this you gotta hear!" a voice called, and

Massan turned to see Trig trotting up, looking furious. "Would you believe this? I mean, don't it beat all?"

"Believe what?" Massan asked, looking around to see how far he was from his favorite wineshop. For some reason he was really thirsty, not to mention hungry.

"My purse!" Trig answered, outrage all through the words. "Some little thief cut *my* purse! Do you believe it? Going after a fair-ward? When I find that little thief, I'm gonna skin him alive, you see if I don't!"

Trig's outrage sent him stamping off through the slowly moving crowds, oblivious to the way Massan was staring after him. It's true, Massan thought, his big hands turning to fists as he stared. All of it was true. The wizard, the trek, the fighting, all of it. To the east, Rothaz had said, my holding is to the east. Somewhere near the Death Swamp, then, but what man in his right mind would ride toward the Death Swamp?

Massan stood unmoving where Trig had left him, but slowly, slowly, his head turned until he was looking east.

"Indelee," he whispered very softly.

MANDRAKE

Caralyn Inks

"Grandpa?"

Though Joss heard his grandson call his name, he concentrated on his fingers. Under them, the hair he'd just carved in the root stirred. The wild magic was working a change! Fear filtered through his awe, fear not for himself, but for the woman trapped in the root.

Joss hooked the carving knife onto his belt, then slid the 'drake into the chamois bag he'd made for it. "Yes, Wairen?"

"Grandpa, we're here."

"So we are." Joss put his hand on the boy's shoulder. During his reverie, they had moved through the Galzar Pass. Ahead, his son Masen's wagon slowed to a halt behind a long line of wagons, peddlers and merchants waiting to pass through the gates of Ithkar Fair in the morning, their lanterns and campfires glowing like gold eyes in the predawn darkness. He felt Wairen bend forward, setting their own lanterns to swaying. Joss laughed. "We'll get there soon enough. Or is it young Tass, the acrobat, you're so anxious to see?"

"Grandpa!"

"I'm sorry. Do you care so much?"

He patted Wairen's back. The boy looked like his dead

wife, Jena, with his bird-bright eyes and his hair as red as the apples they'd brought from the farm. Since discovering the 'drake his mind had turned often to memories of Jena. He'd never loved another woman.

"I do. At the last fair I asked her to bond with me. We love each other, but she's afraid she might not like a farmer's life. Tass loves visiting the big keeps and fairs."

"And she might love it more than she loves you?" At the boy's silent nod, Joss said, "Have you thought about going with her?"

"What would Father, Mother, and you do without me?"

"There's your sister and her husband," Joss suggested. They and his daughter-in-law had not come to Ithkar, as Mari was expecting her first child in the next ten-day.

"What good would you be to us if your heart is elsewhere? Boy, whatever you decide, go for your heart's desire. If you don't follow it, you'll wither like an apple—life will lose its crispness, and it will shrivel and rot until the seeds won't even sprout into renewal. Think about it. Whatever you and Tass decide, you'll have my blessings."

The sun was two fingers high in the sky when Masen leaned out from the wagon he was driving. "Y'ho. Father, Wairen! Catch up. We're next. Old Sanda is Ithkar's witch this year."

Wairen and Joss laughed. Sanda was a favorite of theirs. Off and on for the past forty fairs she'd been one of the gate's protectors.

"Nothing can pass her." Joss chuckled. "She can sniff out illegal magic as a spice merchant sorts his wares by smell alone."

Joss's humor died. He smoothed the bag holding the 'drake, then cupped it close to his side. Why hadn't he thought? He was bringing wild magic to the fair. It was banned by the temple. Rightly so, they believed magic that could not be controlled was dangerous, especially wild magic, for it transformed its wielder and not always pleasantly. Only the mage-priests had the power to destroy it.

The woman in the root was helpless in her present state. Until he could release this child of the wild magic, he must protect her. As if in response to his thoughts, the femaledrake moved inside the chamois bag. She'd been doing that, off and on, ever since he'd finished carving her nose.

Wild magic took many forms. It erupted, spring and winter, during the violent storms that formed over the Tors.

Last spring, during such a storm, he had heard a woman scream his name, though all his family denied hearing it. When the storm blew over, he and his son and grandson separated to check the farmland and the apple orchard for damage.

Joss had felt compelled to climb up from their small valley. On the Tors he had glimpsed a moving light. As he'd approached it he'd realized the light was stationary and that the wind blowing through branches gave the illusion of movement. He'd found a mandrake entangled in the roots of a lightning-struck blue oak. A silvery-gray aura had surrounded the 'drake, as if it had absorbed the electrical bolt that had felled the tree. Joss had known better. It was wild magic.

Old wives' tales said death came to those who heard a mandrake's scream, but he wasn't dead, yet. He now believed this was the source of the voice he'd heard during the storm.

The wild magic had attracted him. He'd reached out. Its aura had twisted outward, threading his fingers. The power had pulled him. Unable to do otherwise, he'd grasped the root. The stored magic had exploded up his arm!

When Joss had regained consciousness, daylight was gone. His son Masen was holding him, asking what was wrong. Awe had held him still for a moment. The wild magic had tossed him several yards away from the blue oak, and clutched in his hand was the mandrake.

It wasn't until Masen had taken him home and his daughter-in-law had finished fussing over him that the chance had come to examine the strange gift the wild magic had given him.

The smooth, bifurcated root was a hand and a half long. Its magic-hardened, silver-gray body was akin to wood; a pale grain flowed throughout it. Years of whittling had told him it would take well to a carving knife.

As Joss had studied it, knowledge had flowed into him that it was not a mandrake, but a femaledrake, and a woman was imprisoned in the root!

"Grandpa!"

"Hmm?"

"We're at the gate, and here comes witch Sanda," said Wairen. "What were you thinking about? I called you three times."

"Nothing. Old people's minds often wander."

"You're not old!"

"Wairen," Joss said, "I'm eighty-seven winters old. My life is nearly over. Look at me. Do not hide from the truth. You'll only cause yourself undue pain if you do."

Joss slipped the chamois bag into his shirt, then tied up his vest lacings. He caught Wairen watching him. Making no comment, the boy looked away.

Thinking rapidly, Joss sat back and forced himself to relax as Wairen pulled their wagon alongside Masen's.

"Y'ho, Sanda," called Joss. "Are you ready to sample some fresh cider? Or"—he lowered his voice and winked—"would you like to sample some that has aged for a while?"

"Hello yourself, you old fool," she answered, laughing. "You only want to get me soused so you can lift my skirts!"

Joss watched her as she approached. They'd been good friends for many years. But friend or not, old Sanda was a witch. The moment she paused he knew she sensed magic.

"What's going on here, Joss?" she asked. Sanda rested her hand on his boot, which extended out over the wagon's side. "Since when do you hire a wizard's protection for apples?"

"Now, why would we do that?" asked Masen, who had followed her. "We have never resorted to magic!" He said "magic" as if the word tasted foul. "Is there something wrong here?"

"Is there, Joss?" she asked.

He lifted Sanda's hand from his boot and climbed down, hoping the tremors in his hands would be attributed to old age and not to fear. "Sanda, I don't know what you're talking about. What's troubling you?"

"There's a smell of magic on this wagon," she said, walking around it and the horses.

Sanda nodded at Wairen but continued to run her hands over the wooden sideboards, then over the horses' harnesses. "I'll have to go inside."

Masen stepped up beside her, half lifting her until she perched beside Wairen. "Ever was our tent open to you, so, too, our wares. No magic has been used to enhance the produce, be they from the apple tree or made by our hands."

When Masen's eyes met his questioningly, Joss shrugged his shoulders, turning his hands in an outward motion.

"Here, help me down," said the witch. "No magic has been worked on the wagon or its contents. Still, there's something here. A strange magic. What it is, is beyond my experience. Because I know and trust you folk, you're free to enter Ithkar Fair.

"I will have to report this to the priests. I'm sorry. Leave the barrel of cider I've marked at the temple." When Sanda passed Joss she whispered, "Later I'll be over to sample the aged apple-fire I saw under the rugs!"

"Do," said Joss, winking.

As he began to climb back up to the wagon seat, Masen grabbed his arm. "What was that all about?"

"She just plans to come by later and share some hard cider with us."

"By the Three, that is not what I meant. This magic business. What do you know of it? You have been acting odd ever since I found you on the Tors. I ask you again—as I asked you then—what happened to you?"

Joss evaded the first question, answering the second. "Nothing happened to me," Joss said, letting irritation show in his voice. "I was tired and fell asleep."

Sitting down, he asked, "Are you ready, Masen? We're blocking those behind us."

When the wares were unloaded Joss left Masen and Wairen digging post holes for the tent's key poles. He climbed into the provision wagon and began tying the tent to its high sides. He would do the same to Masen's wagon, which he had drawn up at right angles to this one. At eventide the tent's sides would be let down and lashed into place. He tugged on the tent ropes, checking each before fetching the hard cider for Sanda. If not tonight, then on the morrow she would stop by for drink and gossip. Hearing Masen speak, he paused.

"Watch Grandpa. I'm worried. There's been a change in him."

"I will," said Wairen. "He's been frail since spring and getting more so, though he tries to hide it."

"I don't know what to think since Sanda sensed magic in his wagon," Masen said. "I'm sure he knows something. But I've never been able to get my father to talk unless he wants to. Well, I'm off to take the horses to the boarding pens."

Joss waited until the sounds of Masen's leaving faded. As much as he didn't want to agree with Wairen, he realized he wasn't as strong as he had been. He glanced down at his hands. The backs of them were riddled with brown spots. They were nature's way of warning the mind the body was giving out. He carved with his left hand, and after each carving the spots grew larger on that hand. When he wielded the knife he felt the wild magic stored in him course from his brain down his arm to his fingers to meet with the 'drake. It was as if the magic in the femaledrake and the magic in him communicated with each other through the knife and his fingers. It wasn't an unpleasant feeling, but each time he put his tools away he trembled with weakness.

Joss stepped down from the wagon. "Wairen?" He met his grandson's eyes.

"You heard?"

Joss nodded. "You seek your destiny at Ithkar Fair among the acrobats. I, too, seek. It may bring me death or something else entirely. Give me the dignity of choice such as I give you." He watched his grandson nod. "I'll mind the wares." Joss laughed as Wairen hesitated. "Go on. See if she's arrived yet."

In between letting his customers sample the cider and selling apples and hearthcrafts, Joss whittled on the 'drake. He was a firm believer in the old saying, "If you want to hide something, put it out in the open."

Joss thought about what he'd said to Wairen. When the wild magic had revealed that a woman was trapped inside the root—he'd committed himself to freeing her. He could have fought the power and been transformed into something unpleasant, but he'd bent his will to its. He was also curious.

Joss believed some rare and strange life force would die if he didn't make the effort to save it. Once before he had failed to save a life, and he'd spent his lifetime trying to bury grief.

His wife, Jena, had died in his arms when Masen was two winters old. He'd done all he knew to save her. Even if a healer had been there when the wood viper struck, she still would have died.

In remembrance of her he carved the 'drake in Jena's likeness. In some way he felt if he succeeded in bringing forth the wild magic's child, he'd have made restitution for his powerlessness to save Jena.

Joss wielded the carving knife deftly, finishing the face. He moved downward, shaping its throat, shoulders, and small, pert breasts. Never before had he carved wood that parted so willingly for the blade. It was as if the magic-hardened root eagerly sought the sharp edge giving it birth.

He held it out to see if his work was in balance, and the 'drake bent at the torso and bit his thumb!

Shocked, he dropped it. It fell into the small barrel of cider he'd been dipping samples from.

"By the Three," he exclaimed, wondering why it had bitten him. Joss bent to fish it out, halting when he heard his name called. Looking up, he saw Sanda walking toward him with a priest at her side. The priest's silk robe proclaimed he had reached third-level attainment. Joss thought for a moment, then sucked in air. That meant the priest was a mage.

"What are you doing," Sanda asked, amused, "fishing for a drink without a cup? Have you sampled the apple-fire without me?"

He fumbled for the ladle hanging on the far side of the barrel, hiding the excitement he knew was reflected on his face. The 'drake was sentient! He'd thought so but had had no proof until now. When it bit him it was protecting itself. Unlike normal wood it did not float but had sunk out of sight. Joss filled the ladle and offered it to Sanda.

"Now, would I do that?" he asked, winking at her. "I was so startled by your beauty I forgot what I was doing."

"Hush, you old fool." She laughed. Sobering, she turned to the priest beside her and offered him the brimming ladle. When he shook his bald head Sanda said, "Ta'xel, this is my friend. He and his kindred have been coming to Ithkar Fair for generations. In all that time they never manifested magical abilities. It is passing strange that some power now surrounds one of their wagons. There is a taste about this magic I cannot place."

"So you have said before," Ta'xel replied, walking toward the wagons.

Joss shivered. The force of the priest's personality frightened him. He'd need all the wits he had garnered in his lifetime to face Ta'xel down. Though invisible, power surrounded the priest. His search was more methodical than Sanda's. When the mage-priest stepped down from the last wagon, an aura was shining about his fingers, a silvery-gray glow like that which surrounded the femaledrake when he'd first seen it.

"Who is he?" he asked Sanda, nodding at Ta'xel.

Sanda leaned her head until her mouth touched his ear. "Ta'xel is a gatherer and sorter of power. Given time, he will discover what kind of magic hides itself in your wagon. Then he will destroy it."

Joss fought his growing fear. He moved away from Sanda and forced himself to face the mage-priest.

"Joss, is something wrong?" When he didn't reply she added, "If there is, I'll help all I can, but if you've involved yourself in forbidden magic, there's little I can do."

"What could possibly be wrong?" he prevaricated, keeping his eyes on the priest.

"Goodman Joss," Ta'xel said, wiping the silvery-gray magic from his fingers and rolling it into a ball. "This form of magic is unknown to me. What is unknown is unacceptable to the priesthood. You will accompany us to the temple."

"A judgment?" Sanda asked in shocked tones, reaching out to grasp Joss's arm.

"Questioning," replied Ta'xel, looking down at her. "I hold back on sentencing judgment only because no wares are enhanced by magic."

Ta'xel removed from his robe a clear glass ball. The mage whispered over it. The glass split in two. He placed the magic into it and spoke an inaudible word. The sphere once more became whole.

"Come," he said.

Joss found himself wanting to defy the priest. He hadn't disliked someone on sight for many seasons, but he did now.

"Grandpa!" shouted Wairen, bursting in among them, pulling Tass with him by the hand. "What's going on here? Where are they taking you?"

"It is in regard to the magic Sanda sensed." Joss saw the fear in Wairen's and Tass's eyes. They knew full well the danger of being brought before the temple priests with the suspicion of using illegal magic. The least that could be done to one found guilty was banishment, but sentence sometimes was to be hung naked by the thumbs outside the fair gates until dead.

"Mind the wares until your father returns. I'll not be gone long," he said, forcing an air of confidence he did not feel. Joss moved off with the mage and the witch. Casually, as if in afterthought, he turned back to the young couple still holding hands. "Reseal that barrel of cider, and mark it. The flavor is a bit sour." He ignored Sanda's surprised glance. The cider wasn't bitter at all, but he had to protect the femaledrake. Silently he expelled the breath he was holding when Sanda said nothing. Old loyalties and friendship still held true, but not for long if the truth willed out.

Though the way to the Temple of the Three Lordly Ones was short, it seemed to take a long time to arrive. Ta'xel led them through the temple to a small door.

"Wait here," he ordered Sanda. He led Joss inside. It was a small oval room, empty except for a long table and benches placed on a raised dais. "I will return with the judge-priests," Ta'xel said.

Joss relaxed for a moment. He rubbed his face with his hands and through his hair, pulling it hard. The pain helped him focus his thoughts, and he whispered, "Wild magic within me. You got me into this. If you want the femaledrake to be born, get me out!"

Behind the dais a panel slid open; through it filed two men carrying an old woman in a chair. Joss straightened and nodded his head in respect. The woman was Ra'nar. He had thought her dead. The priestess was ten winters older than he. The simple purity of her robe proclaimed her rank, chief priestess. To his surprise, she inclined her head in return. They'd been friends until their lives went in different directions.

Behind her Ta'xel and Sanda came through the panelway and stood behind Ra'nar and the other two seated priests.

Ta'xel stepped forward. "Goodman Joss, you have been brought before the council to be questioned about the magic brought to Ithkar Fair in your wagon. Please answer each question with a yes or a no. If judgment is weighed against you, then you may speak in your behalf. And, if you so desire, have witnesses brought before us to speak for you. Do you understand?"

Joss stepped forward. "I am your elder. If I choose to speak more than one or two words, I will."

Before Ta'xel could reply he looked Ra'nar in the eyes and bowed low. "Greetings. I am pleased to know you live. I thought you had passed over the Threshold of Life. If I'd known otherwise, I would have visited you. Are you well?"

Ra'nar smiled. "As well as bones nearly one hundred winters can be. Joss, the mage-priest meant no disrespect. All questionings are handled in this manner. Will you, for what we represent, answer as Ta'xel stated?"

Joss looked at Ta'xel and shivered inwardly. Rage burned in the man's eyes. Joss thought in passing, Pride will be this man's downfall, in spite of his obvious power.

He glanced back at the chief priestess and said, "Yes."

Ra'nar nodded and motioned for Sanda to step forward. "You will do the questioning." Behind her Joss saw Ta'xel stir in protest. "Goodman, these priests on either side of me are Pevan and Itor, truth readers. Witch Sanda, you may begin." Gone from Ra'nar's voice was the warmth in which she spoke to him before. Now he faced an implacable judge, the chief priestess.

"Goodman Joss," asked Sanda, "when you left your home for Ithkar Fair, did you purchase magic protection for your wares?"

"No."

"Do you know of anyone who would place a sending on you or your kin?"

"No."

"Has any member of your family ever sought out people of power to perform magic for illegal motives?"

"No."

"Does any of your kin have the ability to perform magic in any of its forms?"

Joss felt tension loosen as he answered the same again. He didn't use the wild magic, it used him. If she asked if he could identify the magic, he could not answer no. The truth readers would immediately pick up the lie.

"Did you willfully and knowingly bring magic to Ithkar Fair to use it in a manner to enhance your produce or wares?"

"No!" he answered, unable to hide the anger that rose in him. He and his kin had always been honorable in presenting the fruits of their labors.

Sanda turned to the chief priestess and bowed. "Is there more you wish me to ask?"

"Priests," Ra'nar asked the men sitting beside her, "did he speak truth?"

"He did," they answered in unison.

"Then you may go, Joss," Ra'nar said.

Joss bowed and went out the door. Shutting it behind him, he leaned against it. Eavesdropping was not his intention; even so he listened. He recognized Ta'xel's voice.

"Why did you let him go?" demanded Ta'xel. "Unknown magic rides his wagon, and the stink of it is on the old man! He should be kept here until we know what kind of power we're dealing with."

"And where do you think he will run to?" asked Ra'nar dryly. "He's an old man. A spider can scuttle faster than Joss's swiftest pace."

"Pevan, when we're finished here carry to the gate-ward this command: Neither Joss nor his kindred may leave Ithkar without permission from the temple."

"Ta'xel, I want Joss's kin brought before me."

"His son is waiting in another room," Ta'xel responded. "He approached the temple this morning and asked to speak with someone about his father. Masen is much concerned about the change he's seen in Goodman Joss this past season.''

"I'll see him on the morrow when the sun is seven fingers in the sky.''

Joss hurried out of the temple. Masen had come to the temple out of concern for him, not to betray his father. Yet, unwittingly, that was exactly what Masen was going to do. Joss knew that at some point in Ra'nar's long life she had dealt with wild magic. All the chief priestess needed to hear Masen say was that his father's strangeness had come upon him after a violent storm on the Tors, and she'd identify the magic.

As Joss weaved through the chaotic yet rhythmic activity of Ithkar Fair, he thought about wild magic. It was rare that one heard of it outside the high Tors. The magic was elusive, wild, and canny, as if it had an intelligence all its own.

Wairen and Tass rose to meet him.

"What happened?'' asked Wairen.

Joss put an arm around each and led them to a bench. He didn't have much time to finish the 'drake. He needed help. Sitting, he pulled Tass down beside him.

"Wairen, bring me the barrel of cider I asked to be put aside.'' When the boy hesitated he added, "I'll explain in a moment.''

Wairen set the barrel before him and popped the lid. Before Joss could reach down through the cider, the femaledrake bobbed to the surface. Picking her up, he wiped her dry. The 'drake's body stretched like a cat being stroked. He heard Tass whisper, "Whaa . . . I must be seeing things!''

"No, Tass. Your eyes work just fine.'' Joss tried to tease in his old manner. "Fine eyes they are, too!''

Wairen sat down opposite them.

Before Wairen could speak, Joss asked, "Have you two come to a decision?'' Seeing them look at each other as if each represented the world to the other, Joss didn't need to hear their response. He watched Wairen reach out and run his hand down the side of Tass's face.

"I'm going with her, for a time."

"And I," said Tass, "will go to the farm, every other harvesttime. We'll do this until we decide where we want to have our home."

"You are each other's home," Joss said. "Remember that in the years to come. So many forget." He laid the 'drake down and placed a hand on each of their heads.

"I give thee both my blessings . . .

"May the Three Lordly Ones guide your hearts with courage and daring as they themselves risked the void between the stars to come to Ithkar.

"May the fertile earth bless you with young and the renewal of the commitment you made to each other before me this day.

"May the roots of your love delve deep into bedrock and reach high to the burning sun . . .

"Blessings." It wasn't going to be easy for them. Masen was a loving man, but he could be hard. Joss didn't think he'd take well to the idea of Wairen's leaving. He'd better, or he would lose the boy. Joss looked over at Tass. Masen would also lose the joy of knowing Tass and the young that would spring from her womb.

"Now," said Joss, "I need your blessings and your help."

"We'll do anything," Tass said.

Wairen, more in tune with his grandfather, raised his eyebrows and said, "Without question you have my blessing and my help. What is the need?"

Joss picked up the 'drake. "To finish carving this and to be uninterrupted until the sun is at seven fingers tomorrow."

"You could stay with my family."

"Thank you, Tass, but no."

"You must hide because of that?" Wairen asked.

"I must."

"Why? What is it?" Wairen pointed at the root.

Joss thought a moment. He couldn't tell them the truth, or the priests would charge them with concealing illegal magic. "Would it be enough if I say this is something I've grown to love? I'd like to finish it before I die."

"Grandfather," said Wairen, panic in his voice, "you're not dying!"

"But I am," Joss answered him gently. He held out a hand, palm downward. "See those brown spots? They are the body's sign that living time is almost gone. Remember our talk in regards to the dignity of choice?" He saw understanding dawn on Wairen's face.

"This is my choice," he said, lifting the 'drake. "Let me go."

"Oh, Grandfather!"

As the boy reached out, so did Joss. They held each other. Joss felt Tass's hand on his back and knew she was touching Wairen, too, trying to offer comfort.

Wairen stood and raised Tass. With their backs to him Wairen said, "I wonder when Father will get back from the temple."

"Try not to worry. Haven't our difficulties worked out?"

Joss sat for a moment and looked at the femaledrake, wondering if she was worth all this effort. The late afternoon sunlight glistened on the gray-silver root, touching it with light points of fire. The long hair he'd carved in the root wrapped around his fingers. This was the finest piece of work he'd ever done. Putting the 'drake into his shirt, he went to his pallet and got his carving tools. He climbed into the wagon.

In the back of the wagon was a patch of sunlight. Joss settled there. Rotating the root, he examined it, checking his work for flaws; something about the face bothered him. "It needs a dimple!" he whispered. Jena had had one at the corner of her mouth. It had flashed provocatively when she smiled. He put one in. Satisfied, he started shaping the hips.

"I am not your wife, though you carve me in her likeness."

Joss started, dropping the 'drake. It did not fall. She clung to his fingers with her hands.

Her eyes were a compelling gray and met his boldly. "Why are you surprised? You knew I was sentient."

"I don't know," Joss answered, turning his hand to cup her. Not knowing what else to do, he resumed carving. "Does this hurt you?"

"Not at all. It feels good to be born. What are you doing?" The 'drake curved her torso in the palm that supported her and rested her arms on his thumb.

"Shaping your navel."

She cleared her throat. "Is that really necessary?"

"I don't suppose it is, but I have the need to put one in. You'd look strange to me without one." The wild magic within him coursed down his arm to meet that stored in the 'drake. He glanced at his hand. The brown spots were spreading, soon no white skin would remain. Curious, he pulled up the sleeve of his shirt. It was as he thought, the splotches were now moving up his arm.

"What are you looking at?"

"The marks of age," he answered. "As I deliver you from the root, I wither."

The 'drake was silent for a moment; then she asked, "Are you afraid?"

"A little, but then I've lived many years. Your birth will give meaning to my death."

"But aren't you too young to die?"

Joss laughed. He was enjoying himself and the 'drake's questions. He imagined, though he gave her the body of a woman, she would approach life with a child's bright enthusiasm. "My dear, I am an old man."

"That cannot be!" she argued. Shifting closer, she rested her chin on her arms. "Your spirit burns as bright as Red Eye."

"Red Eye?"

"That's what we call the sun."

Arrested by what she said, Joss asked, "We?"

"Others like me. The wild magic's children."

Joss thought while he shaped her thigh. "Are there many of you?"

"No. If there were, your kind would try harder to destroy us. They think we're evil—mischievous we are, maybe, but not evil." She squirmed about.

"Hold still!" he said. "If you don't, the knife might slip and gouge a chunk out of your body."

"Sorry. Ah . . . ah . . . Joss?"

"Hmmm?" he answered, concentrating on shaping her knees. The patch of sunlight had moved. Dusk would soon give way to night. He must get as much done as he could before full dark.

"Would you give me a name? I do not like being without one."

His first thought was of Jena.

"No!" said the 'drake, hitting his thumb with her fist. "I want my own, not your dead wife's. Joss," she said more gently, "all through your carving of me you saw your wife. I am not she, though from your memories I know Jena was a woman who knew how to love and enjoy life."

"You can read minds?"

"Of course. Can't you?"

"No."

"Would you like to?"

"It might be interesting. But first, a name." He looked at the femaledrake with new eyes. Yes, here and there, there was a look of Jena, but he had to really search for it. It resided mainly in the dimple. "Would you like me to smooth it out?" he asked, placing the blade point near her lips.

"No! I want a name."

"Persistent, aren't you." He chuckled. "The color of your body reminds me of a flower that only blooms in full moonlight. I'll name you Kalanthe. Do you like it?"

"Yes," she said, then laid her head down and shut her eyes.

Tenderly Joss ran a finger over her head. "It's fatiguing work being born," he whispered, leaning his head back. Exhaustion weighed on him, too.

Outside he heard Masen exclaim, "Where is Joss? Isn't he back yet?"

"He's been here and gone," said Wairen.

"By the Three, where is he? I want to talk to him."

Joss could hear the slight quaver in his grandson's voice. It was hard for the boy to lie.

"He said he was going to spend the night by Sanda's campfire."

Masen snorted. "Sanda doesn't live outside, but in the temple."

"That's what I said, but he said there's fire and there are other types of fire. When he left he was laughing."

"Well," said Masen, sighing, "he can't get into much trouble with her, and I am too tired to go looking for him. How were today's sales?"

Joss shut his eyes. He was too tired to listen. Just for a moment he'd rest.

"Joss. Joss!"

Hearing his name called, he struggled to open his eyes. He couldn't ever remember being so weary. Slight but insistent taps on his thumb brought him completely awake.

"At last!" Kalanthe sighed in relief. "Sanda was here looking for you. When she discovered your lie, she and Masen left to get Ta'xel. They've also set the fair-wards to seeking you, so we don't have much time! You've got to finish me. I can't run the way I am."

Joss looked at the sky. He had slept through moonrise. "It's too dark! I can't carve without light!"

"But we have light, see." Her body began to glow silvery gray. "It's the wild magic. You have it in you, too. Call it forth."

"How?" Joss asked. He was so tired, too tired to even be amazed he could call on magic.

Kalanthe put a finger in her mouth and chewed on her nail. "I do it by looking into myself until I see a reflection of the wild magic, then I ask it to share its light. There are other things you can call from that source. Later I will teach you."

Joss didn't say there'd be no later for him. He did not have to; she'd take the thought from his mind.

He shut his eyes and tried to see as she told him. To the left, if there could be such a direction in one's thoughts, a light began to glow, and his mind was filled with the familiar tingle that came only when he carved on the 'drake. He had come to recognize it was the wild magic moving in him, seeing its purpose fulfilled.

"Open your eyes and look."

His hand glowed, and light shone through the shirt-sleeve. He rolled up the sleeve. His arm was no longer white, but deep brown. It felt hot and dry, and the thickened skin was taut. The wild magic was working a change in him, too!

Joss picked up his knife and began working on Kalanthe's calves. He'd committed himself to this and would see it finished.

"Grandpa?"

Not looking up, he answered, "What is it, Wairen?"

"They've gone to get the priest. They'll be back soon. Sanda said Ta'xel thinks it's wild magic you're hiding. Is that true?"

"Yes."

"Grandpa, it's dangerous!"

"All life is dangerous. Wild magic lives, though differently than we do. What the people and their priests do not understand, they often fear," Joss said, sliding his knife carefully over the wood, delicately forming an ankle.

"You've got to stop! I didn't understand what you were doing!"

"I didn't intend for you to understand." Joss drew a deep

breath. "Did you or did you not give me your blessing? Or was it merely words?"

He waited out Wairen's silence while he finished the other ankle.

"I gave it with all my heart."

"So did I," said Joss. "Try to delay entry into the wagon. And Wairen," he added, hearing him move away from the wagon, "I love you."

"Me, too, Grandpa."

In a small voice Kalanthe asked, "Do you love me, too?"

"You know I do. You only have to look into my mind to see the truth."

Kalanthe laid her head on his hand, and a small tear fell, tracing its way down a knuckle. "I needed to hear you say it. You're giving up so much that I might be free." She stretched, looking down at the knife. "Don't cut those off! I need them."

Joss had started to pare away some of the fine, long hairs at the bases of the bifurcated root. When the 'drake had lived in the ground she'd used them to draw nourishment from the earth. "Some must go, so that I can carve your feet." He continued to work. Nearly finished on the last foot, he heard Ta'xel's loud voice. "The wild magic is here. Even you should be able to smell its stink!"

Joss muttered, "By the Three, I dislike that man."

"Grandpa's not here. The tent is open. Do you see him anywhere?"

"Good for you, Wairen," Joss said. He opened his palm, setting Kalanthe on it. He smiled as she climbed rapidly up his arm to sit on his glowing shoulder.

"Joss," she said in his ear, using mind-voice as well. It felt strange having words form inside his mind. "Open your shirt." Using the knife, he slit the laces of his vest and through his shirt. His chest was nearly covered in the thick brown skin. As he watched, it spread farther. Weakness washed over him, and he slumped, then slid to the floor. He no longer had the strength to hold himself upright. Joss watched the femaledrake scamper around him, then climb up on the arm supporting his head.

"Come with me," she asked.

"What?" A fog was beginning to cloud his thoughts and to obscure his vision, but he could still hear.

Outside the wagon Wairen, Masen, and Sanda were arguing with Ta'xel, but he was no longer concerned with them. His task finished, Joss knew he was dying.

Kalanthe was pulling his hair. Why hadn't she run? Joss opened his eyes. He hadn't realized he'd shut them. She was still standing on his arm. Surrounding them were several strange creatures; a few looked something like Kalanthe.

"These are the wild magic's children," she said, answering his unspoken question. "They always come when the wild magic gives birth. I am the first to be born in many years." She paused and touched him between the eyes. "Joss, you haven't answered my question. Will you go with me?"

"I cannot. I am dying."

"Yes, you are, but the wild magic is in you. You can use it. It gifted you with itself. Try, Joss. Let it give you life."

Did he want to die? Joss thought about it. His vision had narrowed until he saw only Kalanthe's glowing form. He knew what she wanted from him, to be her mate. The wagon-bed jostled under him.

"There!" shouted Ta'xel triumphantly, in an I-told-you-so tone of voice.

Anger sparked in Joss. He hadn't liked the powerful mage-priest; now what he felt was akin to hate. By the Three— No—by the wild magic, he'd win out over that prideful fool. Focusing the last of his strength, Joss looked within himself and immediately found the silvery glow of power. "I want to live," he told it.

He felt hands grappling with his body and clothes. Fear drove him to try and move. Ta'xel would not have him!

"Lie still while we set you free," Kalanthe said urgently.

She and her kindred were climbing all over him, stripping off his clothes. Kalanthe picked up his carving knife with two hands, holding it like a spear. He saw her tremble under its weight. She brought it down, hard, stabbing his flesh.

He yelled. The wild magic exploded all about him. Joss heard his skin pop. Dazed, he couldn't move.

"Joss, get up."

He looked down. Kalanthe's hand fit perfectly in his own. Surprised, he leaped up. His body was compact and silver gray! They were standing in the brown shell of his old body.

Vaguely he could hear the beginnings of a chant. It was Ta'xel.

Joss smiled. The mage-priest had lost.

Around him, Kalanthe, and the other creatures was an opening in the middle of the wild magic that flamed about them. Through it he could see the Tors.

As if from a great distance Joss thought he heard his grandson call his name. He half turned back.

"No, Joss!" said the 'drake, pulling him back toward her. "We only look forward to the wild magic. Never back. If you turn from the power, you will be lost. The wild magic will reject you, and you'll be trapped, forever, between the gates of life and death, unable to enter either."

Joss met Kalanthe's eyes. At this moment nothing frightened him. A sudden, mischievous joy swept through him. He kissed her lips. Holding the femaledrake's hand, he ran, a mandrake, following the wild magic's children.

TO TRAP A DEMON

Ardath Mayhar

Belkor came down from Galzar Pass bearing a bale of furs that would have wearied a pack horse. He carried the weight high on his shoulders, and his back was straight, his thoughts upon other matters. He had trapped the forests of the lower ranges for half his life, and carrying the fruit of his labors was a trifle, no more.

The demon, it was, that worried him.

Galzar was infamous for its dangers. Some considered those to be caused by men who pretended to be evil spirits. Some thought them to be spirits of rocks and winds and terrible winters. Whatever they might be, all too many weather-whitened bones could be found at the bottoms of clefts and amid tumbles of stone. Belkor had traveled that way many times, and his mind was still unconvinced by any of the explanations.

He had been harassed, once, in the midst of a storm, by accurately aimed stones, shrieks and catcalls, and trip-ropes arranged artfully in the most precarious places. That spoke more, to his mind, of human ingenuity than of demonic abilities.

Because of his huge size, he felt, he had been untroubled in most of his coming and going. He had become used to a sort of unspoken truce between himself and whatever force troubled Galzar Pass. Now, on his way to Ithkar for the fairing, he had not expected to encounter trouble. Had not wanted that, indeed, for he was carrying upon his back the cream of the crop of furs that he had harvested so carefully over a period of three years. This bale should enable him to retire from his trade, to buy the nook of land in the end of a valley, complete with hut and garden spot, which would enable him to marry his Hulla.

They would grow foodstuff for the village nearby, rear a dozen vigorous youngsters, and live to ripe old ages . . . if he could rid himself of the thing that had followed him from the pass. The worst of it was that he didn't quite know what it was that was tagging after him, just out of sight.

When he paused to resettle his burden, there were slight sounds, as if someone—or something—stopped just after he did. He felt a gaze fixed upon his back, just between his shoulder blades. The fact that the bale came between seemed not to dilute the effect at all. When he camped at night, quick glitters, as of eyes in the dark, watching his fire, kept him alert and edgy.

Even after he reached the principal road, lying across the steppes for the convenience of those who traveled to Ithkar, he still felt that dogged presence. The jests and songs and ribald talk of the traders and vendors and supplicants who also traveled the way were very welcome. They took his mind from his problem. But when he rolled into his own lush fur for the night, he felt something there, in the darkness, watching.

They went with some speed, laden as all the travelers were. The fairing came earlier every year, and they all wanted to find likely spots to set up their booths and stalls before their competitors could beat them out. The long Valley of the Ith stretched before them in a matter of days after Belkor joined the train.

He had bought, after some haggling, a small pony to carry his furs. It was a matter of status—no matter how fine the furs, the best prices came to those who made a show of prosperity. He hated to part with the coin . . . it could have gone into the store that Hulla kept safe in a stone jar buried beneath her father's hearthstone . . . but he knew he must. And the beast, too, felt the presence that had pursued him down from the heights. This told him it was not his fancy that had made him so uneasy on the journey.

As the train approached the palisade, with its controlled gate, Belkor found himself wishing that he had brought with him one of his traps. The weight would have been trouble-some, true, but even a demon, he felt, must succumb to his wily methods. To trap a demon would be a fit climax to his career.

He waited in the long line before the gate as the fair-wards inspected the incoming wares, impounded the weap-ons, and allowed the attendant wizard to survey each party. The feel of that . . . thing . . . was like an itch that couldn't be scratched. If he had only brought a trap!

But his traps were clumsy things, made of wood and rope and wire. Heavy and awkward, they were the worst of things to transport. He stored his, in off season, in a secret cavern near his trapping ground.

A priest came along the waiting line. Peddling spells, most likely. Or doing a bit of minor blackmail upon those he knew to be questionable. Many were not allowed into that gate, if they were identified as banned persons. The man approached Belkor.

"A most interesting pack you have beside you," said the insinuating voice. "Furs?"

It was not as penetrating a guess as one would have thought, for Belkor dressed himself in the prize of his catches, and his raiment would have stunned a barbarian emperor into instant envy.

He smiled down his great length at the small priest. "Indeed. Of the finest. Would you like to purchase one?"

"We are not allowed money," the small one said with a sigh. "But I might trade something . . . valuable . . . for the smallest fur you have. A mere tippet or muff worth of fur. For I know of a trap . . . one whose design has come to us from the Sky Lords themselves . . . which can catch a shadow or a breeze.''

He might have named a thousand other things and been heard with a smile of contempt. But the word ''trap'' caught Belkor's instant attention. ''A trap . . .'' he mused. ''Now that is a thing always interesting to one in my trade. It is, you guarantee, a good trap? Light and easy to handle? And humane to the creatures it catches?''

The priest's eyes widened at the last question. ''I have never before met a trapper who cared about the feelings of the things he traps,'' he said. ''Yet this trap, indeed, does not injure the thing it catches. It clamps padded jaws upon any limb that trips its plates, and if the trapper arrives before the creature starves or chews off its leg, he has a living beast with which to contend. Not always a comfortable matter, which is the reason why other trappers use it little, if at all.''

''Perfect,'' said Belkor, for he had not the heart to give pain even to a demon. ''I will trade you a snow-fox fur large enough for a muff—or a tippet—that is the gray of storm cloud, tipped with the silver of sun on ice. If that tempts you to trade . . . ?''

The deal was struck at once, and the priest named a place and hour for the consummation of their business. Then the line moved up, and Belkor waited while the fair-wards poked through his bale and took custody of the quarterstaff that was his only weapon. They could not remove his tremendous hands, or his oaken arms, or his granite-hard head, which were almost always the only weapons he needed.

He moved away slowly, one ear cocked to hear if the wizard had any comment about a demon trying to creep into the fair. But nothing was said, and he moved away toward the area allocated to those who sold furs and leathern goods. As he went, he felt those alert eyes fixed upon his back.

It took most of the day to set up his tiny stall. He bought

screens of light wood and deployed them to show off his wares to best advantage. The furs, treated with the skill he had learned from generations of trapper-forebears, glistened in the light of torch and lantern as he completed his task and fastened his seal across the entryway. It was time to meet that priest . . . if, indeed, he possessed the secret of the trap he had described.

He did. At the appointed place and time, the small priest appeared. He was lugging a large bag and cursing under his breath as sharp corners of the box inside it banged against his ribs.

Belkor drew from beneath his cloak a packet wrapped in thin leather. Stepping beneath a torch that flared atop a post, he drew out a silken fur that glinted in the ruddy light. Gray and silver, it seemed almost alive between his huge hands. The priest looked, and his breath caught at the beauty of the thing.

"I have brought a trap for you. It was not easy to take it from the stores—nobody wants those things, but they are counted and tallied as if they were used every day. I was almost caught, and to be caught would mean . . . punishment. But for that fur, it would have been bearable. Here. Take the trap. Look at it. Oh, do *like* it!" He thrust the bag into Belkor's arms and took the fur into his own hands, stroking it with trembling fingers.

Belkor untied the mouth of the bag and carefully removed a square wooden contraption from its folds. The box itself unfolded, each side unpegging from its neighbor, to reveal a strange-looking thing made of metal. It was light. But how did it work? He could see no way in which a beast might be caught.

The priest saw his dilemma. "Here. You press here. Catch the jaws apart so . . . and set this plate into position." The thing unfolded into sprung halves, with a palm-sized plate between. Each lip of the halves was padded thickly with something that was almost as yielding as flesh. He looked about for something with which to trip the thing, found a strip of wood, and touched the plate cautiously. Not enough, he would have sworn, to trip it.

There was a creak and a soft thump. The wood was held firmly between the lips. A chain fastened to the rear of the trap could be hooked to a stake or a tree to secure the prey. Properly concealed . . . it just might catch that demon of his.

"Trade," he said.

His stall was provided with a cubbyhole for sleeping, and he returned there with his prize. At this remove from the main body of the fair, there was no traffic this late. Shrubs and vines grew among the trees that shaded the horse pens and stables as well as the stalls. One who approached him as he slept would most likely come from the rear of his place, trying for the narrow window that ventilated his tiny sleeping quarters. To look into that window, one would stand . . . there. Belkor surveyed the strip of soil closely.

Someone had stood there . . . the ground was scuffed. As far as he knew, no demon would leave a track, however blurred. He knelt and dug into the ground with his eating-knife, making a hole large enough to hide the trap. He covered the thing carefully, fearful that the lightest thud of a clod might spring the thing, but he was lucky. He got it covered with a light layer of soil without mishap.

Once he was within his sleeping spot, he lay wide-eyed, thinking. Was it wise for such as he to meddle with a demon? Should he have, instead, asked the priest for a blessing—or a spell? Yet he had no faith in anything of the sort that that particular priest might have offered.

Was the thing that followed him a demon at all?

He turned restlessly and rearranged his fur coverings. It was beyond belief that a man might have followed him so closely and so long without his glimpsing him. Belkor was famous among trappers and woodsmen as one who was difficult to foil. So it had to be a demon. Yet why had the wizard-of-the-gate not sensed it when it entered? He turned again.

He had neither expected nor intended to sleep, but he drifted into a doze. The slight commotion outside his window woke him at once, and he peeped from his tiny window. Something was there. In the trap, he had no doubt. He hurried out and around to see what he had caught.

It was small. He had not thought that a demon might be so little. He moved toward it warily, catching dim glimpses of motion in the almost complete darkness behind his stall. Something snarled.

Belkor pounced, catching the small shape into his bearlike embrace. A shrill shriek was stifled in his fur robe, but claws raked his face and neck. He tightened his hold, folded the struggling limbs into a bundle with the rest of his captive. Panting, he carried it into his stall and struck a light.

He almost fainted with the shock of it. No demon sat there on his earthen floor. A child! A child was there, its foot still held by the trap, which he had unhooked from its stake. He couldn't tell, so filthy was it, so wild its hair and tattered its scanty clothing, if it might be male or female, but it indubitably was a human youngling.

He held the lamp close and examined the face. Eyes blazed back defiantly . . . but they held a hint of fear. He had, after all, some ten times its weight and more than that its strength. He smiled, tentatively.

The eyes widened. The worst of the terror subsided. The thin lips twitched.

"If I take away the trap, will you sit and talk with me?" he asked softly.

The little creature was watching him as warily as any wild thing in a trap had ever done. But it nodded, very slowly. He knelt by the stool on which he had put it, upon realizing that it was human. Carefully, he pressed on the springs that opened the jaws, and the trap opened. It looked as if those padded sides had not even bruised the grimy skin of the ankle.

The child jerked its foot free and cradled it in both hands, glaring at Belkor all the while. "You . . . hurt!" he said.

Belkor sat back on his heels. "I thought you were a demon. You came all the way from Galzar Pass, where demons are reputed to live. What else could I think? Be fair, now!"

The boy—it was obvious now that it was a boy—frowned. "It's how we live," he said. "Howling and frightening people until they drop their goods or fall into a ravine. But sometimes they fight back. That's how my dam was killed. He forced her over the edge."

"And your father?" asked Belkor.

The boy looked blank. "What's a father?" he asked, which told Belkor much.

"Then there are no demons at all in Galzar Pass," pursued Belkor.

"I'd not say that," said the child. "No. There be something there, indeed. But it be what gave the notion, you see? And it be not there all the time. When it comes, all us run very fast and hide."

It would have made Belkor happier if the child had agreed with his suggestion. However, with luck his trapping days were over, and he would not have to brave that pass again.

He was not overnice in his habits, was Belkor, but the state of the child was beyond belief. He made a decision.

"We shall find a pump," he said, "and wash you off. See what you are made of besides grit and grime. Come with me."

He held out his hand, and the child took it timidly. That reminded the trapper of something.

"Why did you follow me?" he asked, bending over to see the small face as the child answered.

"You be big. Strong. And you be covered with fur, all

soft and nice. Nobody care for me there. I think I follow you. Maybe . . . you care for me, like my dam used to.''

The unsuspected (by others) soft spot in Belkor's heart twinged. Instead of caring for the poor orphan, he had trapped it. A nice way for a man to behave! He had always hated to kill the creatures in his traps, avoiding their eyes as he slit their throats. He had avoided hurting the smallest thing, when it was possible. And he had hurt a child. It troubled him.

They found a pump, deserted at this hour, and Belkor washed the lad there in the street, pouring streams of water over him, scrubbing him with a rag, rinsing him again and again. When the job was done, a fair-looking boy stood shivering on the flagstones about the fountain.

Belkor removed his robe and wrapped it about the child. ''We shall see, in the morning, about finding you a home. The priests and priestesses in the temple will know. But for tonight, you shall sleep with me, and I shall keep you warm and safe. Are you hungry?''

The child nodded.

''I have half a meat pie in my cubby. Bought it at a cookshop this afternoon. You shall have it, with a nip of wine.''

It was morning before he thought to ask if the boy had a name. He looked up blankly.

''Name? What be that?''

''What do they call you? Your dam, and the others?''

''Boy.''

''Won't do. There are too many boys hereabout. I shall call you Haral. My brother was Haral. He would like to have his name passed along. Does that suit you?''

Haral nodded.

''Then come. We shall seek out a priest . . . a real, honest priest . . . and see what he says.''

It was more easily said than done, but at last they found a young priestess who seemed willing to listen. She was fascinated by the tale.

"We shall go to Andrell. She will be amused by your tale, and she will probably know what to do. She always does."

The way to the priestess Andrell was complicated. Belkor couldn't have found it again, even with all his skill at finding his way in the forest and mountains. But they stood before a slight, veiled shape at last and told the story again.

She went off into a peal of laughter that sounded very young. "A wonderful thing, my friend Belkor. So. You wish to retire from trapping and take up farming, with your charming Hulla. And rear a dozen children? A laudable ambition." She paused, as if thinking.

"If your furs equal those on your back, then they are wonderful. I shall buy them."

"All?" Belkor was stunned.

"I offer a thousand silver pieces for the entire bale. I saw the fur you traded to Emphis for that trap . . . yes, we knew what he was about, and we have faced him with it. It was a minor misdeed, compared with some he has done. But we can use those furs. And you can use the money to buy your land and house, to wed the fair Hulla. And why not begin with a ready-made child? One large enough to help? I suspect that Hulla would as lief bear eleven rather than twelve."

Belkor began to smile. More and more of his teeth came into view as he thought upon her suggestion. The thought of turning his captive over to someone else had begun to bother him a great deal, and here she had removed that necessity.

"It sounds . . . possible. If Haral agrees."

Haral stared at them both, alternately, as the proposition was put into simple words for him. But he did agree, enthusiastically. His tall, furry friend had been his choice from the first.

Belkor turned to go . . . then he looked back. "You truly think that Hulla will like this?" he asked, his tone doubtful.

"Hulla came to the fairing two years ago. She is one I

met while attending to a task in hand. She will agree. Take my word for that.''

Belkor straightened his shoulders and reached down for the small hand. Haral caught hold and held on.

Together, the trapper and his son, the demon, walked away into the fair. There was much to do before they could go forth to find their new life and their new trade.

Belkor had a strange feeling that, behind him, Andrell was smiling.

TRAVE

Shirley Meier

Trave's booth was the third to be vandalized in as many days. She stood in the wreckage and wondered where to begin.

"Dorven, I thought that this is what I paid all those temple taxes to prevent." She looked up at the fair-ward leaning on his bronze-bound staff, the wind blowing his blond hair into his face. The man reminded her of his sister, lady of EastHold, south and east on the edge of the swamp that lay many days' travel away from the Fair at Ithkar. Nervously he swept a hand through his hair, holding it clear of his eyes.

"Trave, you know we're doing our best. Marjalene and Coutou both had trouble."

"Yes, but . . ." She bent over and picked up the shredded remains of what had been one of her better pieces. Instead of floating gently above her hand, it hung limp, dragged down by the weight of dirt ground into it. The destruction was both thorough and vindictive. Even the racks of windforms had been wrenched open, each bit of cloth torn carefully in half.

The slight figure drooped within the folds of the voluminous cloak she wore, and for a moment even the bright wash of color that showed her status as a weaver seemed dull. The acid taste of the destruction trapped her. For a second the fear and suspicion caged her, tied her to the ground, and she struggled to slow the hammering of her heart. Their fear of her did this. Fear of her. And her kind.

"Dorven, you know as well as I that a few knife marks on the outside of a locked booth, and this"—she swept a hand around at the splintered wood and torn cloth; no two bits joined together—"have no comparison."

The hand was only exposed for a second before it disappeared back into the robe. I should be used to them, Dorven thought, but I'm not. EastHold should never have allied with them. Against us . . . He cut the thought off and looked down at Trave, who barely came to his shoulder, blond hair cut in a short fuzz over her skull and enormous green eyes set into the triangular face. Not womanly at all, he thought, but still a friend, or at least not an enemy. He shifted uncomfortably.

Trave looked up at him dithering and realized that he could, after all, do nothing except listen to her complaint and try to find the vandal. Not thief, for nothing was gone. The sun was warm on her back, and she fought off the drowsiness that the heat brought on.

"Go on," she said. "You've heard me out, and that's all you're required to do. You'd better find the criminal, or I'll take you instead."

He laughed at the idea that this tiny creature could touch him and left, angling toward his patrol area along cooks' row. She sniffed and choked slightly at the odor of cooked meat drifting from that direction as she began to try salvaging something. A shame to spoil good meat like that, she thought irrelevantly.

In the bright, noisy air of the Fair at Ithkar the destruction was wrong, a sour note in a piper's song. To the right and toward the river Ith dust hung heavy, shuffled into the air by the penned horses, cattle, draft beasts, performing animals, and the people around the enclosures, haggling.

She stood a second, the torn weaving still hanging from her hand, looking up into the rustle of the maple tree her booth had stood under and wishing she wasn't here. She had been lucky to get this spot, in the second ring outside the Temple of the Three Lordly Ones, shaded by that tree. Trave laughed at herself, bitterly. The space was not the problem, not with temple taxes paid. With nothing to sell from that space, she was ruined.

It was darkening rapidly, the twilight taking on a dusty rose tone that muffled edges. This close to the end of the summer the heat was still thick enough to cut, especially at the end of the day, but cooler breezes were making themselves felt. The night would be cold. Trave leaned her head back against the tree, listening to the sounds of the animals settling for sleep. The wreckage had been cleared away, and the remnants of her wares bundled together into a surprisingly small case. A vagrant wind off the Ith ruffled her plush hair, bringing with it the smell of mud, reeds, tar, and new wood from the docks. What a lovely form to weave, she thought.

She looked around quickly at the food and beverage stands that were already brightly torch lit, catering to early celebrants. No one seemed to be near enough to see her in the shadows under the tree. Perhaps she could indulge herself in a small freedom that traveling among humans denied her.

She reached out and caught the breeze in one three-fingered hand, snapping it up and around the other fingers, as a human child plays with string. She breathed between her hands and watched, feeling joy in simply seeing it happen, even now when her attempt to begin trade was in shambles.

A faint strand glistened between her hands, then a second, third; faster and faster like frost-on-water or glass. Deep green for river depth, milder greens for reeds and plants, brown and warm blacks and blues for water, mud, and sunlight. A tiny image hung in the air over her hand, floating there with streamers gently writhing in the next wind to rise from the river. The small Maesim would continue to grow and gain texture, feeling, and, very slowly, size every time a wind from the river struck it into motion. At the upper range of her hearing she heard the quiet bubble of a river and smiled.

A human weaver could never replace or repair weavings so thoroughly torn; not cloth. But could the shape of the wind ever truly be changed? Perhaps I can salvage more than anyone believes, Trave thought, and stretched slowly as she got up, opposite arm and leg, feeling herself start to wake up and put some snap into her movements. I have all night, she thought. But I'd best sleep some if I want to stay awake all day.

Next morning Trave sat under the tree again, dozing slightly as the day began. She squinted her eyes against the brightness and pretended to ignore the whispered speculation from booths around her.

"Child!" she called. "Don't touch! In fact, go away and take your brother with you." The children had been hanging about all morning, trying her patience sorely.

In the clear morning air, her wares floated, tethered to branches, small stakes in the ground, and the open lattice-work of wood that had replaced the small, closed-in booth: lengths of bright cloth that never stopped moving even in still air. She had restored her goods.

Trave lowered her head to shade her eyes with the edge of her hood when she heard the footsteps stop in front of her. The muffled sputtering was something she had expected. Without looking up, she said, "Did you just repeat your offer, Twill? I couldn't hear that."

The man standing before her booth area was small and dark, weasly thin and nervous, a slight tremor in his hands. "There, there was talk of trouble. They said you needed help."

"They?" Sarcastically polite, she continued, "Not your help, thank you."

"But . . . this is still indecent! Spinning is acceptable for women, but weaving? No, this is an abomination of . . ."

"Of the craft and dignity and pompous, overblown self-importance of the master weaver of Riuff. The only weaver that the master of guild here in Ithkar refused to see." She matched his tone exactly, mockingly. "Is that why Marjalene's stock was also destroyed?"

"Coutou of my own clan was also attacked," Twill said huffily. "His wares suffered most grievous damage. Do you accuse me of crime, Trave?" The whiny voice suddenly smooth. False accusations were a serious thing.

"Naturally not. It just seems that Coutou's best was sold all on the first day. Strange, wouldn't you say?" She allowed one corner of her mouth to twitch upward slightly, but the face she lifted toward the master weaver was solemn. She gave respect only to the master's black that edged his robes. The man himself she despised.

A dark flush was creeping up Twill's neck. "You say you do not accuse me. Well, I accuse you. Magic to enhance shoddy wares is forbidden. And any woman must resort to magic, therefore." With that he turned and stalked away. She called after him, angry rather than contemptuous.

"I will not spin to your weaving, Twill. No matter what you do!" She spun around. "And I told you children to go away!"

She was shaking, but not from anger alone, and struggling to control her threat reaction, holding her arms in close, tensely. The man always affected her like that. He had the gall to offer to buy thread from her and weave it into something decent! To be allowed the great honor of having her thread purchased, she would have had to become part of his guild/clan and subject to his control. She smoothed her fur down surreptitiously under her cloak. At least on her face and hands it was thin enough not to invite comment, unless it was bristled out.

She looked around at her Maesim-na, windforms that billowed out to create illusionary walls, and realized that her other venture had to be begun now, before Twill could cause trouble. But there was no one to watch and sell during the day. She cursed herself and wished she had been able to talk the Ancients into risking another Younger of the Iystria-khym. Lack of funds and time fenced her close, and her arms kept wanting to spread.

The ragged girl peered timidly around the edge of one of the hangings, her dirty brown hair brushing the head of her brother, who peeked out below. Trave opened her mouth to chase them away again when a thought struck her, and she chuckled. The Ancients wanted some human contact? Well . . . "Come here, girl. I want to talk to you."

"Trave Iystrian. You have been formally accused of using magic to enhance poor work by one Master Weaver Twill Sluagh-Cland of Riuff."

The wizard's voice was brisk and businesslike, but there was an undertone of curiosity in it. Trave looked at the young man flanked by a fair-ward escort, accompanied by the accuser Twill, who was doing his best to be unnoticed. He was having trouble keeping the smirk off his face as he thought of the fine that would be imposed on her, making his offer her only way out. Gloat, you offspring of a diseased squirrel, she thought.

"Wisdom, my goods and keeping are yours to inspect. Freely and without let. If good Master Twill would also care to inspect? I have nothing to hide."

She stepped back to allow the wizard access to her wares, bumping into Sayonda, whose hair was now clean and neatly tied back. The dirty, ragged caravan follower had cleaned up nicely, as had her brother, Naim.

"Trave, are you crazy? If you just let him look, he'll confiscate it all!" she hissed in Trave's ear.

"Hush," she whispered back, "let Atad judge as he is

supposed to. Any wrongdoing of mine is just in Twill's head. Besides, I could afford to be the injured party . . .''

The wizard had stepped forward and begun to inspect her wares. They were mostly hangings meant to be displayed in the gardens and conservatories of those who could afford them, with smaller ones for indoors: luxury items. There were tiny ones as well that almost anyone could afford.

They weren't strictly lengths of cloth because each one had its own shape, some long and coiling, others compact with feathery edges that fluttered slowly in the sunshine. Colors blended seamlessly in swirling patterns that suggested people, things, images that whispered and spoke with voices and sounds just under the edge of hearing.

The wizard inspected several with care, then moved to the center of the display, closed his eyes, and concentrated on the hands he spread to either side. There was an itchy feel in the air, a reaching, seeking feeling like a man searching in the dark with outstretched hands. Trave blinked as it went away, smoothly like the outsurge of a wave, as the wizard dropped his hands. His face was grim.

"There is crime here." He turned to Twill, who hastily wiped the smile of triumph off his face. "Master Weaver, I find against you for false accusation and insult. The good journeyman's wares are untainted. The fine is the value of''—he looked around—''that work, to Journeyman Trave, and two ounces of silver, to the temple.''

Twill, who had had his eyes on Trave in anticipation of her plight, sagged in shock, and his mouth dropped open. "But, but, this, but I, but—''

"Fair-ward, escort the master to the temple to record payment of his fine.'' As the three left, the wizard turned to Trave and smiled, suddenly looking much less formidable. "I wish I could make him apologize as well, but envy speaks falsely, whatever it says.''

She smiled back. "No need, Wisdom. I know several such folk. You approve, then, of my work?'' she continued.

He laughed. "I wish I knew how you did it, almost as

much as the master of Riuff. But the fact that they *are*
magical as opposed to being enhanced by magic doesn't
make the method clear to me!'' He reached out a finger to a
green-blue hanging that needed the tether spot or it would
have blown away in the wind of people passing by. "This
one makes me think of late spring, just after rain." For a
second his eyes looked far into his own past. "I can almost
hear the drip of water from the trees in the garden, and
birdsong." One of the tendrils blew across his face, catching
a moment on his short, dark beard. He started and came to
himself, becoming formal once again.

"Journeyman, I bid you good day," he said, and strode
off into the crowd.

Trave turned to the girl child. "See, Sayonda? My gam-
ble paid off."

The girl sniffed more like an old woman than a child of
some twelve years. "But you weren't sure." She rubbed
her hands against the new smock she wore. "That's why
you sent Naim around to the blacksmith's booth by the
fountain so early."

"Yes," was all Trave replied. "Now I can talk to the
smith since you've learned so quickly." She pulled her
elbows in close. "Bundle the blue hanging and send it to
His Wisdom, Atad. I can afford to gift him with spring."

"But, isn't that . . ."

"Unwise? Yes. But no one can falsely accuse me of
bribery if there is no name on the gift. Don't argue, child!"
Ironically, the girl was probably only a few years younger
than she was; Trave wondered what it would be like to live
as long as humans did.

She watched as Sayonda took down the blue Maesim and
began to wrap it. She had indeed learned quickly. Perhaps
she could even learn Trave's weaving, if any human could.
"I'll be back in a while, Say, and I'll bring Naim with me.
If the business goes well, we can close up early and attend a
performance of some kind." She turned away, missing the
smile Sayonda threw at her back.

Trave had been outraged at first when she'd discovered that no one cared about the children. The clerk who had made up the papers had even said, quite casually, that any city or gathering had lost children, and why should Ithkar be different? Then she had had to think of all the Youngers who didn't come back to the Iystria, and many more that never lived to become Ancients.

Trave dodged around a family deciding where to go next, the one boy tugging in one direction while his brother clung to his mother's skirts, thumb firmly in his mouth, eyes wide. Well, she thought, every kind has its own method of culling.

The air was full of the smells of cooking, sweets, hot people, dust, and here, deeper in the craft quarter, oil, smoke, glues, resins, and other odorous things. Some craftsmen continued their work at the fair, taking orders rather than bringing stock complete. Several rows over she could hear the clangor of hammer blows on metal, and she knew that Naim, deafened but still fascinated, would be standing as close as the smith would let him.

The first time she had felt secure in leaving his sister to manage her booth and had gone to give the smith a commission, the boy had been at her elbow, at least at first. When she'd looked around for him he had been standing by an apprentice watching intently as a window grill had formed out of raw metal, oblivious to the sparks burning pinholes in his tunic.

The odor of hot metal welled out around her, making her sneeze as she stepped into the shop. Erythan was settling an account with one of his customers, listening to the scribe's recounting of the bill, when she entered.

"Good day to you, Mistress Carine, the harness fittings will be delivered to the tanner today. Jodai, see the lady out. Still not used to it, Trave? You should be, considering how often you've been here over the last few days. Worse than a rooster with too many hens!"

The smith rose and followed his comment to Trave across

the shop to where she stood. As the man's bulk loomed over her, Trave was again glad that this man was her friend, at least as much a friend as a fairing could make him.

"Still busy as ever, Erythan. Is Naim here?" He grinned and indicated the boy, who was visibly not asking questions. She smiled back. "If he becomes a nuisance, send him back to me."

"No trouble, that boy. He's not learning guild secrets." The smith turned to open a chest by one wall. "I believe that I finally have what you want." He beckoned her over to the window, where it was brighter. The smithy was, for all intents, a permanent building and so was both safer than wood or canvas—but also thereby darker.

Erythan unwrapped a pair of slim metal darts, perhaps two spans long, each with thin vanes that curved slightly in a smooth spiral.

"There you are," he said. "Much point heavier this time." She picked one of them up and tested the weight. "If I didn't know any better, I'd say those weren't for throwing but for dropping from a height. Castle height?"

"Hmmm." She looked up and placed the dart carefully back into his hand. "No, not castles. Would it be unreasonable to ask ten score? As well as the knives."

"Ten? Are you starting a war?" he asked, surprised.

She shook her head quite seriously to his question. "No, finishing one. Erythan, I am expecting more trouble from a certain person quite soon. I . . . I need to ask a favor of you, just for an evening, but I hate to fo—"

"Nonsense!" He tapped her firmly on one shoulder, staggering her slightly. "You are a friend and need not excuse yourself. Out with this great favor you want me to do!"

"I had hoped that you and your lady wife could take the children this one evening, perhaps the night."

"This isn't a great deal," Erythan said. "Why make a fuss? Of course we can take the children, but . . ." He thought a moment, then his bushy eyebrows drew together in an ominous frown.

"Now what is this? You have not had problems protecting those two despite the troubles they've given you since you kin-bonded them. Why should they not be with you, unless you expect worse than vandalism?"

She shrugged. "A feeling I have. That's all. And I find puppet shows and duels with silvered wood swords tiresome."

"Ah." He wasn't deceived. "Of course we can take them." He reached out as if to forestall her leaving, wanting to speak of the possible trouble further, but the stare she gave him cut him off. "As long as Sayonda doesn't take my two out on the roof again!" he continued. If Trave didn't wish to speak of it, then he could not, for friendship's sake.

She laughed and promised to speak to the girl.

With a start Trave woke from a light doze. She still found it strange to be tired enough to sleep at night. The leaves around her rustled softly, scattering sharp-edged patterns of moonlight across the ground. Below her was the faint sound of someone creeping up to her booth area.

The light wickerwork stood out against the night, and the strangely silent Maesim coiled in the moonlight, their presence felt more by the shadows they cast than any other means. Trave held her breath as the noise was repeated nearly under her and she heard, barely above a whisper:

"Here, cut that one down."

That was enough for her. She swung down to a lower branch, snagged the rope she had specially coiled there, beginning the shriek that was the battle cry of her people.

There were two of them. They froze for a second at the eerie whistle echoing off the booths and buildings around them and turned to run. One made it away, and the pound of retreating feet faded rapidly while the other one went down. Light though she was, all her weight came down on his shoulders. He twisted to throw her off, and she clamped one of her feet on his throat. At the unexpected strength of her grip, he froze, struggling to breathe.

"That's good, despoiler. Lie still," she said. A rock was digging into one of her elbows, and she could feel the grit driven into her fur. Her back felt bruised. The rope had been dropped in her plunge and lay just beyond her reach. She untangled one hand from the robes that had gotten twisted around the both of them in the short tussle and reached for it.

At her motion, he lunged to free himself, clawing at the foot clamped around his neck. She rolled, the robe pinning her to the ground, and the man's full weight descended on her other foot.

There was a sickening crack, and Trave bit through the inside of her cheeks to keep from crying out. Hot saltiness flooded her mouth, and tears squeezed from the corners of her eyes. She levered herself up and consciously unclamped her unbroken foot. The holding reflex had cut in as the pain seared through her, and she had almost strangled the man unconscious. Somehow, she managed to struggle to a kneeling position and tie him.

At last she pulled away from him and hiked up the edge of her robe. "This is what you get for trying to do it all yourself!" she muttered to herself in disgust. A whimper kept trying to crawl out of her throat. "Trying to be a warrior rather than, sssssaah!" She hissed through her teeth as she pulled the broken half of her foot straight and sat, panting, for a long moment. "A diplomat." She looked down at the two toes, one pointing straight forward, the other back, each tipped with a talon. The one would never be quite straight again. The disturbance would bring other merchants, hire-swords, and the fair-ward, but she should have several moments to catch the other.

Hastily she tore the hem of the offending robe and bound the foot tightly, glancing at the man she had tied. She would have a few moments to catch the other vandal, having seen enough of the man to find him again. She gritted her teeth against the pain throbbing through her foot and leg and launched herself after the vandal, the illusions of the Maesim fading behind her. The real Maesim-na one would have heard, but the visual image was enough to protect her valuables, drawing the vandals, even if she couldn't afford to buy the illusion of sound.

Dorven, the fair-ward, wheeled about and peered into the darkness behind him. Had that been the scuff of a footstep? He turned again and froze in the act of reaching for his staff. Between his outstretched hand and the bronze-bound oak stood Trave. He cleared his throat.

"Trave. Ah, what can I help you with so late? I mean, the ah . . ."

She spoke quietly, but the sound of her voice was enough to silence him. "Why, Dorven? You of all the people in this place would have no quarrel with me!" She took up the heavy staff, leaning on it casually. Pain was shrilling through her body, ringing through the bones of her head. The eyes she fixed on Dorven's face were a darkness that he felt he was about to fall into, green lost in black.

He turned away from those eyes, his fists clenching. "Why did you have to come here?" he said. "Here I could have made a place for myself."

"Your sister offered you a place of honor. Even after what you did with her holding."

"Yes! But not of war lord! Not even of adviser! Steward was all I could beg for!" He swung around to confront Trave. "And her allegiance with your people, when she took the holding back with their help. Your grandmother's help. Do you think I could bear to live under her rule or that of your inhuman matriarchs? The priest was right!" He took a step toward her. "I should have taken what was mine rather than steward for a woman!" His hands reached for her.

"And what do you here?" Trave asked quietly. "Steward for all the fair and the Temple of the Three Lordly Ones.

That priest, of the hated one, who died at our farewell fire, by our hands, led you about by your manhood. When you seized EastHold.'' She watched his hands, clawlike, tremble before her face and guessed at something she believed. ''And how much did Twill pay you?''

For a long moment his hands stilled. She could see the hard calluses, yellowed on his palms, before her eyes. Those hands could snap her neck in an instant. A moment only, then they began to tremble again and moved to cover his face, a harsh sob tearing free.

''I don't know. I don't know who to believe. He was right. You are right. My honor is sold, and what EastHold believed is true. I am a coward and forsworn.'' He was down on the dusty road, hidden in the shadow of the tents and booths. ''I am forsworn. Trave, believe me, I did not touch thy things when all was destroyed. Twill approached me only today through the priests of—''

''Name me no names!'' She cut him off, hearing him slip into the softer tongue of the EastHold he grew up in. She had meant to give him to the fair-court for the justice he deserved, but . . . he was her wind-sister's brother, led by evil though not truly evil himself.

''I swear to thee, Trave! I—''

''Here!'' She swept the staff, the symbol of authority, into the hand he reached to her as, in the distance, a man began to scream. ''Be the first at my booth. The vandal will be babbling by the time you arrive. Hide the rope, and no one will give credence to his accusations of you. For your sister's sake and my grandmother, who was her first-friend among the Iystria.'' He looked up, incredulous. ''Go!'' she cried, and saw the pale flash of his hair as he ran, this time to redeem his honor.

The world was graying out around Trave, then she could no longer see. As she sagged to the ground she heard another scream and smiled. The wind from the slaughter grounds made a rope that even the most insensitive felt. The wind roared darkness through her head.

• • •

It was fair's end, and Trave clung to the tips of the tree where her booth had stood, the night wind ruffling her fur. The twigs clenched in newly healed feet swayed, first one way, then the other.

Twill had paid for many things—for arranging vandalism, as well as being banned from the fair, and guildless. Sayonda had left early this morning with the caravan going north and east, traveling as humans must. The girl would eventually become a wind-weaver, even being a human, for she had the talent. Trave smiled at the thought of having an apprentice, even if it did tie them both to the Ancients' village, rather than traveling with the Youngers. And Naim. The boy had been ecstatic at the thought of being apprenticed to Erythan. They would see them next year at the fair, for Trave had succeeded and could return home with her success and responsibility for the children she had kin-bonded. Weaving new paths to grow in the wind of years to follow.

She pulled the voluminous robes over her head as she swung, so far above the ground, and laughed, releasing the fine weaving into a wind that curled around her, feeling free for the first time in many ten-days. Trave Iystrian spread her hands wide, letting the wind fill the membranes stretching from wrist to ankle, and soared into the night sky, reaching for a wind from home.

THE BOOK-HEALER

Sandra Miesel

Where was Master Romrad? The old book-healer's booth had been my favorite stop at the fair ever since I was a spindly acolyte barely able to read the manuscripts Romrad repaired and sold. With sometimes strange things about them even that older magic which only the most adept can understand—which delivered all we know. My eagerness didn't age even when priestly robes—and the beginnings of a priestly paunch—slowed my steps a bit.

I rued my present bulk as I tried to move against the stream of fairgoers. Even up here by our temple gate, the first-day crowds were thick enough to clot. Then shouts erupted on my left. A trader named Hansper started screaming for the fair-wards as a thief snatched one of his baubles. Gawkers began to surge toward the captured criminal, and I slipped through the crowd to my goal in the opposite direction.

Master Romrad was too engrossed in his work to heed the commotion, much less me. He was bent over his desk cleaning a choral song sheet with a lump of fresh bread.

Glancing at the manuscript, I reeled off a glib attribution: "Third Nocturne, Feast of the Apotheosis, lacewing borders and foliar initials suggest a school of Maros origin."

147

"Father Tomazio," he greeted me without raising his eyes, "if you take another look, you'll see it's just a provincial imitation of the classic Maros style—a good imitation, mind you." Then he beamed up at me. His crinkled smile was as warm as ever, but he winced as I clasped his hand. Rubbing his gnarled fingers, he said: "Putting on flesh, aren't you, lad? Heading the library must agree with you."

"Since when is gauntness accounted a virtue?" I sucked in my plump cheeks. "A temple functionary is expected to be a man of substance." My voice softened. "Are the twinges in your hands getting worse, Master Romrad?"

He nodded. "I drink extract of mourningtree as other men drink wine. So now I have ringing in my ears as well as stiffness in my joints. As the saying goes, I expected to feel my age, but not so soon."

"Surely our temple heal-alls can find you a better remedy. I'll ask one to examine you."

"At this season? When the great ones of the land will be clamoring for their services? Lords bless your kindness for the thought. Now"—he motioned me closer—"come around behind the counter and sit with me. Mind you don't step on Brindle. He's been downright surly since we arrived." A shadow passed over Romrad's face.

I accepted the invitation, cautiously avoiding the cushion where Romrad's pet tree-cat lay sullenly curled. Although more scarred and less spry than he used to be, Brindle was still a formidable fighter. He roused himself stiffly, yawned, and sniffed my robe. Only after passing that inspection did I dare presume to stroke Brindle's brown-and-gold-striped fur. He gave thunderous purrs and nuzzled my knee.

Meanwhile, Romrad had pulled another gobbet of bread from the broken loaf beside him. He wadded the soft material into a ball, breathed on it, and whispered a word of his craft, then resumed rubbing the soiled parchment clean.

"All this gold and heliotrope does take the lordlings' eyes," he said with a chuckle. "They don't care if the calligraphy's shaky—they won't be chanting these verses. I re-bound a genuine Maros volume recently, *The Maxims of Quaritch*, as I recall. If its owner had only kept it properly wrapped in its book chemise, the damage—''

He broke off as two customers approached the booth. One was a foppish young nobleman, while the other had the suavely sober look of a lawyer. I stepped back discreetly while they bargained with Romrad to unroll a brittle leather scroll. This fragile document held evidence vital to an inheritance dispute. The case was so complicated, our temple's judicial seeress had been asked to intervene. Romrad promised to restore suppleness within three hours, in time for the afternoon session of the court.

After the lordling and his lawyer departed, I shook my head in dismay at their arrogance. "Truly, Romrad, you have the patience of the Sky Lords."

"Only the patience of a craftsman." He waved my compliment aside. "Save your praise for the goods I sell."

Since his stock was not the sort to attract idle interest, no one disturbed us for nearly an hour while he spread out his wares. There were chronicles and romances, almanacs and oracles, manuals of ritual and treatises on war, decorated in all the regional styles of the last several centuries. Some texts were complete, others had been reduced to a few gatherings or even single leaves. One tantalizing fragment of glossy paper was penned in that fluid script used beyond the southern seas. It made me yearn for loveliness beyond my grasp.

Romrad himself grew pensive. "For me," he said, "fine illuminations are like windows on enchanted realms where smooth roads wind past fields of flowers that cannot fade."

But my mind's eye saw a weary old man driving his wagon through a bandit-ridden wasteland. I murmured, "Would that misfortune spared men and manuscripts alike."

"Then how would I get my living? The trouble is, Tomazio, I spend so much time getting my living, I've little left over to read and savor the books I heal. And time, I fear, is running out.''

Trying to banish melancholy by a return to business, I noted those manuscripts whose special beauty or rarity made them candidates for acquisition by the library.

''Sound choices, Tomazio.'' Romrad nodded his approval. ''Advancement has taught you prudence.''

''Not according to our new bursar. To hear her talk, I chase books as hotly as a minstrel chases skirts. It's all too true, I must confess.'' I sighed in mock contrition. ''But if I were spending my own gold instead of the temple's, I'd buy your *Primer of Perfection* here just for its whimsical borders.'' I leafed through the fable book, chuckling. ''Look at this page. Who couldn't laugh at the manticore with the toothache?''

''Master Hansper,'' snapped Romrad.

''The curio seller?'' I pointed to the other side of the courtyard. ''The one who relies on expensive spells instead of a watchful tree-cat to guard his goods?'' As if on signal, Brindle stood up on his hind legs to peer over the edge of the counter.

''The very man.'' Romrad looked about warily. ''Here, Tomazio, stand on this stool. Can you see Hansper in his booth? It's the one draped in red.''

I peered across the crowd as directed and stepped down. ''There's a black-clad figure greeting customers.''

''May they bargain keenly and long. Then even if he has some occult means of overhearing us at a distance, our talk should be safely private for a while.''

I frowned. ''This isn't like you, old friend. What's the matter?''

''I wish I could tell you. Listen and see if you think I'm cringing at shadows. . . .'' His voice trailed off.

I laid a hand on his shoulder and bent closer to hear him.

He continued, ''You realize, Tomazio, that the invasion and other disorders of the past few years have shaken loose all manner of valuables. Even if they escaped pillage, many proud folk found that they couldn't eat heirlooms. Like others in the luxury trades, I've been picking up bargains at distress sales. That's why my stock is so good at present. Hansper has been doing the same, often in the same places. As our paths crossed repeatedly since the last fair, I began to notice a new and marked preference for arcane, bizarre, or even . . . unwholesome objects. Perhaps I'm making more of it than the case warrants, but I keep sensing a profound wrongness in what he buys or why he seems to want it.''

"Have you seen this pattern in your own dealings with him?''

"Nothing really alarming, except the way he hovers about my booth and wagon, turning up when I least expect. I feel I'm being watched even when I don't see him.''

"Anything else?''

Romrad's brows knitted. "As you know, we merchants trade among ourselves before the fair opens to the public. Yesterday evening Hansper bought a mutilated copy of An-Jan's *Everlasting Questions* from me because its margins were unusually thick with variant readings and unique glosses.''

"Do you suppose he's looking for some hidden meaning in a book everyone else treats as nonsense?''

"Exactly. And he offered an outrageous price for my amulet.'' What he drew from beneath his garments was a pendant of mellow brown-and-gold-striped amber carved in the shape of a griffin's paw. "I think this was originally a book pointer to protect pages from readers' fingers. I've put it on a cord and wear it as a charm to keep my breathing easy—amber's good for that, you know. And I've no wish to sell it, even if Brindle would let me.''

The tree-cat flicked ragged ears at the sound of his name.

"Look how the amber matches his coat, Tomazio.''

As Romrad held out the amulet for my inspection, Brindle reared up on his hind legs to bat at it, fortunately with his claws sheathed. To my own touch it felt warm as a living thing. I was loath to return the talisman and continue our earlier train of thought.

"That's not much evidence against Hansper," I said. "Could your instincts be detecting some subtle Thotharn stain?"

"Don't assume that all this world's evil stems from that vile sect. Most of us sin perfectly well by ourselves."

"Do you think Hansper's flaw is greed? They say he boasts, 'When I find a gold piece in the mire, I do not sell it for the price of silver.' "

"No. This new corruption is something other than avarice or even twisted pride."

As we both knew, Hansper was reputed to be the by-blow of some Rhos nobleman. Exaggerated shame at his condition had been the spur driving him to excel.

"If it'll ease your mind, Romrad, I'll try to probe for hidden rot in Master Hansper. But now I'd best be off if I'm to do both that and make an appointment for you with a heal-all."

We parted. I strolled around the area, trying to keep my movements casual. I ignored the bankers and money-lenders with their scales and counting boards, but there was no need to feign interest in the splendid merchandise offered for sale in this section of the fair. Whole fortunes glowed and rustled and glimmered on racks and counters and well-fed bodies.

After a bit of aimless drifting, I looked in on dealers I remembered from earlier years. The first booth on Romrad's left belonged to Lenise and Lensay, jewelers who were twin sister and brother. They had just sold a bridal crown to a beaming family of wool traders. Afterward, the proprietors showed me choice gem specimens—displayed on exactly the right shade of velt—simply for the pleasure of discoursing on lapidary lore.

Then I commiserated with an automaton maker whose perennially popular wares had been eclipsed by another craftsman's magically animated gaming pieces. Apparently, the traditional clockwork images of the Three Lordly Ones hatching from their Egg could not compete with lifelike toy warriors storming across painted battlefields.

At last my leisurely pace brought me to Hansper's stand. Heavy crimson hangings surrounded it like a gaping maw. Just inside sat the merchant, a large man with the fleshy blond good looks of the Rhos. He was attending the same sulky lordling who had earlier brought his scroll to Romrad for healing. The lawyer was nowhere in sight.

"And so, Lord Vingho," said Hansper, "you have but to choose a spell-word from the list, and the figure will enact your desire in the most delightful fashion." His supple voice engulfed the customer but left open the question of price. Since Lord Vingho must still be living on his expectations, what future advantage did Hansper hope to reap? "Do take this pair to your quarters," the merchant continued. "Examine them overnight so you may fully test the perfection of the illusion."

The nobleman smirked. I was glad not to have seen what went into the box Hansper gave him.

After bidding him farewell, Hansper turned to me. He stroked his crisp beard with a ring-laden hand and asked, "What rarities might tempt an underlibrarian?"

"As a chief librarian, I really couldn't say, Master Hansper. Anything you show me is sure to be interesting."

"Now, Father Tomazio, even you devoted servants of the Three Lordly Ones must retain some appetite for novelties." Hansper's smile tightened as he laid out his wares. "Which of these would beguile you best? A shimmershell mask that changes from man's face to dragon's at the twitch of a string? A lead-and-crystal coffer filled with relics from the Death Swamp? Or perhaps this prayer bracelet whose beads are ivory skulls? Notice how they split open." He demonstrated. "Observe the extraordinary carvings within."

The alien images he held up to my eye writhed as I tried to view them, but I managed to match Hansper smile for smile. "Every cabinet of curiosities worthy of the name will be clamoring for these rarities." Except our temple's, I added silently, blessing our bursar's parsimony that would spare us such pollution.

"Let them clamor or not as they please." He shrugged, no longer smiling. "It suffices that I know the value of what is mine."

I pleaded priestly duties and took hasty leave of Master Hansper.

I now agreed with Romrad: something was amiss here. Formerly, Hansper's astute taste had won him a distinguished clientele. Only a few years earlier he had sold our temple a magnificent cloisonné ewer for the jubilee purifications. But what he had just shown me—and what I had glimpsed on his shelves—looked morbid, even blasphemous. Yet personal revulsion gave me no grounds for complaint to the fair-wards.

The next few days passed peacefully. From time to time I spied Hansper within the temple precincts, presumably making deliveries to our guests. He went unattended, carrying packages in his own smooth hands as if distrusting others with their contents.

Meanwhile, our heal-all's medicine had restored suppleness to Romrad's fingers. Now freed of pain, he worked with his old deftness, if not quite his own joy. Fear of Hansper still seemed to haunt him.

The library's needs kept him well occupied. I brought blemished books to his booth in the morning, and he returned them sound to the library at night. This arrangement gave us ample opportunity to confer and browse.

After more than two decades of watching Romrad work, I still marveled at his dedication. His art was his life: he truly was a healer of books. To him, a torn page deserved the same gentleness as torn skin. He would replace crude stitches, mending a tear with a transparent membrane that left only a fine scar at the join. He could close the wounds left by corrosive ink or coax flaking pigment to recover bare spots.

Then, one sultry morning at the end of the first ten-day, I found Romrad in an oddly reflective mood. Wearied by the unseasonable heat, he sat idly stroking Brindle while waiting for paint to reconstruct a damaged initial.

"Tomazio," he began, "do you think that words are somehow alive—that writing outlives the writers?"

"Perhaps. I've heard that there are lands where folk believe each word, sound, and letter of their scriptures is a kind of god."

"But I say more," Romrad continued. "To me, every individual book has a life of its own, cursed or charmed as the case may be. So we should treat even commonplace texts with reverence."

"I fear few would agree with that principle. Parchment gets scraped and reused, pasted into bindings, or cut up for the sake of its illustrations."

Romrad's sharp groan sent Brindle springing from cushion to counter. "Lords! May there be a hell for those who injure books!"

"And a heaven for those who heal them." I touched his bowed shoulders. "If vandals had to face tree-cats, they'd speedily reconsider their intentions."

As I pointed toward Brindle, the animal laid his ears back and growled. I turned to see Hansper stalking away from the booth. How long had he been listening to us? But why should it matter? The oppressive weather must be addling our wits.

A storm continued to gather all day, then broke after sundown. I was watching the first flashes of lightning from the library window that evening when Romrad arrived with a newly repaired volume. But instead of settling in for a session of scholarship and sweet wine, he checked doors and windows to confirm that we were alone. Then he removed a few unbound leaves from a slim leather carrying case and laid them on my reading desk.

"What do you have there?" I asked. "The ruins of some private prayerbook?"

He ignored my question. "Tell me, Tomazio, will you share a burden I have borne for many long years? Can you keep my crushing secret?"

"What ails you, old friend?" I cried.

"Those."

I peered at the manuscript fragments. They numbered perhaps a ten of pages in both single leaves and binions. Except for a few blank sides, they were richly illuminated in a random assortment of styles. Subjects were equally diverse: a garden where noble lovers danced might face a pit where fiery monsters devoured malformed men. All the portrait miniatures were uncommonly lifelike.

"They're splendid, Romrad. But what are they? What's a Zenthal carpet page doing on the same sheet as Delrend line drawings? Those studios flourished two centuries apart at opposite ends of the country."

"I've been asking myself those questions for more than forty years." He sighed and rubbed his eyes. "Tomazio, have you ever heard of a book called *The Scale of Scales*?"

It took me a moment to place the title. "The one legend calls *The Key of Heart's Desire*?"

He nodded.

"It's said to have been written before the Sky Lords came, but I've never seen a copy nor know of anyone who has."

"It lies before you."

"These bits and pieces?"

My bewilderment vexed him. He sighed again and joined me at the desk. Distant thunder rolled as he fanned out the leaves. He spoke like a master scribe with a slow pupil.

"You remarked on the variety of decorative styles, Tomazio. Be more specific."

I inspected each piece carefully and ventured an opinion. "These were all written on the same material, a creamy supple parchment. It's thicker than the uterine vellum used on luxury volumes nowadays."

"Also notice the needleholes down each seam."

"They match. But if these were originally bound together, why is each illumination different? No modern painter could duplicate so many archaic styles. He couldn't even get the proper pigments to try."

"Yet they're genuine, Tomazio, not copies. When I was a lad studying here at the temple, the blessed Illardo taught me how to identify and date manuscripts. I've extended his vision, though only as a dwarf perched on his great shoulders."

"Did you learn of *The Scale of Scales* from him?"

"Yes. I so badly wanted that legend to be true, I vowed to find the book. Other manuscript hunters had met with success, why not I? A few years later, while rebinding an ancient book, I slit open the cover and found this." He pointed to a purple-dyed leaf inscribed in gold ink. "Unnaturally slight effort restored it to the pristine condition you see."

Turning it over, I was amazed to discover that the verso side was unstained. No trace of color showed through on the blank surface.

"So you suspected magic from the appearance."

"The text itself had told me that. For a librarian, you seem to have forgotten how to read."

I blushed. I had to squint to decipher the rustic script of centuries past. Surprisingly, the spell—which I took care to read with eyes alone—did not confer power on the user. Instead, it weighed his soul against the stylus of truth, which is sharper than a word's point.

"What do the other pages say?" I asked.

"Exactly the same thing. Insofar as I can read the various dialects and expand the abbreviations, the spell is simply repeated on each page."

"But how does one cast it?"

"I've puzzled over that longer than you've been alive,

Tomazio. Something more must be required to activate it: disposition, surroundings, a talisman, the time of year? Whatever it is, I haven't discovered it yet."

"Yet with mystery piled on mystery, one expects the magic to work."

"Or perhaps we should rejoice that it doesn't." He shuddered. "Meanwhile, the responsibility for the leaves that I have as well as the hunger to find more are growing unbearable."

"So does the threat of Hansper. Do you think he suspects you have *The Scale of Scales*?"

He nodded sadly and gripped my hand. "Sometimes I wish—"

A crack of lightning sent me scurrying to close windows. Rain and hail beat against the small panes. There was no question of Romrad leaving just now.

As we waited out the storm, he told me the story behind each leaf. He had gathered them over the decades, in the course of ceaseless travels through all the lands this side of the sea. Pages emerged from the oddest places: glued into bindings, rolled up with merchant's tallies, hidden in false-bottomed coffers. One had served to wrap comfits. Another had had a love letter written on its blank side. But ponder as we would, we were no nearer to solving the riddle when the rain ceased.

By this time, Romrad was exhausted. I tucked the box holding *The Scale of Scales* into my sleeve and offered to escort him back to the wagon in which he slept behind his booth.

We walked slowly through a pall of soothing mist. Lenise and Lensay joined us en route. They had been detained by the storm while visiting customers at the guest house.

Praise their grace, we were with Romrad when he found the wreckage. Someone had plundered both wagon and booth. The tailgate was down and the canvas slashed. Tools, clothes, and bedding were strewn about in sodden heaps.

Worse yet, books had been ripped apart and flung into the mud.

"Brindle!" the old man cried. "Brindle, where are you?" His voice rose to a scream.

No tree-cat answered his master's call. I shone my lantern inside the wagon. On a heap of smashed crockery lay Brindle's body. His back was broken, and his claws were clotted with blood.

Romrad clung to me, limp as his ruined goods. His sobs turned to wheezes, but he gripped his amber amulet and his breathing eased. Lenise righted a bench for him to sit on while Lensay ran for the gatehouse fair-wards.

The uproar roused every dealer sleeping in that section of the fair. No one had heard the thief at work because of the violent storm, which had also, of course, washed away footprints. The other merchants closed ranks around their dazed fellow with outpourings of sympathy and rage as well as helpfulness. Even Hansper expressed regret and demanded swift justice. I left Romrad in his neighbors' care.

Only after returning to my own quarters did I realize that *The Scale of Scales* was still in my sleeve.

Early the next morning I found Romrad conferring with a sergeant of the fair-wards, a swarthy veteran armsman, short but powerfully built. His efficient manner seemed to steady the grieving old man.

I listened in silence as the warden asked, "You're sure nothing's missing, Master Romrad?"

"Everything's been accounted for, even my money."

"So the thief mustn't have found what he wanted. Amateur, most likely. Professionals can't afford to make a mess. You say no one's threatened you?"

"No."

The fair-ward's dark eyes narrowed. "By all accounts, you're well regarded here. But you've got at least one enemy. It took special meanness to wreck your property that way."

"Thank the Three no client's goods were lost."

"Now about your tree-cat—"

Romrad winced, but the fair-ward continued in the same flat tone: "The blood on his claws came from the thief. But none of the heal-alls we questioned treated such wounds last night. My men are checking people with bandaged limbs."

"Excuse me," I interrupted. "What if the thief knows how to heal himself?"

"Then a routine sweep won't catch him. You're Father Tomazio, the chief librarian?"

Romrad apologized for failing to introduce us. The fair-ward's name was Rinfer.

"Temple friends are useful," said Rinfer, looking squarely at me. "The hierarchy's taking a direct interest in this crime. They don't tolerate violence at the fair. They especially don't tolerate it within their own walls. Neither do I." He hefted his bronze-bound staff and continued, "So they're lending us a seeress for tomorrow's inquest. You don't see that every day when a commoner's been wronged." He warned us to expect the summoner and left.

Even then we dared not speak of *The Scale of Scales.* Romrad merely touched the sleeve in which I was carrying it. He still had enough wits about him to realize what had become of his treasure. If he chose to keep quiet while the thief was at large, I would do the same.

The fair-court assembled early next morning in a room used the rest of the year as our novices' meditation hall. Fresco images of the Sky Lords stared down upon us, as if measuring our justice against the lofty standard of their own. Traces of incense warred with the smell of closely packed bodies.

Every dealer in the affected section had been compelled to attend. Although a few grumbled about the time lost to trade, most were eager for a speedy solution. They had had two nights to worry over what such a vandal could do to their own booths. I could have been dispensed from appearing by right of my priestly status, but for Romrad's sake I stood penned in with other potential witnesses behind a rope railing.

Discovery procedures are less formal than trials, but any brush with the majesty of the law has a way of making people anxious. I suspect these rituals were contrived with that in view, so nervous malefactors would unmask themselves.

We paid reverence to the magistrate when he and his retinue of clerks and bailiffs entered the chamber. Today's presiding officer was Lord Nacol, by repute an honest man with a questing mind. He would not be today's central figure, however. Instead, attention would focus on our judicial seeress Melha, a serene, dark-skinned woman of indeterminate age. She was rarely seen outside the inner temple except on court duty. Her seeings and showings were matchless tools for revealing truth in perplexing cases. But the high priest did not permit her to exercise her gifts as often as folk would wish, perhaps for fear of exhausting her strength.

Melha took her place in an egg-shaped white chair below the magistrate's bench and crosswise to it. The gold-and-crystal wafers fringing her chain of office clattered as she smoothed her long robes and adjusted the padding of the chair to match the exact shape of her body. Then she caressed the Sky Lords' emblem bound to her brow and slipped effortlessly into a trance.

Romrad was the first witness called. He knelt and placed his hands between Melha's to give his oath. But before he testified, samples of his damaged property were brought in and laid on nearby evidence tables. Brindle's mud-stained sleeping cushion was placed at Melha's feet in plain view of all.

Just as Romrad started to speak, Brindle's image materialized on the cushion. The audience gasped. The tree-cat regarded them with alert eyes and lashing tail. Romrad's voice cracked, but he forced himself to continue. The strong brown hands of the seeress restrained him from attempting to touch the shade of his murdered pet. On the evidence table, a casket flew open and spilled its contents. Fragments of a jar reunited briefly, then smashed. Ruined books left and flapped like landed fish.

Lord Nacol warned the buzzing crowd to keep still. Romrad was dismissed and directed to stand beside the tables. Other merchants came forward one by one to testify in the same manner, but none had seen or heard anything suspicious that night because of the thunderstorm.

Finally, Hansper's turn came. I noticed his lips moving in what could have been a spell. As he strode toward the seeress, Brindle bristled and snarled. Hansper shied from the hissing beast, but a bailiff forced him to his knees before Melha for his oath. Evidence stirred on the tables. It thumped and crashed while the cat snarled. Hansper had to shout his denials.

"I know nothing of this crime!"

Bleeding gashes ripped across his hands. The crowd screamed. Romrad wept.

"Your victims accuse you, Master Hansper," said Lord Nacol in a voice that quelled the din. "What say you?"

Hansper rose defiantly. "You speak of victims, my lord? I am the real victim here, victim of the greedy temple. It means to ruin me by conjurer's tricks and confiscate my goods. Surely this court is too wise to be deceived. What did I possibly have to gain by harming Master Romrad? His trade was no rival to mine."

Full-armored in his pride, Hansper did not even try to conceal the damning claw marks or the red stains spreading through his clothing. I was appalled that Romrad offered no challenge. Hansper's cunning talk might raise doubts about the evidence—and our temple. If Romrad would not speak for himself, I would.

I pushed to the front and cried, "Behold the motive!"

After the bailiffs let me pass, I took the book box out of

my sleeve, opened it, and gave the manuscript leaves to Melha. "A man might kill more than a cat to steal *The Scale of Scales*, the book legend calls *The Key of Heart's Desire*. Somehow Master Hansper learned that Master Romrad had assembled a few priceless fragments of this book and resolved to steal them. He relied on the storm to cloak his crime, but while he was wrecking the book-healer stand, the prize he sought was elsewhere."

Confusion boiled through the crowd.

Lord Nacol signaled for silence. "Are these manuscript pages yours, Master Romrad?"

The old man dutifully identified his property. "Yes, Your Lordship. I had left it with Father Tomazio in hopes my friend could help me unravel the book's secrets."

"What spells does it contain that make it so precious?"

"There is only one spell, Your Lordship, repeated from leaf to leaf. It promises rewards beyond mortal ken according to one's inmost wish."

"Have you tried it?"

"I am no mage, Your Lordship. I simply wanted to study *The Scale of Scales*, not use it."

"A man would have to be very sure of his merit to risk so rigorous a test. By his own testimony, such a man is Master Hansper."

The accused glowered, unrepentant to the last. "I have always known my own worth even when the world denied it. False charges cannot taint me."

Before the magistrate could reply, Melha raised her voice for the first time. She sang judgment on Hansper in notes as keen as flensing knives:

> *"Since you distain this lawful court,*
> *Submit yourself to higher laws.*
> *Now let the book that weighs the soul*
> *Deal out the doom your deeds deserve."*

Hansper took the verdict in silence, his face as hard as a statue cast from flawed metal.

"So be it," proclaimed Lord Nacol. "Let justice be done through ordeal by magic. We shall see if the power that can punish the guilty will also reward the innocent."

The magistrate commanded both Hansper and Romrad to hold *The Scale of Scales* while the seeress chanted its spell aloud. Hansper's bloody fist crumpled the edge of the parchment, but Romrad's knobby fingers grasped it lightly as a lover's.

Mingled fear and curiosity froze us all in our places. The only sound in the courtroom was the old book-healer's raspy breathing. He fumbled for his amber talisman and continued to clutch it even after his lungs had cleared. He bowed and closed his eyes against the coming blow.

Melha's voice struck. We moaned and writhed and covered our ears to escape its awful beauty. The written words I had read without effect now cut to the very bone. My sight blurred. The forms of Romrad and Hansper lost their color. They faded to black outlines.

"Save us, Lords, or we perish," I sobbed, and fainted on the floor.

The ministrations of Lenise and Lensay revived me. Bailiffs were assisting other groggy witnesses. Clerks clustered nervously around the blank-faced magistrate, but no one dared touch Melha, who still lay slumped unconscious in her chair. But Romrad and Hansper had vanished along with *The Scale of Scales*, the ruined goods, and the specter of Brindle.

Everyone gave statements to the court recorder and staggered off to our own quarters.

I slept until evening, mercifully without dreams. When I awoke, I discovered that in my dazed state, I had carried Romrad's book box home. In it lay one last leaf of *The Scale of Scales*, the one with the purple-dyed recto side. But its verso was no longer blank.

It bore a fresh illumination painted in the best modern

style—Orina of Loray could not have done it better. There, within a border of gilded vines and redda leaves, a scholar who might have been a younger Romrad sat reading. Around the base of his book-laden desk curled a guardian tigrigriff with fur like striped amber. But inside the initial letter that opened the text of the spell, a man with taloned hands scrabbled to dig a golden statue out of a cesspit. Both man and idol wore Hansper's face.

So the power that had erased their images in this world had painted them anew . . . elsewhere. Did other lives likewise adorn the other decorated pages?

I breathed the Sky Lords' blessing on my old friend and his tree-cat. Then I slipped the remaining leaf inside an ancient list of temple offerings. There may it rest, deep in our archives, until it is ready to be found again, it and its fellows with pages yet unfilled.

THE DEMON'S GIFT

Kathleen O'Malley

Luca spat the bitter milk onto the ground. The lumpy, yellowed curds that fell from her mouth belied the seemingly sweet liquid sloshing in the cup she still held.

"She witched it!" the merchant Tagus bellowed at the bravo standing beside the woman. "Taste it yourself!" He wrenched the cup from her, throwing half its contents over his own hand. "It's good, mild milk! Taste it, Oskar!"

The fair-ward held up his hands. "It's not for me to judge. I'm only here to see Luca comes to no harm on her rounds."

"Good thing for her, too," Tagus said, "if she spends her time casting spells on the goods of honest traders!"

The short, stocky woman pulled a sweet from her cloth purse and popped it into her mouth. Her graying brown hair blew against her round face, and she impatiently tugged it back into the small bun where it belonged. Her eyes, a soft brown flecked with green, never left Tagus's face. "No one has to bewitch that ewe's milk, Tagus, you ruin it yourself."

She moved confidently to the merchant's sheep, penned in the rear of the stall. A gawky lad of twelve, whose nose and chin proclaimed him unmistakably as Tagus's son, stood in her way, but only for a moment. A little white dog creeping low around the woman's heels suddenly emerged from the curtain of her skirt, lips raised over small, sharp teeth, and darted threateningly at the boy's ankles, forcing him back.

The clean, fluffy sheep clumped together in alarm as Luca approached, then calmed as she crooned something low, except for one old ram who kept a wary eye on the dog. "Be still, Bear," she warned, "there's work here that's worrying me."

"Boy!" Tagus shouted. "Don't let her in there!"

The youngster flinched visibly at his father's sharp command but dared not challenge the dog.

"It's her right, Tagus," Oskar said, laying a hand on Tagus's shoulder, "granted by the high priests in the name of the Three."

"In the name of the Three, what's Ithkar Fair come to that a trader can't sell his beasts without being magicked!"

By now Luca was in the pen, while Bear sat on his haunches outside, keeping guard. The woman held the head of a full-uddered ewe, looked long in the animal's eyes, then breathed into her nostrils. Finally, Luca touched a stone tied about her own neck, stared into it, then finally marched back to the men.

"You're poisoning your sheep, y'bastard!"

"What?" yelped the merchant. "The witch is mad, Oskar!"

"It's in the milk of that ewe, and in her breath! And the Thorn is dull when I'm near them."

The gem was half a handspan long and of a strange, ruddy hue, tied in wicker netting around Luca's neck. It had gone dim since she'd approached the ewe, but even without its usual brilliance, the sharp-edged shard twinkled with power.

"All Ithkar will hear how the priests have countenanced witchery against the merchants that fill their offering chests!" Tagus threatened. "We're forbidden to use spells on our wares, yet she can bend the rules so easily?" He pointed at

Luca accusingly. "And how did the likes of *you* come to own a stone that glimmers of the dark and looks like something from the Death Swamp? No one gets out of the swamp with their wits, so whose widow did you steal it from? You couldn't afford to *pay* for the tiniest chip of a thing like that! That gem should be in the hands of the priests. How is it this woman is allowed to defy the first laws of Ithkar?"

Oskar grabbed hold of Luca's arm, pulling her aside. "Are you so very sure this time?"

"Oskar!" Luca seemed disappointed with her lanky friend. "You're letting this lout's ravings unnerve you. You know very well the Thorn has nothing to do with the dark. He wants to distract us from his animals. His *sick* animals."

"These sheep, Luca? Their fleeces are the finest I've seen, and the milk seemed fine before you drank. I know you trust your stone, but what am I to do with no other evidence? You must understand, Luca."

She nodded. "I understand Tagus brings gold every year that lines the fat priests' pockets—"

"Luca!"

"—and a lamb or two for the pot. He's *poisoning* his sheep, and if my word's worth nothing, then I hope the bitterness in those lambs gives the priests the raging—"

"Luca! Enough! You'll get us all cast from the fair!" Oskar walked back to confront Tagus. "Be warned, merchant. Luca has every right to question the health of your stock. If she finds that you're treating them ill, you'll be cast out from Ithkar. We'll be checking again." He latched onto Luca's arm and hustled her off, his sudden action frightening Bear, who set up a terrible barking, until his voice finally turned into one long, howling note as the friends left Tagus grumbling behind.

"Is it just the grossly sick I'm to help? There's more to ill treatment than that!" Luca argued, huddled over her beer.

The two sat at a center table in the Joyous Goblet,

rubbing elbows and rumps with the tavern's customers. Oskar had finished his duties for the night, content to draw pictures in the sweat of his stein.

"Luca, if you hadn't been so smooth-tongued that day you pounded on the priests' door—and, in truth, if they hadn't been so scared of what they saw in that stone— they'd have snatched your gem and cast you out right then." Oskar drained his mug and signaled the tavern-keep for another round. It was late in the day, and the inn was enjoying good business, filled with customers dressed in all the different costumes of the varied peoples that came yearly to Ithkar Fair.

"I should know!" Oskar continued. "I was there, as usual, running myself into the ground with their fetches and carries. But I can still remember how they buzzed when you showed that rock." He snickered, remembering. "Scared the lot of them into holiness for a week, and made my days easier . . . till they ordered me to guard you during the fair!"

"As you remind me constantly. Well, the fair's only two weeks from finished, and then you can go back to tending Their Holinesses and I can go back to the fen. But if I can't get the priests to give my stone more credence, there's little point in my returning again." She drained the last of her own beer, regarding the bottom sadly. "Tagus is killin' his sleep . . . eh, sheep, and that chicken farmer's up to something as well. Those birds were wild with terror . . ." She clamped one hand over her mouth to stifle a hiccup and the other over her mug as the tavern-keep tried to fill it again. A second hiccup caused Bear to bristle and snarl, fearful as he was of strange digestive sounds, even from his mistress. "Oskar, I'm starved."

"That's no surprise. You found something to complain about at every booth we passed. This one's cheese, that one's milk, eggs that looked clean to me, and beans 'ruined' by a ham bone!"

"That pig died horribly. . . ."

"You cannot live on bread and sweets, Luca!"

"Is it *my* fault most of the traders think so little of the beasts that feed and clothe them, and put coin in their purses, that they cannot give them a fair life, or easy death?"

Oskar leaned near his friend, sharing his beery breath. "Y'should throw away the stone, Luca, and not concern yourself with all this blood and bile of dumb beasts."

Outraged, the woman thumped her fist hard on the heavy table, causing more than one head to turn. "Throw away the Thorn?" Her dog began to howl, and with practiced moves she scooped him up in her arms, clamping one hand around his overactive muzzle. "Live as the rest of you? Stupid and callous and uncaring?" The dog punctuated Luca's argument with muffled woofs while trying to wriggle free.

"Fine thing that!" she spat, contemptuous. "Oskar, when I pulled this Thorn from the paw of the swamp beast, his gratitude filled my heart till I thought it would melt. Every time I help some 'dumb beast' from his hardship, the flood of that relief fills me again. That's worth all the succulent carcasses the world could serve up. I'll keep my Thorn, thank you, and my hungry belly, too, if that's what it takes. . . ." She released her dog's mouth, and he subsided with small grumbles and a passing lick at her chin. She glared around at the customers who gaped at her, and they quickly busied themselves.

The exception was a lean, gaudily dressed woman at the next table who boldly met Luca's glare with her shadowy gray eyes. "If you'd like a clean bit of food, you're welcome at my tent," the stranger said. "I promise you'll taste no pain in it."

Oskar and Luca looked meaningfully at each other but said nothing. The woman stood to leave, moving gracefully though she stood nearly as tall as lanky Oskar. Even Bear was quiet as they all rose to follow her.

• • •

"I'm Gwynngold of the Irfan," she said as they entered her stall. The long, narrow space was kept private from her neighboring merchants by means of woven blankets, rugs, and fabrics draped over ropes strung along the timbers that outlined her boundaries. It made the small area seem like a festive patchwork tent. Her small, ornamented wagon was parked near the rear, where more blankets sat folded, turning wooden chests into comfortable seats that surrounded a clever clay stove. A pot of the same material sat on ebbing coals and gave off an aroma of something wonderful.

Just then, a brace of attractive, shaggy animals the size of small horses stepped out from behind the wagon, chewing cud and gazing at the visitors with large, black, limpid eyes. Gwynngold smiled and touched them with affection. "This is Daras," she said, "and that Basra."

"You must be from far away," Oskar said in surprise. "I've never seen beasts like these."

"We call them the Kaffa, and we live together in the mountains to the north."

"You shear them?" Luca asked, rubbing her face against the luxurious blankets and bolts of plush cloth Gwynngold had brought to sell. So beautiful was the animals' wool that all the yarns were woven in their natural colors of browns, golds, and purest white. Gwynngold herself went clothed in soft trousers and vest of the same fabric, and Luca realized how the varied hues of the yarns matched the Irfan's hair, streaked as it was with browns and golds and white. She realized, also, that touching these clothes did not cause her to erupt in the hideous, itching splotches that the fabrics of many other weavers did.

"No," Gwynngold answered, "their coats shed the softest parts in spring and fall, and we comb it out. These beasts are stubborn and intelligent and strike out if ill treated, which makes them much like the Irfan. The yarn is their gift to us, as is their milk and honest labor. We are nomads, and the Kaffa help us find good mountain pastures, clean water, tubers and plants for food, and flax for homespun."

"And their young?" Luca asked, suspicious.

"Kaffa breed seldom. A calf is only killed if he is maimed and would die in pain. The death of a Kaffa is the death of a friend."

The Thorn had recovered some of its glow while Luca and Oskar were at the tavern, but as they'd entered Gwynngold's tent, it had started to twinkle. Now it was gleaming so wildly that its rainbow colors danced over tent, beasts, and people. The sparkles reeled and swirled even though Luca stood still. Bear snapped at the colors, trying to catch one.

The Kaffa, untethered, approached the strangers with interested snuffles. Oskar endured Daras, who examined him from toes to nose, while Luca shared breath with Basra. Impulsively, the woman threw her arms about the graceful neck.

Gwynngold brought out bread, cheese, and dried fruits, offering the food first to Basra, Daras, and Bear. This forced the dog to reassess his normally suspicious attitude and give her a tentative tail wag.

As people and animals feasted, the dancing colors of the ruddy gem gave the tent an air of celebration. It was only when Luca was sopping up the last of the thick grain and tuber stew that had been simmering in the stove that Gwynngold finally spoke up. "When you were speaking at the inn—"

"Y'mean when Luca was ranting," Oskar interrupted.

"Well, you were saying something about Macao, the chicken farmer. I wanted to talk to you about that."

Oskar looked interested. "You've had trouble from him?"

"I'm not sure. When I was setting up my first day here, he was friendly, offering tools, help, like that."

"Sounds like he's sweet on you, Gwynngold," Oskar teased.

"I wondered myself at first, but he kept asking about the red metal studding my tack and the milky stone we use for decorations. These things are native to our mountains, and I brought some with me to trade, but Macao's no gemsmith, so I saw no point in talking them up with him. Then he questioned me on the taste of Kaffa roast, and I politely sent him on his way.''

''Probably didn't mean to give offense,'' Oskar offered as he settled down on a cozy stack of rugs.

''Perhaps. But that's not the end of the matter. That afternoon I went to the Shrine of the Three Lordly Ones, and returned to find Daras and Basra in a rage. On a hunch, I snuck round Macao's tent, and there, out back, was his jerkin fresh-washed, but still carrying the strong smell of Kaffa cud.''

''What?'' Luca asked, confused.

''The Kaffa can defend themselves very well with their sharp, cloven hooves and their strong teeth, but the most effective weapon they have is their cud. They can spit the stuff from five armspans away, and the odor of fermented food is hard to wash out. I believe he tried to steal my goods, thinking the Kaffa mere draft beasts that would ignore his thievery.''

''Hmmm,'' mumbled Oskar as he patted his full stomach. ''What's to be made of it? Chicken farmers and Kaffa cud, and poisoned sheep still alive . . .'' His voice trailed into sleep.

''Hmmm is right!'' Luca grumbled, realizing that warm food and strong beer had conquered her friend again. Once Oskar was asleep there was no moving him, she knew, as did any regular customer of the Joyous Goblet. He was known for passing many a night next to his supper plate. Now, his fatigue seemed contagious as her own eyes suddenly felt dry and heavy-lidded.

Gwynngold laughed at Oskar's throaty snores. ''You're both welcome to stay, of course, Luca, but I did want to say this. I'll be meeting some gemsmiths before dawn. I could ask some questions, see if there have been any thefts.''

As Luca thought about this, the Kaffa settled themselves

down near her with a sleepy groan, a hint to the humans who burned the lamp too late.

Gwynngold tossed Luca blankets for herself and Oskar. "They always remind me when I'm guilty of keeping guests up late. I'll wake you in the morning after my meeting, all right?"

"With breakfast?" Luca asked, smiling sleepily.

"A man that would ill-treat a beast would not hesitate to steal," Luca told Oskar as she tidied Gwnngold's wares the next morning and started a breakfast of her own making in the Irfan stove. "Besides, it's bad for the fair. If you were Gwynngold and this your first year, would you be so eager to return to a place where your very goods might be snatched?" Gently, she moved the sleeping Bear from the unfolded blankets to the neat ones. The dog gave a noisy yawn and settled back into sleep.

"Luca, thievery's a problem wherever people gather, but I see your point well enough. And here's Gwynngold, back at last, with a look that says she's gotten a good price for her stones."

"My stones, my metal, and some interest in my cloths as well. That's why I'm so late returning. But there's more news, friends. Ah! My thanks." The tall woman reacted with only a moment's surprise when Luca presented her with a cupful of a dark, aromatic brew. After a long swallow, she began, "The gemsmiths talked a lot about the protection of their wares, or the marked lack of"—she gave Oskar a meaningful look—"that seems lately to have befallen the fair. There's talk of thieves stealing fine stones and small jewelry to smuggle out of Ithkar and sell elsewhere at higher prices. Several merchants have suffered losses, and others are talking of leaving the fair early. But there's something that worries me more."

Luca took a lump of rising dough and slapped it onto a pan sitting on the coals while listening to Gwynngold's news.

"The jewelers say that a group of special gems will be offered that throw moving sparkles of fire though the stone stands still. Of course, the jewels are magic and cannot be trafficked in Ithkar, but outside the fair they would bring a fantastic price."

"Is there to be a market outside the gates for the selling of wares illegal here?" Oskar demanded. "This defies the laws of the Three!"

"Oskar," said Gwynngold, "thieves have no respect for the Three. But I'm concerned about something else. Luca, what would happen if your Thorn were stolen and cut into a thousand gems?"

"How can I say?" Luca watched the creamy clouds in her cup as she sweetened her drink with Kaffa milk.

"The Irfan believe that things of power link themselves permanently with their owner. Our elders love to tell stories of people careless with magical things, and the sorrowful fates that befall them. . . . As far as I know they are just stories . . . and never about things with the power of the dark."

Luca could tell that this was Gwynngold's way of asking, politely, the true source of the Thorn's power. She had never even told Oskar the full story, but now seemed the right time.

"My parents were farmers on the fen and our land bordered as close to the Death Swamp as could be farmed safely," she began. "I'd always had a way with creatures, and worked as an animal healer after harvesttime. One day Bear chased a rabbit across our wheat lands. I found him near the border sitting quiet, looking out toward the swamp. Then, I heard the call."

Her eyes stared at nothing as she recounted the tale, but the warmth in her voice was unmistakable to her listeners. "I'd been warned from that place since I could toddle, but the calling drew me in. I'd been told the land was odious and rank with murky pools and dark weeds twisted in strange shapes, but as I walked, the place looked to me only interesting, not evil. Strange animals scurried around, and I wished I had the time to watch them, but I couldn't stop. I had to find the caller.

"When I did he took my breath away with his beauty. Oh, I know others would have called him hideous, but to me . . . well, it didn't seem that way. His scales seemed like tiny crystals, and there was a glow around him, but it was dim. He was in pain. That's why he called me. His hand was pierced deep with a shard of greenglass, and he bled freely. I sat there in the swamp and pulled that huge hand onto my lap and worked as carefully as if it were the smallest kitten. As soon as I removed the shard his bleeding stopped, as did his pain, and his glow became so bright I had to cover my eyes. The gem was my reward. I called it the Thorn, having pulled it from this creature that others fled in terror. His very blood is what gives it its strange color and, no doubt, its power." She took a long swallow from her cup to wet her throat before going on.

"I know how others feel about the Death Swamp, but I can't agree with their judgments. I didn't feel the presence of the dark when I was there, and thinking about it over the years, I've decided it was because I'm not open to that power. Maybe that's why others go mad in the swamp, because they come for the wrong reasons—to take, to hurt, to steal. I went to aid someone in pain, just as I would anywhere. I saw no evil in the creature, or in the other beings I encountered. They were just as you and I are, with all the same wantings and gladnesses and sorrows."

They all sat quietly for a moment, until Luca realized she had never really answered Gwynngold's question as to the consequences of her losing the Thorn. "I use the Thorn in my work here and outside the fair, but I don't know what other powers it might have. So, I simply can't say what its effect might be on others, especially if *they* were open to the dark. If I thought it might cause them to be more kindly to their beasts, I might happily give it up . . ."

"But Luca, if you lost the gem, what would happen to *you*?"

"It's a magic thing, that's true. The tales of the Irfan may have much truth to them, but I cannot worry about something that may not ever happen. I'm much more troubled over the condition of Tagus's sheep or Macao's fowl. I believe that Tagus is selling sheep that will die not a month from the time their new owners drive them home. And Macao's fowl have trays filled with food—untouched food . . ." Luca spread her hands in a gesture of confusion. "Yet their crops are also full. They sit in their pens fluffed out, eyes lowered . . . and the Thorn dims."

"What's stranger yet, the man won't part with them," Oskar agreed, seeming more comfortable now that the conversation had moved away from the Death Swamp and back to things he might have some control over. "Claims Tagus has bought the lot, and he's just holding 'em till the fair's ended. Tagus should be able to buy some good hens locally, and healthy ones at that, so why would he want those? That shepherd had a keen interest in the Thorn, too. I don't like it; something's cooking here besides chicken stew. But what am I to worry about first, ladies? Gem thieves or sick stock?"

"Well, Oskar," Gwynngold said, "the sick stock is quite puzzling, but I wonder if there isn't something you might do directly to catch the thieves. Couldn't you set a trap?"

"With what bait? Your stones?"

"We could try that. We could let it be known they're in the wagon, but that we have business elsewhere. I'd tether the Kaffa behind the wagon so they were out of the way, and we could hide ourselves right here in the stall and wait them out. We'd just have to hope the right people were interested."

Luca interrupted, suddenly excited. "No! Not your stones. Something we know they already want." She fingered her gem and watched the dancing colors spill between her fingers.

Gwynngold's face darkened. "You could be harmed," she warned.

"What are you two scheming?" Oskar demanded.

"We can't keep waiting for others to play the game their way," Luca told them.

"*Your* stone?" Oskar blurted, suddenly realizing what the women were debating. "Leave *that* stone for thieves?"

"*You* told me to cast it away!" Luca reminded him.

"But what if we can't get it back?"

The woman stared at the ruddy gem. "Anyone who would take it has no way of controlling its power. Let them try to shatter it. I have a feeling the Thorn can take care of itself."

Turning, Luca looked through the open tent-flap at fairgoers coming and going through lanes outside the stall. Never having set a trap for any creature, she was unsure of the rules. "I should collect my salary from the priests," Luca said, her voice pitched loud enough to carry through the tent walls. "The stone makes them so nervous between their wanting it and their fearing it, I think I'll just leave it here."

"I must take my weavings to a dealer in rare cloths I spoke to this morning," Gwynngold said, then lowered her voice. "Daras and Basra will protect the Thorn, so I'll tether them loosely and leave them food. They'll stay put and not be too much of a threat for a thief more clever than the last one."

"Well, make sure you take that cur," Oskar growled in disapproval, "since he'll never keep his yap shut. And before you go running off, give me some time to gather my comrades and set up watch. It'll be easier to follow a thief back to his lair, won't it, than to trace the culprit when it's all done? I hope this doesn't go wrong." The bravo looked at both women to see if they were taking his words seriously.

"It's a chance that's true," Luca agreed. "But so was going into the swamp."

• • •

"This is madness," Oskar hissed, hugging his knees to his chest. The three conspirators were cramped together in a hideout created from stacked crates and piled blankets. It was hours past suppertime, and they had sneaked into this carefully constructed hiding place inside the tent while it was still daylight. Now, large torchlamps along the fair's aisleways threw crosshatched shadows across the stall. It would be almost impossible to see anyone who might slip between Gwynngold's draped fabrics. "They're just not taking the thing tonight, that's all. Remember, there's many days before fair's end."

He peeked through the chinks past gaps in the draped blankets to make sure his old friends Haiduks and Roanne were feigning sleep where he had left them. Yes, there was Haiduks, propped against his heavy stave, snoring gently some distance away, and the hefty Roanne so deep in the shadows Oskar could barely see her or her short cudgel. They were close enough to answer a call, but far enough not to be obvious. In fact, they were feigning so well the fair-ward began to worry their sleep might be genuine. After all, the two bravos had been easy to find—"protecting" the Joyous Goblet from a lack of customers.

"Shhh!" Gwynngold warned as Bear's ears pricked up and his hackles raised. She grabbed the dog and held him tight.

"I think we've finally got what we want, Oskar," Luca said in a dull, hushed tone. Her friends looked at her, worried, then shared a glance, trying not to think of Irfan legends or the paleness that had gradually overtaken Luca in the hours she had been without the Thorn.

Clamping Bear's muzzle shut, Gwynngold and the others listened to the soft, shuffling sounds of the restless Kaffa. The animals were not accustomed to being tethered for so long, and the steady, grinding noises of their cud chewing had often been interrupted by impatient snorts.

Oskar glanced up, his heart gladdened as Roanne and Haiduks both gave him a short sign, their attention riveted.

Bear's eyes roved wildly from Luca to Oskar to Gwynngold, who held him tight, keeping him from attacking the intruder creeping around Gwynngold's stall. Soon there came the slow creaking of wagon springs as someone climbed in over the tailgate. The wagon swayed slightly as the intruder rummaged silently about.

Basra and Daras stared, ears up and noses twitching. When they realized the intruder was a stranger, they began to snort and stamp and pull at their tethers. All at once there was a clatter of pots, the sound of angry Kaffa, and the frightened yelps of a child. Bear gave one great wriggle, freeing himself from Gwynngold's grip, and exploded out of hiding, determined to save their goods and enjoy himself, too. Bear hated children.

Gwynngold signaled to the others to stay as she followed the dog. With mixed emotions she realized the thief had escaped, and a quick perusal of the wagon's interior showed the empty hiding place that had held the Thorn.

The little terrier marched stiff-legged around the perimeters, snarling and anointing the farthest posts, while carefully avoiding the cloven hooves of the irritated Kaffa, finally loosed from their ties.

"Well, the thief may have gotten the stone, but he hasn't escaped unscathed," Gwynngold said as she took a towel to the delicate muzzles of the Kaffa. She looked around her, expecting someone to respond.

"Gwynngold! Come quick, help us!" It was Oskar's voice coming from the hideout, and he sounded frightened.

Inside Macao the poultryman's small tent sat a gemsmith, looking at a crystalline shard and turning it over in his palm. All the while he gazed into its murky interior he considered reneging on his agreement. There were no dancing sparkles or flying colors, but deep in the heart of this dim jewel he saw the glimmer of real power. Theft was one thing, the gemsmith thought, but tampering with power . . .

"Will you be cuttin' that thing, or whilin' our time away dreaming on its facets, old man?" Tagus snarled.

"Let's get it splintered and packed into these chickens so we can be on our way," agreed the poultry man. "We're to meet the buyers at dawning." He took bright yellow gems and force-fed them to a protesting hen. "There won't be any trouble getting through the gate, and we'll kill the birds away from Ithkar."

"I've still got to hand over my sheep to their buyers," Tagus insisted. "But I can meet you then."

"Still givin' those sheep that powder?" asked Macao.

The shepherd nodded. "It did just what you said, made them old ewes look better'n any others here."

Macao chuckled. "Too bad they won't live past the new moon."

A loud snuffle interrupted them, reminding Tagus of his forgotten son. "You'd better not be sobbing over those damn sheep again, boy," Tagus threatened. He snatched his son up from where he sat cross-legged on the ground and shook him hard. "You've been whimpering and sulking and defying your own father for two months now, and I'm damn sick of it!"

"Not so, Da," the boy argued brokenly. "Didn't I do all the spying you told me to? Didn't I manage the stealing after Macao almost got caught? Didn't I snatch that big rock just now, and get nipped smart by that mutt and puked on besides? I just don't know why you've got to go and sicken the sheep, Da."

"To get rid of them, I keep telling you! I'm not spending my time chasing them all over the hills anymore. I'm going to live like a lord!" He cuffed the lad sharply, making him howl. "You're as stupid as your mother."

"Here, now, Tagus, the boy has earned his keep," Macao said. He tapped the lad with a long, dirty finger. "But if he doesn't stop snuffling and take his stinking self out of sight, he can smuggle stones the way the hens do . . . how's that, son?" He jiggled a few sharp-edged gems in front of the boy's horrified eyes. The lad slithered out of his father's grasp and cowered into a corner with silent tears as the men laughed.

"Hush, you two," snapped the gemsmith. "Think I can divide this stone with all that prattle? I need quiet to work on a thing with power." He lined up his tools in precise order. Securing the Thorn in a fleece-lined vise, he placed the point of a gem-cutter against its center. Taking his mallet, he tapped it lightly. A spasm struck his hand and arm, and the mallet clattered to the ground.

"Losing your touch, Quito?" the poultryman asked, laughing.

Shaken, but not wanting to seem a coward, the gemsmith took hold of the mallet securely, determined now to split the gem.

"It's just taken me some time to get used to it," Luca insisted.

"We need a heal-all!" Oskar nearly shouted, holding his friend in his arms as Gwynngold ran to them.

"Stop, Oskar," Luca told him over the din of her dog's terrified howls, "you're scaring Bear out of his wits!"

"She grabbed at her eyes and fell over like the dead," the bravo told Gwynngold all in a rush, "and now she's blind! Haiduks, Roanne, a heal-all, find a heal-all!"

Luca clamped a hand over Oskar's mouth and countermanded him. "Don't you dare, we've no time for such silliness, and we'll need them to help you make the arrests!"

"She's not blind, Oskar, look at her," Gwynngold insisted, realizing what it was Luca could see.

"Help me up, hurry! Bear, don't get underfoot. Oskar, hold my arm." She stared straight ahead, unblinking. "It's all ruddy and dark . . . we're heading for Macao's stall."

"I know where that is!" Roanne announced. "Come on, Haiduks!"

"Go quick, but hide when you get there," Luca told her.

"We don't know how many are there yet, we're still in a pouch. . . ."

"She's seeing through the Thorn, Oskar," Gwynngold told him. She took hold of Luca's other arm, noticing Bear was carefully hidden beneath his mistress's skirt, only the tip of his tail and the occasional grumbling comment revealing him.

"I never should've let her do this," Oskar complained as they helped Luca through the dark aisleways past the last of the fairgoers wending their way back to their own tents.

"We can smell," Luca was mumbling as they sped her along, "and see . . . Macao! He's forcing gems into his birds!"

"We're almost there, Luca," Gwynngold told her.

"That smell, it's awful!" Luca complained.

"Kaffa cud," the Irfan woman decided, "on Macao, no doubt."

"No, it's on the boy, Tagus's boy . . . who weeps from his heart for his dying sheep." And Luca began, herself, to cry.

"If they cut that stone, she'll die!" Oskar hissed through his teeth. "How did I ever agree to this?"

"Turn here, this is near enough!" Luca ordered them, and reached under her skirts to extract her terrified dog. "Don't come any closer, no matter what happens!" She thrust the dog against Oskar's chest. "Don't let loose of him, Oskar, promise?"

"What now, Luca, what are you planning?"

"*Promise,* Oskar. Even if he nips you."

"Do it, Oskar!" Gwynngold shook the man. "She's got to do as she's bid."

Luca jerked suddenly as though she'd been struck and yelped in surprise. "Oskar, *please,* I can't stay here . . ."

"All right!" shouted the perplexed bravo. "All right, I've got him!"

Luca turned blindly in the direction of Macao's tent and called, "I'm coming! Don't worry," and stumbled away even as Oskar clutched her dog, who lay surprisingly calm in his arms.

To Luca, the world seemed a dark, ruddy place, fractured into dozens of repeated images. It was hard to balance herself, place one foot before the other, while at the same time watching a multiple group of Quitos and Macaos and Taguses mill about her. The Thorn was showing her the world through all its many facets, and gradually she was learning how to focus. Any moment now, she knew Quito would land his next, sharp blow, shattering the gem.

The mallet hit its mark when Luca was just behind the tent. She threw her arms across her face as the jewel exploded into a billion fragments. The thick fabric of the tent was shredded as the minute sharp shards swirled up and up into a mushrooming cloud that roared and boomed and blossomed flame.

Luca was dimly aware that the eruption of sound and light had roused every fairgoer across the length and breadth of Ithkar. As if from far away, she could hear the shrieks of frightened people shouting for heal-alls and wizards to fight this terrible magic. Somehow, she knew that all the priests were leaning far from their windows and seeing all too clearly this formidable demonstration of true power.

The cloud of tiny gems began to coalesce into the shape of a gigantic snake-headed demon with razor teeth and burning eyes. Luca was framed by the glimmering creature, shading her eyes against the rainbow light and grinning. Her vision was her own again, and she could see the cloud beast as he formed with huge clawed hands and flaring hood. As his rainbow hide sparkled with all the tiny shards of Luca's shattered gem, he pointed a finger at the three cowering and terrified thieves.

As one person, all the converging fairgoers halted and fell silent as the guilt of the thieving conspirators crystallized within each and every mind. As soon as this knowledge was shared and understood, the unnatural quiet was shredded as Macao began screaming and tearing at his throat, even as Tagus clutched at his belly and fell over and Quito clapped his hands over his eyes and moaned. Before the crowd of astonished onlookers, Macao vomited a cascade of gems and sprouted a soft down, Quito revealed eyes that had become the milky stone found in Gwynngold's mountains, and Tagus began growing a luxurious woolen fleece, his hands and feet becoming small, cloven hooves. His son fled, shrieking, back to his own stall.

Luca walked calmly over to the chickens caged near her. She was not at all surprised to find that the gems sitting leaden in their crops had been spewed from the gut of their owner, and the birds, now healthy, were scratching at their feed. Macao's shrieks were sounding more like chicken squawks, and his legs were becoming scaly. Luca somehow doubted he would end as a rooster. She also knew that when Tagus's son finally looked at his sheep, he would realize they were now freed of the poisonous powder. The drug enhancing their fleece swirled in his father's blood, forcing wool from his pores, even while the demon's magic transformed the brutish man into a large but gentle lamb. The dishonest jeweler could still see out of his gemstone eyes, but the images were opaque and multiplied through each tiny facet.

Finally, the cloud beast turned to Luca. Bringing his massive hand down to her, he held his palm up, and it was bleeding. She pulled the hand into her lap gently, then plucked something from it and held it aloft. As the demon dissolved into shimmering dust that fell slowly to the earth, Luca turned to her friends and showed them her Thorn, restored to her again.

"Tagus's son is a fine lad," Oskar told the women as they relaxed around Gwynngold's fire after a few hours' sleep, "cruelly forced to do his father's work. He's returning home with his ewes all cured and a new flock of hens—including one big, ugly one. He canceled the sale, and he'll have no further trouble from his father, who seems still not quite used to . . . well, being a sheep!"

"I suspect he should produce quite a fleece once he's shorn," Luca offered, and the women burst into giggles.

"I thought it was noble of you to cure him of his own poison, Luca," Gwynngold said, knotting a new holder for the Thorn from colorful strands of Kaffa yarn. "He didn't deserve such kindness!"

"He's just another beast now," Luca reminded them, "no different from the Kaffa, Bear, or us." She gave her dog a gentle hug.

"Oh, it's funny now," Oskar grumbled, "but some of us were damned worried! And I don't know if I'll ever be able to call on Haiduks or Roanne for aid again. They were scared nearly witless. Roanne's even threatened to take the veil!"

"That reminds me," the Irfan woman asked excitedly. "Tell us, Luca, what the priests had to say about all this!"

"Oh, they said they had visions of the Three and their blessings upon my Thorn. They've decided I should be checking the beasts as they enter the gates from now on— and if the gem dims, well, that's all the evidence I need."

Suddenly, Gwynngold cleared her throat and blurted all in a rush, "I've been looking for the right moment to ask you this, Luca. The Irfan have never had an animal healer come to our mountain. I thought perhaps if your work on the fen might be left for a while, you could come home with us after the fair and train me—you would never want for decent food, remember. We'd return next year for the fair, of course. Oskar, wouldn't you care to see the mountains?"

"Gwynngold, I've seen all the wondrous things I'd ever care to this very day. Luca is my dearest friend, and I'll miss her, but I'll be following her on her rounds next year at this time."

"Leave Ithkar?" Luca looked down at Bear, but he declined to comment, choosing for once to remain silent. "And Oskar, what would you do all year without me?"

The long-limbed man folded his arms behind his head as he rested against the placid Daras. "Earn my pay carin' for the priests, as usual, and eat plenty of succulent carcass, my dear!''

The guttural sound of rising cud brought Oskar scrambling to his feet faster than a hot coal, and Bear's baying only punctuated the women's laughter as Daras slowly chewed with lidded eyes.

THE GENTLE ART
OF MAKING ENEMIES

Claudia Peck

Nimrod Beangh would have been notable in any gathering with his perpetually wind-tossed brown curls shot through with gleams of auburn and premature silver, his dark brown beard, and his maverick eyebrows, one light brown and one white. And were he the type to be overlooked, still cek mounts would have caused some stir on most of the well-traveled Ithkar roads in areas other than the south. Ceks, much admired by northerners for their fleetness, their stream-lined appearance, but not for their lumpy and almost wartlike noses, were rarely found beyond their natural boundaries. And one could scarcely miss a voice that carried for lengths down the trail.

"I saw a maid milk a bull," Nimrod roared out in fine baritone. "Fie man, fie. I saw a maid milk a bull; who's the fool now? I saw a maid milk a bull." His voice lent a peculiar emphasis to the remaining lines. "Every stroke a bucketful. Thou hast well drunken, man, who's the fool now?"

Nimrod let the song trail off unfinished. He couldn't understand it. He had not seen anyone since he'd left home, despite the fact that he was on his way to one of the most popular ceremonies in Ithkar. A knot on that edderman, he thought, the man's cast something on me.

He leaned back and laughed. Trouble had driven him out of town, trouble for serenading the edderman's house with that tune and getting the old man in trouble with his mate. For all the edderman's pomp, he had been a humorous sight then.

A more thoughtful, and perhaps more sober, man, Nimrod decided to leave until the edderman was in a better temper. One trick meant ill temper, but two . . . It would be late fall spinning at least before the leader got over his discomfort. And if Nimrod's other escapade came to his attention—as no doubt it would—it could only be a matter of time before his visits to the edderman's sister became known.

It was a matter of little time to gather his weavings, tapestries, and handmade hair saddles, to capture his half-wild pair of ceks, and to be off to Ithkar Fair.

Ah, well . . . He sighed, settled even deeper into the broad cek-traveling saddle, and opened his mouth to sing the chorus. Just then he saw a wine-gold flicker off in the underbrush. He drew in his breath and quietly stopped his mounts. He dropped the cek's weighted tethers.

Dismounting as quietly as he could, he left the trail to slip into the underbrush. The blurred glimmer moved ahead of him in erratic darts, and he followed. It didn't take many attempts to close with the creature for Nimrod to verify his hopes: it was indeed a hyn he pursued. If he could catch it, he could sell it for enough to pay for several trips to the fair. In that case he needed to adopt different tactics. The hyn, he knew, was a clever magical. It had the ability to both change shape and transfer location. Rumor was that the creature had a third power; however, they were so rarely seen that some of their lore had been forgotten. A witch or a priest might have known more of them, but he did not. Still, if he could but catch it— Ah, but there was the difficulty. Hyns had been captured, but how?

Patting his pockets in search of a pipe and brownmir,

Nimrod sat beneath a tree and stared at the hyn thought-fully. It hovered just a few lengths away. If a ripple of color could be termed a jeer, then it did so. Nimrod chuckled. The hyn dipped twice, then settled to the ground, still safely distant, and began to run through a series of transformations, almost as if to amuse itself. It seemed to be able to adjust height, width, or features without any difficulty.

The weaver's chin itched; he raised a hand to scratch it. The hyn was off, flitting around the trunks of two small trees.

Two things, then: the hyn was curious, and perhaps it couldn't move farther than a short distance. He seemed to recall vaguely that if one could ever touch a hyn, it would not be able to transfer.

Nimrod settled down and pretended to yawn and nod. Closing his eyes, he peered at the hyn beneath his eyelashes. It fluttered in indecision and moved a little closer. Nimrod realized the creature was larger than he had first thought; it looked to be about the size of his forearm in length and the width of a medium-sized tree. Stilling his breathing to a slow rise and fall, he watched the hyn approach. If he left, he'd be kicking himself for want of sense. If he stayed, there was no guarantee he would capture it. He relaxed his shoulders. It would not matter if he delayed his journey for an afternoon. . . .

Cursing under his breath, Nimrod walked back to the ceks. They had strayed down the road since he had last checked them, but not too far. He was hot; he was disheveled; and he had wasted the better part of a day using all his woodcraft. Traps did no good; he had known that from the beginning. However, he thought surprise might work. None of his choice food had interested the hyn. Its color had varied more than ever—Nimrod was certain by this time that the color flicker was the hyn's form of laughter. He scratched his chin. Perhaps only one versed in magic can capture such a creature. . . .

Shrugging his shoulders, he called softly to the ceks as he approached. Then he stopped in astonishment. He had pursued that variegated, four-limbed imp of a hyn all over the area, and here it hovered just above his pack animal. As he watched, it calmly alighted and blinked its membrane-covered eyes at him.

"Now can you fathom that?"

Nimrod gathered up the tethers, looped one over the neck of a cek, mounted the other, all in one smooth motion. His cek moved reluctantly. Glancing behind him, Nimrod saw that the hyn rode along without any hesitation.

"How long will you stay, my fine friend?" he murmured.

Soon Nimrod took up a song once more. "I saw a Nim chase a hyn, fie, man, fie. I saw a Nim chase a hyn; who's the fool now? I saw a Nim chase a hyn, far into a wicked fen. Thou hast well drunken, man. Who's the fool now?" He laughed heartily and winked at the creature. "Now that's a good sign," he said, "for the beginning of a journey."

Nimrod groaned. These ceks were bony creatures. Even if they grew as large as barrels, still their bones would protrude to give a rider pain. He'd forgotten how far it was to the Shrine of the Three Lordly Ones. Here it was wellnigh dark and no sign of the fair boundaries.

They rounded a curve, then the lights of the fair-wards shone, dazzling his eyes. Nimrod heaved himself upright, banishing the weary slump of his shoulders, and waved his hat at the wards. He could barely see their outline through the glare. "Ho," he yelled, "and a fine meeting."

"Fair wind at your back, Nimrod Beangh," was the reply. "Have you weapons?"

Nimrod replied, "A minimum," wondering all the while how they had known it was he.

"Toss them behind you. Stand for search."

Nimrod dismounted and waited patiently while they searched his clothing, patted him in places he'd have cried insult another time, and looked with care through his packs. They were stern-faced and spoke little. Nimrod stared at their leathern-covered backs and brass helmets. It was only then that he noticed a cloaked figure off in the shadows. The wizard-of-the-gate, no doubt, searching for concealed magic. A huge angry bellow reached them, possibly from the tent of the Vardos, who were prone to ill temper and battles among themselves. The wizard, his attention distracted, glanced in their direction.

One of the wards spoke abruptly. "Enter. Keep the peace, Nimrod Beangh." Nimrod's eyebrows rose. "Yes, we still recall you. Were it up to us, you would not be granted admittance. Do you think it was chance that you rode alone from the south?"

Then he recognized the fair-ward as one who had risen to an officer in the last fairing. They must have marked him well to have an officer awaiting him, he mused.

"Keep the peace and all will be well. Good fairing to you." The fair-ward inclined his head.

Nimrod avoided his eyes with the ease of long practice. "I'll not be looking for trouble; I can promise you that. Good fairing and less trouble *to you*." He moved toward his cek, but the clerk at the ward's side stretched out his slate. Reluctantly Nimrod scribbled his name, dropped his fee into the waiting palm, and remounted. "See that you give me the table I have marked."

The scribe's eyes flashed.

It bothered the priests not at all if two weavers purchased the same spot, although they were less likely to pull that sort of play on the wealthier cooks.

Nimrod passed through the great gates with a slight inclination of his head to the small carved likenesses of the Three Lordly Ones in the upper niches. His nod was as much to annoy the fair-wards as to pay respect.

It was not until they rounded another curve that he looked back behind him. The hyn was just settling onto the bundle-laden cek. Its color glowed brighter in the half-light. As he watched, it altered its appearance until it looked a rough copy of himself—a much younger self. The image wavered. The hyn winked a membraned eye at him. Those eyes. He shivered. It was disconcerting to look at large, slant-orange eyes through clear membrane. Then the image settled into place. Why *had* the hyn accompanied him? . . . It was a strange little thing. . . . He shrugged. It was a mimic, nothing more.

They reached the middlemost section of the fair, and Nimrod tumbled from his saddle. He tethered the ceks, pulled his sleeping robe from the left pack, took off the heaviest of the bundles, and promised himself an early rising. Looking around the section, lit by the glowing crescents that marked cooks' tents and the softer light rods that marked the weavers', he could make out the glint of the skyreaches of those lucky enough to have dwellings. He pulled out two of the weavings he had marked for the thank-offering to the temple. No matter that it was night; the doors of the temple were always open for offerings. He could safely leave his wares to the guardianship of the ceks—they were less than courteous to strangers—though in the morning he would have to move them to proper quarters.

Nimrod trudged up the pathway toward the temple. Fine gravel crunched under his feet, and he guided himself by that sound and by the feel of the night. It was early yet, the fair not properly begun, and the preparations were not complete. Later the pathway would be well lit. Nimrod tossed the guard at the outer wall a bribe, crossed the cobbled stones to the inner gate, and bribed the second guard as well. Fairing was always expensive due to the need to bribe the fair-wards, pay for tables, *and* give a thank-offering. And if his offerings were not acceptable, he knew from experience that one of the temple members would accompany him to search his pack for a better. The two weavings he carried with him, however, were worthy offerings, colored by rare dyes.

The area around the temple teemed with life even on the

first night: ladies in long, stiff robes and intricate tabards; soft-voiced eastern men in dark clothes and darker skins; women in softer fabrics; money-lenders, scribes, and jaded collectors; converts of Thotharn with coarse robes and close-shaven heads; Sisters of the Moon, now-empty scabbards at their belts, their faces half-painted in ceremonial tracery, the other half without. Above them all, on the temple steps, those birds of ill omen—the priests—their smoky eyes held silence, and more than silence, captive. The temple that loomed overhead, square save for a round tower in the center, made the large crowd look minuscule in comparison. As he approached, the vague unease that always filled him at the thought of the priesthood increased. Nimrod never enjoyed this obligatory trip, and he hoped that the ceremonies would soon be over.

As he joined the offering line, he felt a large hand clasp his shoulder, and a voice boomed, "Welcome, Nim, I've not seen you in a fairing or two."

"Senshal! How goes it in the north?" He turned and clasped the large, hairy man to him, smacking him on the shoulders with the palms of his hands. Both men ignored the glares of those around them.

"Well enough, though I hear you do better."

"I can't complain," Nimrod said while eyeing the huge sypal ring on his friend's hand and the matching one on the armband that circled his left arm. His friend had been a fool to wear this sort of finery before he'd made his thank-offering. "Lord Gismael has commissioned a weaving from me this turning. I had intended to send it with someone from a village near my own, but at the last moment I decided to come instead."

Senshal pulled his large mustache. "You haven't heard, then? Lord Gismael died this last ten-day."

"Nay! But I had counted on that weaving. Full sorrows to his widow," he added hastily.

"Perhaps his family will hold to the bargain. His son's here, I understand, and a bad business it is, too. Celebrating

and his father barely covered with stone.'' He lowered his
voice as a man just in front of them turned to stare. The
stranger's clothing marked him as one of the followers of
Thotharn, a minor religious sect of which there were rumors
of strange practices. ''At any rate, the pledge may still
stand.''

Nimrod's face brightened. ''I'll look for him tomorrow.''
The line moved closer to the priest's table. ''I see you come
late, as I do, so that we don't have to enter the temple and
waste the day with their ceremonies. These priests do not
please me. Their sifting of thoughts . . . it leaves a trail.''

Senshal laughed. ''I like them not much, either, and their
torches make me gag. Guard your thoughts. I've heard
much the same from others.''

Nimrod looked toward the table. Just behind the sleepy-
looking scribe who received the offering, he could see a
young priest, robed in black with gold trim. The priest's
dark-rimmed eyes regarded him steadily. Nimrod could smell
the torches even from the steps, and their perfume had a
narcotic effect. He moved up to the table in his turn.
Thotharn's follower brushed by him with a glance of dis-
taste, and Nimrod marked him to memory. The fellow had
pale, dishwater hair and a pasty complexion.

''What offerings do you bring, sera Beangh, this fairing?''

''Two weavings, priestly one, of a surpassing fine dye.''

''Of your weavings we have plenty, man of the south.''

''Not the likes of these.'' He heard Senshal snort. With
an effort he kept a straight face. ''Examine the dyes, look at
the richness of the scene and the loft of the thread. This
tapestry will cover half of one of your inner walls. And it is
the scene of the arrival of the Three—''

''Yes, yes.'' The priest behind the scribe waved a languid
hand. ''We will require an additional two kars.''

''*Two kars!* Why that is fully twenty-four ithlings!''

''Two kars.'' He smiled at Nimrod, and the tips of his
teeth glinted as the smile widened. ''Or perhaps you would
prefer to enter the temple and consult.''

"Two it is." Nimrod spilled the coins out onto the table and began to count them hurriedly. As he counted, the priest stared just over Nimrod's shoulder and asked, "What brings you to the fair, sera Beangh?"

"I come to sell, to sing, and to take a rest from my keep."

"And perhaps give them a rest as well." The priest's eyes were shrewd. Nimrod heard Senshal suppress a laugh. "See that you keep the peace, sera Beangh." He touched the tips of his fingers together and bowed quickly to Nimrod, who returned the favor before he moved back through the crowd to await Senshal. Two weavings and an additional two kars. Saddled with a hyn that loved the taste of lrna, a not inexpensive drink. I'll regain that money, he vowed. They'll not find me such an easy pocket.

"These priests grow too fat," he muttered as Senshal rejoined him. "Why, by the forks of the road and the fast wind in my face—" He broke off as a fair-ward strolled by. Senshal pulled his mustache and said nothing. "Senshal, will you need a helper in your stall? I must recoup my losses, what with Lord Gismael's death and these robber priests—" He broke off again and doffed his hat at a passing fair-ward.

"Meals and five ithlings a day."

"Done." They clasped hands.

"It may be that we can pull these priests' whiskers for them. Eyes open, wits about us." Senshal's brown eyes held a hint of glee.

"The last time you said that, they threw us out of the fair."

"And have we not learned from that?" Senshal's voice was complacent.

Nimrod winked. "I'll help you set up in the morning."

"I begin not so long after sun's rise."

"I do recall."

Senshal left him then, in front of the largest styeach, a true cook's tent indeed with its soft leather flaps gleaming in the moonlight. Its crescent light guided Nimrod back to his own gear. He pulled a few more bundles from the ceks and stretched out on his bedding. Placing his hands beneath his head, he glanced at the hyn, which had settled on his largest bundle and was regarding him with unwinking eyes. It never sleeps, he pondered drowsily. And with that he fell asleep himself.

He awoke in the morning only to discover the hyn was gone and the ceks were unburdened. The remainder of his wares were neatly stacked like a wall to his left. Most of the tents showed no sign of life, no morning fires. Nimrod wondered where the hyn had gone. It would be difficult to detect the creature if it changed shape. Ah, well . . . the imp had come at its whim and would stay or go at its whim. It seemed all his plans were going awry.

Nimrod patted the nearest cek absentmindedly on the rump. Finally he decided to take a stroll around the section before brewing the lrna and joining Senshal.

Steam rose curling from the pool in a great billow until it was difficult to see even the thick-packed grass squares, droplets hanging from them as dew on a spider's web. Nimrod leaned back and felt the heat of the stones beneath him sting his back, and then his skin grew accustomed to it. Men around him grunted, and one hummed an idle tune under his breath. From the distance came the roar of the festival crowd, now grown as large as any Nimrod had seen, in one mere day.

This was the feast, then, with the steam in your nostrils, the stones at your back, and soon a good measure of liquor in your mug. The day could have been better: he could have sold his weaving to Lord Gismael's son; nonetheless, a while in Senshal's cooktent with food and drink to spare was not so bad after all. He lifted a dipperful of water and trickled it over his calves. It was a matter of joining in the fair, of feeling that your hand fit the filled mug, your glance those that passed, and a certain tight cord of emotion that wove even as those who came eased. And with the ease came a feeling of mischief running within him until he scarcely needed wish to unleash it. On a night such as this, when the cool brisk air wrapped the shoulders like a brother's cloak, one would *scarcely* need one's clothes. He stole silently from the inner room of the heatra to the dressing closet and dressed quietly. He stuffed the clothes lying in five careful piles into his shoulder sack. A mere jest and a bit of skin between fair-brothers. Grinning at the thought, he closed the tightly sealed door even more firmly with his foot and moved to open the door flap that broached the outside. As he did so, a woman with dark curling hair and liquid, mocking eyes swept through with a tray of mugs. He lifted one from the tray as he tossed her the change. She caught it deftly in one hand, still balancing the tray with the other, and gave him a curtsy. He lifted his hand to her shoulder. She brushed by him and made for the sealed door. Nimrod left without haste and with a slight swagger. He chuckled as he thought of those still in the heatra and the journey they would make in their skins.

A slight figure slipped from the crowd to walk beside him, and he looked down at it in surprise. Flaming red hair, a dusting of speckles across the nose, a young stripling looked up at him. And who are you? he wondered silently, until looking at the fellow's eyes, he detected for a moment the slant-orange glance of the hyn.

"So and so, you grow better at it; but, my friend, if you seek to go for lrna in the taverns with me, you'd best change your form to one somewhat older."

The hyn's face took on an older cast with swiftness, and he grew a span or so even as Nimrod watched. "Do you talk as well?"

The brown eyes the hyn had assumed were as inscrutable as its own.

"Ah, well, I'll say you're my own cousin from Varya,

who's not spoken since birth. I wonder what you've been playing at today.''

They proceeded to the Irna booth. Nimrod brushed past the throng with practiced ease and one broad shoulder; the hyn kept pace with him, a little of its hovering grace even in this form.

It was not until they neared the booth and Nimrod heard a rippling swell of laughter behind him that he remembered his joke. The heatra was at the edge of the fair that bordered the outer wall. The men had no way to slip from it quietly to their lodgings. Those he had left without clothes had to walk through at least a small part of the way he had just come and past the booth. The laughter he heard behind them was likely from that passage.

He paused, the hyn standing just behind his left shoulder, and watched. The crowd parted in front of him, and he saw three men who wore little more than bath towels push aside those who laughed. Nimrod chuckled and slapped his knees. A hand grabbed his right shoulder, and a quiet voice said, ''Be you silent, Nimrod Beangh, and give me back my clothes. I have a mind to keep them.''

Nimrod turned with a grin and a flare of the eyebrow to face a tall man in clothes that strained at the seams. The fellow's level eyes stared into Nimrod's, green-flecked with gold and a faint, black circle around the edge like the eyes of a feline. Nimrod held the man's gaze in faint inquiry, and then the echo of his grin lit the stranger's face.

''With pleasure to a man who likes a good jest.'' The weaver rummaged through the bag and then tossed it to the stranger.

The other's grin widened. ''And how could not a jest please the jester?''

''What do you mean?''

''I am called Wyr, which means 'jest' in my land's tongue.''

''How did you find me?''

''The woman who entered as you left has somewhat of

the sight and a liking for me as well." He flipped a wave to Nimrod and turned away, then shouted back over his shoulder, "If you seek good entertainment later, come by the circle. Look for Wyr the juggler."

Nimrod turned back to find the hyn regarding him with inquisitive eyes. For the first time it showed some sort of expression, though what it was he couldn't tell. The crowd surged, and the two of them made their way to the booth.

It was only with slight surprise that he found a quiet table in the corner served by the selfsame woman who had spoken of his tricks to the juggler. She tossed her hair braid back over her shoulder, her eyes mocking, as she poured the lrna. Nimrod waggled his hand at the hyn to no avail, for it quickly drank the contents of the mug and handed it to her for more.

"Faith, *cousin*, I'll soon be without an ithling if you drink so much."

Her eyes widened as she looked at the hyn, and her eyebrows lifted. "You should not have brought him here."

"Cousin Hynlin? Why, he's harmless enough, though he drinks too much. He can't talk, you know, silent from birth." Nimrod spoke to gain time. The hyn smiled charmingly and drained yet another mug.

"You know well what I mean, Nimrod Beangh. What a combination you and that will make! I tremble for those who do not know the pair of you. Though perhaps it will not be so bad if you can do more than feeble jests this fairing." Her murmur was soft and barely reached him.

"Mellowed I am, perhaps, or distracted." He swept his arm around her waist and whispered in her ear, "What do you know of these creatures?"

"Little enough, save that they don't often partner with men. The sight does not look into them, but keep it away from the priests. They would have barred it from their walls had they known. You didn't know they posted a ban on these?" The hyn grabbed her pitcher and refilled its mug. "There are few seen anymore, so they have relaxed their guard this past fairing or two, or I should think you'd not have gotten in. They can keep them beyond the walls, but once inside . . ." She shrugged. "You're fortunate I have little love for the priests."

"You are wise in your choice of friends. . . ."

She snorted.

"The hyn seems harmless enough."

"The grim and proper sealhs *seemed* harmless enough until they breached the holds of the north and so brought down a whole way of life." She tossed her head. "The priests can't ward the hyn's magic. Did you not hear me; they cannot *see* into a hyn."

"Yiertha!" A man at the other corner roared for drink, and she slipped from Nimrod's grasp.

"So they like not what they cannot ward, eh, cousin? That may prove useful." He clapped the hyn on the shoulder and rose, tossing coins on the table. "Let us go see Wyr juggle. I have it in my mind to sing this night until the morning's frost tickles our ears."

The hyn downed another mug and rose somewhat unsteadily, brown eyes blinking and in the center a flicker of orange. They walked to the door. When they were in the dark and well away from the booth, Nimrod turned again to speak. But the hyn was off in a luminescent, clumsy waver high above the crowd. Nimrod stood watching it. "Ah, well, I think that even a drunken hyn would be some little trouble to capture."

The fire burned almost smokeless with the bright glow of the coals. Three dancers in gaudy costumes whirled around the flames to the staccato beat of a leather-covered instrument, while at the next fire other voices lifted in atonal harmony. Fires stretched still farther down the entertainment row.

Nimrod danced the light and stately rhythms of the Veha Mûr, the great music, with half-closed eyes and outstretched arms, catching and twirling each woman as she passed, enjoying the feel of the rich fabric sliding through his hands and the mixture of scents that wafted as they passed. Feet scuffed toward fires, and occasional spurts of flame shot up from kicked debris. The awakening was rough when pairs of hands seized him from behind and broke the chain of dancers.

"You can't mistake those eyebrows!" shouted a small, dark man.

"I saw him with a large bundle on his back," said another with a large patch over one eye. "I think it had our clothes in it." They shoved Nimrod ahead of them. "We'll haul you before the fair-wards and let *them* deal with you!"

"Softly, softly." Nimrod turned to face twenty men or more, all gesticulating excitedly. "And how could I be stealing the clothes of all of you when I've been here dancing and singing the night through?"

His eyes shot a puzzled glance toward Wyr, who stood back in the shadows. Wyr's quiet voice cut through the crowd. "I'd be slow to accuse this man if I were you. The priests do not deal lightly with those who raise voice without proof. Beangh has been here half the night, trailing from one circle to another. If your clothes were stolen during that time, he isn't your man." The hands dropped with reluctance from his arms. The large man left off only when the others pulled him away.

Wyr winked at Nimrod. "And I can attest he has been here during that time. Is it not so?" He turned to the crowd of dancers.

"We saw him here," several murmured, and the musicians began lightly playing the Veha Mûr. Nimrod backed away, but a hand drew him into the circle once more. Turning, he saw Yiertha, the goblet wench, eyes sparkling in merriment. As she drew him away, he heard one of the men muttering about a strange little creature that wouldn't stay still.

"It was all we found when we searched," he said.

Under cover of the argument, she whispered to him,

"Did I not tell you? If you are not careful, Nimrod, your stay at this fair could be difficult indeed."

He smiled at her and curled a hand around her waist. "You're very perceptive, Yiertha; but it seems that the hyn has elaborated upon my 'feeble jest.' I have you and Wyr to thank that the crowd hasn't yet turned ugly. It takes but little to stir them up, it seems, this fairing."

Nimrod turned and watched the men, their voices quieter now and their movements less emphatic. He judged it best to remain within the circle, so he moved with the dancers and then slipped, at Wyr's signal, from the circle at the other side of the fire. He left to go in search of the hyn.

It was with some relief that he found it resting on his extra robe. All he could see was the rise and fall of the hyn's breathing and the gleam of its eyes, although its breath was punctuated with an occasional half hitch, almost a hiccup.

"You'll be rationed if you don't learn more discretion. What if they had searched my bag?" The hyn's color flickered feebly. "And what of the clothes you stole? What need have you for clothes?" The color flared a bit brighter.

Nimrod lay down. He reached over softly and smoothed a coverlet into place. Surely the hyn could not be stealing into his heart? He put both hands underneath his head and stared at the clouds drifting overhead. He had found no woman who could stay his feet, surely he would *not* saddle himself with a little bump of a creature? Nah.

A picture crossed his mind of every Beangh trick done twice or thrice again, and a small chuckle escaped him. "That *would* ruffle the fair-ward's feathers for certain; but by the Three, they would never let me hear the end of it." Faint strains of music drifted on the air, and he hummed the tune idly. Every now and again he glanced at the hyn and smiled.

Nimrod slapped the table. "You're mad, Senshal. There are those who say I am, but in the name of the Three, it's quiet, gentle Senshal who holds the title undisputed."

"Softly, softly. Lower your voice, or we may find ourselves with unwanted meddlers." The roar of the lrna booth
had lowered, and several looked toward their table with
curiosity.

"*I* may wish to regain my two kars from those priests,
perhaps with a little interest. But I don't think it wise to lose
my neck doing so. This scheme of yours could get us
drummed out of the fair!"

"I've bribed the outer and inner wall guards. The cousin
of the inner guard wishes to sell the items once we obtain
them. He's provided us with neophyte robes."

"Why not priestly robes? If someone stops us, they'll
realize right away that—"

"Then you will do it!" Senshal's laugh boomed.

Nimrod leaned over the table. "Well, it would be a
tale," he conceded. "And I wouldn't mind having a magical item or two. I wonder what trinkets are so powerful that
they led the priests to confiscate them at the gates. How will
we know what to use them for once we have them?"

Senshal winked. "We can sell them all and let the buyer
beware."

"Done, then." Nimrod laid his hand deliberately in the
middle of the table.

"Done, then," echoed Senshal, and laid his hand over
Nimrod's.

"Softly now, here comes the goblet wench I told you of
with the sight. Think of her curves or a game of snakes and
bones or anything else if you will; but drop this for now. I'll
meet you outside the gates at dark."

Senshal nodded and left. Yiertha approached and smiled
at him. "Lrna?"

He tossed a few ithlings on the table. "Not now. But why
don't you meet me at the circle?" He pulled her close to
murmur, "We'll dance the Veha Mûr together."

"And a few other things?"

"And a few other things indeed. Those most of all."

She grinned, and then a puzzled look replaced the grin. "What do you plan, Nimrod?"

"What we talked of."

She frowned. "No, something . . . it comes and it goes."

"Someday I'll tell you . . . over a mug of lrna." He smiled and pulled a lock of her hair. "I'm looking forward to this evening—*all* of it."

She slipped past him and said over her shoulder, "Have a care."

"I assure you I intend to."

He met Senshal in the gathering shadows of the temple gate. The glow that lit the pathway was muted there, as though some of the lights had been purposefully dimmed. A cloaked figure waited for them at the door.

"Quick, man, put on your robe." Senshal shoved it in his hands. The two of them dressed hurriedly before stepping through the door. Nimrod had a sudden wild feeling that they had attracted all the attention of the priests. He even had the sensation that the Three were standing at his back, their unwavering gaze upon him. Shadows flickered across the courtyard and followed them in through the second gate, where they saw no guard at all.

They entered a small, narrow passageway to the left of the inner gate. A vibrant hum shattered the silence, and Nimrod froze.

"That's the choir, you fool," hissed Senshal. "All their energies will be centered on singing the feast night lays into shape. That's one of the reasons I chose tonight." He pulled out a map, flicked a finger glow, and muttered irately to himself. "Here it is. Next corridor, veer, and then take a second way to the lower level."

"Lower level? You said nothing about that! I've heard rare tales about the bowels of this temple, and I've no desire to test them."

"But now that you're here?"

Nimrod glanced back along the dimly lit corridor. He

turned back to Senshal. "Now that I'm here." His tone was glum.

They reached the lower level without encountering anyone.

Senshal touched Nimrod's arm. "Be quiet, someone behind us."

They pressed up against the wall and looked in vain for a safer hiding place. Whoever was coming walked with a heavy tread. They could hear the echo of footsteps. A figure rounded the corner, and Nimrod cursed softly but fervently. "It's that thrice-blasted, double besliced hyn!"

"What do you mean?"

"I brought the imp with me from the forests in the hopes of selling it, and it's been nothing but trouble. We don't need it here; I can warrant you that!" Nimrod called, "Get out of here—or by the very—"

The hyn stared at them.

Nimrod groaned. "You damnable beast—"

A second pair of footsteps sounded farther down the ramp. The pair froze. The hyn remained unconcernedly in the center of the hall, its eyes blinking in the light of an approaching torch. The bearer's robe marked him as high priest, one who looked vaguely familiar to Nimrod. Then he recognized the choirmaster, doubtless on his way to take over the singing from his assistant. With one hand shading his eyes, the priest paused as though puzzled. Then he called out, "Who is it, who— Beangh and Senshal the cook . . . what do you here?"

The hyn shot up into the higher reaches of the corridor, hovering over the priest's head, while Nimrod and Senshal took to their heels in the direction of the upper reaches. The priest called after them.

Noise came from the direction of the choir. Nimrod beat Senshal to the upper reaches, and they both clattered into the courtyard. No place in the fair will be safe now, Nimrod thought, even though he continued to run. We'll need a rare trick even to win beyond the fair's outer gates. As though he had caught Nimrod's thought, Senshal nodded to him grimly, and the two of them doubled their speed.

They reached the temple's inner gate and were through it without a hitch. It swung closed behind them, the gate master either not quite quick enough to answer orders or giving them a chance to escape so that he wouldn't be involved in an all-too-obvious failure. Nimrod slipped on the cobbles and cursed.

"Senshal, go on."

Senshal picked up the weaver and lifted him to one shoulder. Even with the extra weight he still moved quickly. They reached the outside gate, the noise of the temple fainter now. The inner court was ominously silent. Senshal lowered Nimrod to his feet. Nimrod tested his ankle, which seemed sound. The tender of the outer gate had left it ajar, and as they looked out, they saw him taking to his heels. With a quick, puzzled glance at Senshal, Nimrod moved toward the nearest shadows.

Somehow the voice at their back was no surprise at all, almost comforting, when compared to the unknown horror they feared at the hands of the priests. "Halt there, Beangh. And Senshal. My, what company you keep. The pair of you inside the temple means no good."

"The fair-ward captain," whispered Senshal.

"We've done it now," Nimrod said.

"It's that hyn of yours that did for us, you mean," Senshal snarled. "I'll not forgive you for getting me drummed out of the fair."

"Once again," Nimrod muttered.

"Once again, and perhaps for the last time."

"I've waited for an excuse to rid the fair of you." The captain chuckled. "Wyr and Fendek, escort these gentlemen to their lodgings and encourage them to pack quickly. Then return them for the haling."

"Wyr!" Nimrod exclaimed.

"Even so." Wyr took Nimrod's arm and began to walk

with him past the outer gate. "Not all of us dress to fit our positions."

"Or act the part . . . at all times?" Nimrod queried softly.

Wyr's voice held only a trace of regret. "A jest and a foray into the temple are widely separate acts." He slapped the weaver on the shoulder. "No, you're well baited and hooked, my little fish, doubt it not."

They moved through the fair, crowd parting slightly for the fair-wards and casting curious glances at the two they escorted. Senshal and Nimrod looked at each other from time to time, but it was plain that neither of them had any particular hope of escape. In order to reach their camp they had to pass by the entertainment circle, and Nimrod played idly with that thought. He had forgotten that Yiertha would be there. And, at any rate, she was as much a friend to Wyr as—

When they neared the row, the first two circles were quiet, but they could hear sounds of some sort of fray coming from the fourth circle. Wyr curtly directed the other fair-ward ahead. He warned Nimrod and Senshal, "If this is one of your tricks, Beangh, I'll have your— We'll wait for Fendek to return."

"Mine? I've been at the temple."

Senshal flicked an expressive glance at Nimrod. Nimrod gave a bare nod. These fair-wards were not like the officers, he reflected; if the commotion gave them an opportunity, they might have a little time.

They were there for quite a while, and Fendek had not returned. Wyr gave a suspicious nod. "We'll go past the circle, but you'll not make a move without me."

The Veha Mûr circle was filled with small groups rolling on the ground, women fighting women, women punching men, men punching women, and across the circle Yiertha, perched on a stump safely apart from the fray, was laughing at it all. Nimrod looked across to her in amazement. She mouthed, "The hyn," and shrugged her shoulders. Just then a woman jumped up from the ground, kicking a man to one side. Her eyes widened when she saw Nimrod.

"There he is, that limb of the devil." She ran toward Nimrod, shooting her fist out in a right jab. Nimrod ducked, and the blow fell squarely upon Wyr's chin. Nimrod and Senshal took to their heels. The weaver dashed around the circle toward Yiertha, whom he could no longer see. Senshal darted away in another direction.

Nimrod yanked Yiertha from her rock. "Come on," he said, and kept running. A priest of Thotharn brushed up against Nimrod, muttered, "You'll not wait long, Nimrod Beangh, for your reckoning," and was gone almost before what he said registered.

"What bites his ear?" Nimrod panted.

"Who knows? Perhaps your hyn has been there before you as well."

Nimrod looked back over his shoulder and saw Wyr weaving through the crowd. The fair-ward was gaining rapidly. "Why don't you leave the fair with me?"

"Leave the fair?! What *have* you stirred?" Then she stopped. He yanked her on. "You've brought my father's choir about your ears as well."

"Your father?" As they rounded the corner of the lrna booth, they heard the sounds of an upset cart behind and loud cursing. If she goes with me, he thought, I'll have the pleasure of good company *and* I'll prick those priests, or at least one of them, after all. "Later you can tell me about it. Will you go?"

"Yes," she gasped. "It will not please my father. There should be no half blood from the priesthood. He does not acknowledge me, but he would not like me from under his thumb. Are you sure you want me to go?"

"What do you mean?"

"I'm not too sure that your hyn will like it."

Nimrod shook his head impatiently and said, "Leave that to me." He pushed aside two clowns and a tinker, shouting as he passed, "Delay the ward who follows!"

Anger forgotten, they nodded and winked. Duck the nap was a game they'd played before, he thought.

"Run to the livestock section. Pack my gear. If you can, go by the stall and pick up my weaving. If not"—he shrugged—"they're lost. I hope in the confusion that they've neglected to check there. Whatever you get away with, even if nothing at all but the ceks, take that and go by the side pathway. Skirt the bravos' area. I'll look for you there. Stay with the ceks, they'll keep off unwelcome attention for a while."

"And you?" She looked at him quizzically.

"I'll divert them. I've got an idea," he shouted as he ran. He darted around the corner and ran square into his double. Nimrod's hands grabbed the hyn by instinct, and he exclaimed in triumph, "At last I've got my hands on you, you imp!"

A shout raised behind him, and he turned, holding on to the struggling hyn as it changed from man into its own form. Nimrod tucked it under his arm.

"Stay there, you beast!"

Wyr moved toward him, though Nimrod saw no look of recognition in the man's eyes. "Duck the nap!" Nimrod shouted as he jumped over a low railing and darted behind a booth. He could hear others roar with laughter and move in to intercept the fair-ward. This can't go on much longer, he thought, or the priests would locate him by noise alone. He looked up. Two priests stood in front of him, eyes searching the crowd. Yet it was as if they could not see him. The hyn— Nimrod smiled. He paused, then ducked around another nearby booth and away. Locating a path, he ran steadily now, shouting every so often as he ran, "Duck the nap!" while confusion boiled behind.

He reached the bravos' area with seconds to spare and made his way through their training center, shouting as he went. The bravos poured into the area, obviously spoiling for a fight. "A hive swarms behind me," Nimrod gasped to the first bravo who reached him. He paused to gasp for breath.

The bravo dismissed Nimrod's comment with a quick wave of the hand, as though it were too obvious to note. "What do you have under your arm?"

Nimrod looked at the hyn, whose color had dimmed to a dull gray. "A rare magical, would you purchase it?"

"What manner of magic?"

"A hyn." He reached down to rub his sore ankle.

"A hyn . . ." The man's eyes widened. "Will you sell it?"

Nimrod glanced back over his shoulder, but he heard nothing yet of pursuit. "Gladly." Nimrod's tone was wry. "Four kars?"

"Done."

"Done. I'll hand you the hyn as you hand over the money. Hold on to it tightly, or you'll regret its loss." The creature looked up at him with unblinking eyes, and Nimrod felt a twinge of guilt. "Be good to it," he whispered softly as he handed the hyn over, pocketing the coins. The creature's color flickered feebly, and it blinked its eyes.

The sounds of the chase grew louder. "Good journey, little cousin," Nimrod shouted as he entered the overgrown path, the alternate route he had spoken to Yiertha about. It was a long and twisty way. He rounded a curve in the path and stopped short as the bushes rustled. Then out stepped Yiertha, muttering to the ceks.

"I had the worst of it."

"Perhaps." He grinned, then mounted the nearest cek, tossed the tether over its neck, and drummed his heels at its sides. "Do you have the ability to ward?"

"Imperfectly."

"Better than none. Let's try the gate."

They rode rapidly through the pathway, and Nimrod clenched his teeth as the bushes whipped back against his legs. Yiertha rode on ahead, and he heard her exclaim. He kicked the cek, setting it to a bone-racking pace. When he arrived, he saw only wildly whipping bushes.

"Yiertha," he called, and heard a faint, muffled:

"Fly!"

He looked at the bushes in indecision. "Haste, fly, I'll follow!" he heard her yelling at the cek. It had bolted, he thought. He whistled to it and heard it stop and then move back toward the path.

She caught up with him several lengths later. He glanced at her. Her hood was over her head. She looked at him impatiently and with a hint of embarrassment, then nodded for him to continue. They heard shouts from the bravo camp. Fair-wards at the camp and fair-wards at the gate, Nimrod thought grimly.

"By the Three, I hope you can ward their sight."

She did not reply but kicked the cek. It moved ahead of him. They broke through the underbrush and were upon the gate before Nimrod realized. There were fair-wards standing by the pathway, gates open, some travelers arriving with rows of wharf carts and tumbled finery leaking from the top bundle. The fair-ward in charge was telling them to move aside, no entry at the moment; but they seemed unwilling to stop. One of the escorts pushed heatedly at the gate, and it swung wide. The entrance looked enough to scrape through. The two rode for it, lashing the ceks as they ran. The fair-wards did not seem to see them, and Nimrod called on all the saints of every religion he could remember in gratitude. He noted with relief that there was no witch or wizard in sight.

The gate fair-ward, making a point to the escorts, stuck out his hand and struck Nimrod's arm. He shouted in surprise. Nimrod pushed by, and they were outside the gate, guards still yelling behind.

The ceks thundered off the pathway and into a side stretch of woods. They located another path and were several lengths down it before they ventured to stop.

Nimrod looked at Yiertha. "By the skin of our skin, I would say, we are free; but we're still not home."

She did not reply.

"What is the matter with your tongue?"

She looked at him and grinned. In the center of her eyes there flickered for an instant a bit of orange. Then he knew. "You—"

Words failed him. You've met your match, Nim, he thought, and kicked the sides of his cek in discontent. The hyn changed, its colors a riot of merriment. They rode along the trail in silence. The weaver gave a disgruntled laugh, then another, more honest one. He looked back at the hyn and roared.

Patting the shoulder of his cek, he began to sing, "I saw a Nim chase a hyn, fie, man, fie. I saw a Nim chase a hyn. Who's the fool now? I saw a Nim chase a hyn, far into a wicked fen. Thou hast well drunken, man, who's the fool now?"

DAY OF STRANGE FORTUNE

Carol Severance

The used-clothing dealer waved a hand in front of his face and frowned at Eliana. "Phew, boy! You smell like rotten fish! Keep your hands off my merchandise."

"I smell of *fresh* fish, merchant," replied Eliana. "And if you care to hawk your wares, I advise you to keep a civil tongue in your head." She met the man's stare boldly for a moment, then returned to her inspection of the clothing pile. She ran her work-roughened hand over a woolen coat sleeve, noting that the fabric was worn thin in places.

"Dead fish," the clothes dealer muttered.

Eliana ignored him. Her hand strayed toward a soft brown cloak, lying in loose folds beneath the coat. It, too, was made of wool, but it felt like the softest of furs under her fingers. She wondered for a moment if the shopkeeper was enhancing his wares magically and ran her fingers across the soft fabric again. She could sometimes detect an illegal spell by the touch of it on her skin. But the cloak seemed to carry no taint of dishonesty. She turned back to the coat.

The shopkeeper stepped closer and settled his fists on his hips. His tight leather breeches pulled at the lacings and forced his bulging stomach to hang in folds over his hands. His startlingly green shirt was richly embroidered at cuffs and neck but frayed along the edges as if it had come from among his own secondhand wares.

"I want no thieving wharf rats in my tent," he said. "Go elsewhere with your dirty hands."

Eliana watched him without appearing to shift her attention from the clothing; it was a survival technique she'd mastered as a child growing up on the docks. With a seemingly casual motion, she brushed back her stained overtunic so that the man could see she carried a money pouch.

Immediately the merchant's dark eyes took on a look of interest and cunning. "Ah," he said in tones falsely respectful, "and what would a lad like you be seeking to buy?"

Eliana met his look, eyes flashing. "I am looking for a decent coat," she said. "One suitable for a long sea voyage. And I'm not a lad."

Eliana almost smiled at the merchant's startled look. For she knew that he had thought her a boy and not a young woman. Her blacker-than-black hair was cropped short, and her skin was dark, tanned by exposure to wind and sun, and she wore the trousers and overtunic of a dockworker. Even her stance was that of a man. Her eyes, however, filled now with challenge, revealed the truth of her claim. The merchant's voice became patronizing.

"You've come to the right place, madam," he said with a covert glance toward her waist pouch. "My name is Harad, and I have here some of the finest new and used clothing in Ithkar."

Eliana glanced around the crowded enclosure. The only thing new she could detect was the smell of freshly salted fish. And she had brought that in with her.

Harad stepped around the table and lifted the coat Eliana had first touched, pressing it into her hands. "This garment is made of the best Warin wool," he said. "You can see there are few stains. It was owned previously by a highborn noble who parted with it only because of the changing styles. It's in top condition. A true bargain.''

"It's worn thin and has a badly mended rip under one arm," Eliana said, tossing it back. "And judging from its odor, that nobleman must have worked in the horse stables." She ignored the merchant's feigned look of insult and glanced toward the brown cloak. She was drawn to it even though she had little use for such a loose, heavy wrap. Its apparent richness might attract more trouble than it was worth in the dark corners of the docks.

The merchant caught her glance. He reached for the cloak. "Perhaps this is what you seek," he said, stopping his hand just before it touched the brown wrap. He hesitated for an instant, then pulled his hand back, frowning. Again Eliana was minded of magic but could think of no reason for the man's reluctance to touch the cloak. Had he laid an enhancing spell on it, surely he would not hesitate to hawk it in his best manner.

"I've no need for a nobleman's cape," she said.

"Ah," replied Harad, and he began pulling other garments from the pile, carefully avoiding the brown wool. Curious, Eliana examined each of the offered coats carefully, paying no mind to Harad's sales pitch. Several of the garments, she was certain, were not quite what they seemed, but she could not prove they had been tampered with magically. She carefully set those aside and moved on to others. She needed a coat that was sturdy and warm, not flamboyant, but certainly not shabby if she was to succeed in her plans. This was not a time to allow herself to be cheated.

Her aged and ailing uncle had died just weeks before, leaving her the sole owner of their thriving fish dealership. And while the business was not large, it had over the years provided her and her uncle with a decent profit. Eliana had managed to save much of her wages, all but what they needed to live on, and was now ready to seek her dream.

For as long as she could remember, Eliana had wanted to leave Ithkar to seek trade and adventure in the lands beyond the Western Sea. She planned to lease the fish business, or sell it if she must, and purchase a stock of trade goods. Then she would join the crew of the trading vessel *Alakai* on its upcoming exploratory voyage across the Western Sea. Once there, she was sure she could achieve a large profit with her trade goods and return to Ithkar a wealthy woman. Even if she lost everything, she would at least have had the adventure of trying. She thought that a suitable goal in itself.

The greatest difficulty now was to convince Captain Sturming to take her on as crew. Women were sometimes taken on exploratory voyages as cooks or washerwomen, but Eliana had no intention of seeking her dream in the blinding steam of a washtub or the heat of a shipboard galley. She must find a way to convince the captain that she could be as valuable to his ship as any male member of his crew. She was too well known on the docks to successfully hide her sex for long. And besides, she did not wish to begin her great adventure with a lie. Not that lie, at any rate.

"You like the cloak, it seems. Why don't you try it on?"

The merchant's smooth voice pulled Eliana from her thoughts, and she found that she was again running her fingers over the brown woolen cape. She frowned, wondering again about magic, then dismissed the thought as impossible. No merchant this close to the temple precinct would dare dabble in spells to make his goods sell; the priests would surely find him out. Besides, while the cloak seemed strange, it did not have the feel of illegal magic.

She pulled it from the clothing pile, then shook it to release the wrinkles and held it up with both hands. The wool was good quality, still firmly woven, though the garment was made in one of the older styles. It was plain except for a small line of embroidery along the edge of the hood. The fine embroidery threads were only a shade darker than the cape itself, and in the dimness of the tent she had difficulty making out the pattern. A closer look showed it to be a line of small fish, swimming head to tail around the edge of the cape.

Eliana laughed at the symbol of her own profession and swirled the cape around to settle it on her shoulders. It felt more like silk than it did wool. When she hugged her arms around herself, the fabric clung sensuously to the shape of her shoulders and hips.

"Have you a glass?" she asked. Harad jerked his thumb toward a dark corner. Eliana walked there, then stared for a moment at her brown-wrapped figure. She frowned. In the glass she looked more a man than she had ever intended. Even her face seemed somehow different. Shivering, she doffed the cape and tossed it back onto the pile.

Pointing to two of the coats she'd examined, she asked their price. She dickered with the merchant, refusing his first three offers, countering with lower ones of her own. She had just decided to try the ploy of leaving without a purchase when Harad lowered the price yet further. He grabbed the brown cloak and thrust it into her hands.

"Take this as part of the bargain," he said. "It fits you, and I've no use for it here. It . . . it was worn by a friend of mine who died recently, and the sight of it makes me sad. I'll give it to you as a gift."

"No gift," Eliana said quickly. She was sure the man was lying about his "friend," but the cape was still a fine garment. She could find some use for it. "I'll take the cape as part of the bargain."

"Done!" cried the merchant, and he stood rubbing his fingers together as he waited for her to count out her coppers.

When Eliana left the clothier's tent, the air had turned cool, and in a fit of good humor she swung the cape to her shoulders, carrying the coats she'd bought under her arm. The cloak was as warm as a living thing on her back. She caught people staring at her from time to time as she strode through the crowded fairgrounds and grinned when she realized that most of her admirers were women.

Perhaps the cloak was not such a useless thing after all, she thought. She'd always found it more expedient to wear male clothing. There were few women in her profession, and customers who believed her to be male took the bargaining more seriously. Besides, fish dealing, from the catch to salting and sale, was hard and dirty work; skirts and ribbons would have made it more so. Eliana had found also that strangers to the docks paid her less heed when they thought her a boy; there were fewer times when she was forced to show how well she could protect herself.

As she approached the wooden stall where her fish dealership was located, Eliana saw two men just turning away. She broke into a run, not wishing to lose such prosperous-looking customers. Skidding to a stop before the men, she gasped in recognition and tried to catch her breath. One of the men was Captain Sturming of the *Alakai*, the other was his first mate.

"What's this, lad?" The captain laughed and put out a hand to steady her. His hand rested for a moment on the brown cape before it dropped back to his side. "Why are you darting across the docks like a fish in a feeding frenzy?"

Eliana was torn between her desire to beg the great sea captain for a place among his crew and her fear that by doing so now, she would ruin her chances forever. She decided on the safer course and pointed toward the stall.

"It . . . it's mine," she stammered. "The fish, they're . . . I saw you looking inside." She cursed herself for a fool, unable to utter a single clear thought. The captain would surely turn away.

"Speak plainly, boy." The first mate scowled. "What do you want? The captain is a busy man." He moved to push her from their path.

Captain Sturming motioned him back. "I think the lad's trying to tell us he's the proprietor of the fish dealership, Talmont," he said. "And I'll wager he's not keen on losing customers." He turned back to Eliana and lifted a brow in question.

"Aye, Captain," she agreed quickly. "Please, pardon my rush. I was called away to the inner fairgrounds. If you are seeking fish, I can provide you with the freshest on the docks."

"I'm in need of both fresh fish and salted," said Sturming. "I've a crew to feed and a long voyage to provision."

"I've both in plenty," Eliana replied, and waved the men back to her stall. She breathed a sigh of relief when they followed. Inside the long narrow storage shed, barrels of salted fish stood in rows along the walls and in neat stacks across the floor. The salty tang of her wares permeated the air, even though the unshuttered windows allowed a constant breeze to pass through. She led the way to the back, where the daily catch was displayed.

"I see you keep your fresh fish iced," the captain said as he pressed his thumb onto the skin of one to test its firmness.

"That'll raise the price, Captain," mumbled the first mate.

"But it'll save your crew from many a sore belly," Eliana said quickly. "Fish poisoning is no small thing, as you know, Captain. You can see by the clear eyes that these fish are safe to eat."

"It takes little enough magic to keep the eyes of a fish clear," Talmont said. "How do we know your goods are not altered?"

"I give you my word," Eliana said, frowning at the insult. "And if that isn't good enough, call a priest and have the fish checked. The river fish were caught by my own hand, and the rest were purchased from only the most reputable deep-sea fishermen."

The captain lifted his hand to stop Talmont from speaking further. "Your word will do, lad. Anyone with eyes to see would know these fish are fresh." He lifted the lid of a salt-fish barrel to examine its contents. Grunting in approval, he turned back to Eliana.

"What would you take for the lot?" he asked.

"Fresh or salted?" Eliana tried to hide her excitement.

She had never sold her entire stock at one time before. It had always gone barrel by barrel or fish by fish.

"Both," said the captain. "Plus whatever more you can provide before my ship sails."

Eliana swallowed slowly, taking the time to calculate an offer that would be fair but still provide her with a goodly profit. Finally, she crossed her fingers beneath her cape and named a price to begin the bargaining.

"Done," said the captain.

Eliana blinked at the speed of his decision, then broke into a wide grin. This was, indeed, a day of good fortune. She thought of the additional trade goods she could purchase with this final sale.

"Captain, what of the fish dealer I brought you this morning?" Talmont cried. "His offer was far lower than this thieving youngster's."

Eliana spun around to confront him. To be accused of ill-using magic she would endure in silence, but to be called a thief in her own shop was more than she was willing to bear. As she moved, an edge of the cape lifted and brushed across the display table, knocking loose one of the biggest fish. The slippery creature slid from the iced pile and landed with a splat on Talmont's polished boots. Eliana gasped at what she had seen and felt happen and quickly folded the cape's front edge out of sight. Clutching the soft wool in her hands, she watched in horror as the seaman jumped back and cursed in anger. Beneath her fingers, the brown fabric twisted.

"Enough, Talmont," broke in Captain Sturming. "The offer is fair. Your friend of this morning was selling tainted goods, as any fool could see." He turned to Eliana. "Two of my crew will come for the fresh fish this afternoon, and the barrels of salted can be moved to the *Alakai* tomorrow. Is that satisfactory?"

Eliana nodded in agreement. She was eager now for the captain to leave. Some magic was at work in the cape, there was no question of it now, and she dare not let Captain

Sturming think she dabbled in such things. He would never agree to take her on. The bunched fabric beneath her fingers felt like a hand trying to clasp her own.

"Will you join me for supper on the *Alakai* this evening, madam?" the captain continued. "I can have your price ready for you then."

Eliana's mouth dropped open, and she almost let go of the cloak's edge. The captain had recognized her for a woman, and a fumbling woman at that. He'd never hire her now. She glanced toward Talmont, who was irritably brushing fish scales from the front of his trousers. He certainly would not speak on her behalf. Talmont glanced up at her, pausing for a moment to stare at the front of her cape.

Miserably, Eliana nodded her agreement to the captain. At least she would get to go aboard the ship of her dreams, even if it was only for a few hours. Her day of good fortune had turned to salt.

"Good, then. I'll look for you at eventide," the captain said. "Come, Talmont, let us move on to that clothier Harad you spoke so highly of."

When the men had left, Eliana quickly dropped the cape's edge and fumbled with the neck clasp to remove it. The clasp was worn, and it caught several times before she got it open. Finally she had the garment off.

"Fine lot of good you are," she said as she tossed it across a salt-fish barrel. "The *Alakai* is the last ship of the season to make for the Western Isles. They'll never take me aboard now." She bent to retrieve the fish that had fallen. Been pushed was more like it, for she'd felt the cape move with a will of its own when it brushed against the fish. She had even seen the misty image of a man's hand just as it touched the fish, then later felt the hand's shape and warmth while she hid it from the two seamen. Eliana was disgusted that she'd fallen for the clothier's ruse; he must have known there was something wrong with the cape and gotten rid of it by passing it on to her. A "gift" indeed.

"I should take you right back to that thief," she said, and

jumped back when a place on the cape's hood moved in response. She waited, frightened, but not enough so that she wished to call for help. She wanted no more entanglements this day, and she knew enough of magic to recognize that whatever was trapped in the cape could not escape without her help. If it could have, it would have, and long before now.

"What do you want?" she asked. "Who are you?"

Again the fabric moved, straining as if to reply. The vague shape of a lip formed, misted, disappeared again into the cloth. The place hung limp over the salt-encrusted rim of the barrel.

"Of course!" Eliana cried suddenly. "The salt is what brings you out. The fish was from the ocean waters and must still have had sea salt on its scales." Carefully, she readjusted the cape so that the place that had moved was resting on a small patch of brine. Immediately, the lips began to form again, then the teeth behind them. When a tongue appeared, she said, "Well? What do you have to say for yourself?"

The lips moved stiffly, and the tip of the tongue ran along the edge of the upper teeth. The thing's breath was stale, but not unpleasant. It cleared its throat and spoke.

"Let me out!"

"Not until I know what's going on," Eliana replied. "And maybe not even then. I've no wish to become embroiled in someone else's spells." She sat on the floor and settled back against the rough wooden leg of the fish table. "What are you?" she asked. "And how did you come to be trapped in this cape?"

"I am a man," said the mouth. "Marcus is my name. I placed myself in this cape three days ago when it appeared my life was endangered."

"I've been in danger many a time," Eliana said dryly, "but I never avoided it by hiding in my clothes."

"No?" said the mouth. "Then why do you wear men's clothing on that female body of yours?"

Eliana sat up straight, blushing when she remembered that the cloak had been wrapped around her shoulders, its hood draped over her hair. She could still feel the soft nap of the wool and the warmth of the cape's flowing folds.

"You are right," she said after a pause. "I do hide in my clothes. But only to avoid the trouble that can come of being a female working among men on the docks. I, at least, have sense enough to know how to escape my disguise." She grunted and leaned back against the post, arms wrapped around her upraised knees.

The lips were silent for a moment, pressed tightly together, and Eliana began to wonder if she had angered the trapped Marcus too far. Then, suddenly, he spoke again. "You, too, are right, fishwoman. I should have taken more care. Still, I don't know what else I could have done. I was in the clothier's shop, trying to determine if his goods had been tampered with, when—"

"Are you a wizard?" Eliana cried, panicked suddenly to think she might be holding such a dangerous person captive. This day could hold not only the end of her dream, but the end of her life if that were true.

"No," Marcus said with a sigh. "Would that I were. Then I might know how to break this spell. I am a mere nobleman, foolish enough to attempt a wizard's job." Eliana relaxed again.

"I own a fleet of sailing ships," the mouth went on, "and of late my captains have been complaining of tainted goods. Whatever spells are cast on the provisions are so well hidden that they escape notice while still in Ithkar. It is only after the ships are well away that the spells fall off and the bread grows quickly moldy, the salt fish rancid. Even the crewmen's clothing develops rents and faded colors."

"So, nobleman wizard, how did you find the good Harad's wares?" Eliana asked with a smile.

"You know well what I found in that shop," Marcus replied. "You easily separated the good coats from the bad, although I can't imagine how with just a touch. It was only after I entered my cloak that I saw clearly which of the clothier's goods was true to its outward appearance. You must be a witch as well as a fish dealer, for that was no ordinary magic.''

Eliana laughed. "My mother was a witch, so they say. She's long dead, but I still carry a few of her skills. I can usually tell honest wares by their touch. I could not be sure Harad's coats were spelled, for as you say, the magic in them was strange. But I knew something was not aright.''

"Aye. Indeed," said Marcus. "The magic used to alter those goods was brought from afar, perhaps even by way of the Thotharn priests. I know little of such things, but I heard Talmont speak of it when he and his companion entered the tent.''

"Talmont! Captain Sturming's first mate?''

"Aye, the same.''

"But Talmont was taking the captain to Harad's tent this very day. Could the first mate be one of those responsible for the tainted supplies aboard your ships?'' Suddenly Eliana caught her breath, realizing what she was saying. "Is the *Alakai* one of your vessels?''

"Aye. And aye," replied the mouth.

Eliana groaned at the unfairness of it all. First, she had acted like a fool before the *Alakai*'s captain, and now she held the ship's owner captive. Would this run of bad fortune never end?

"Talmont and the others must be stopped before they do further harm," the mouth went on. "The temple priests and mages must be told of this new magic before it spreads too far to stop it. All of Ithkar might be at risk.''

Eliana sighed. Her bad luck had multiplied.

Marcus was still for a moment, then asked, "Fishwoman?''

Eliana remained silent, sunk in misery. With one hand, she picked at the crusted salt on a nearby barrel.

"Won't you at least release my eyes?''

Eliana started. "Why? So you can identify me later and cause me harm? You came into my possession by accident, nobleman, and now I must hold you captive for fear.'' She groaned again. ''This is not how I intended this day to go.''

''How *did* you intend it?'' he asked. The voice betrayed his impatience.

''I was to buy a fine coat and present myself aboard the ship of my dreams,'' she said, suddenly angry enough not to care what the trapped nobleman heard. ''I was to sell my fish and buy trade goods for the voyage to the Western Sea.'' She sagged against the post. ''Instead, the ship's captain now thinks me a fool, and I have acquired a cape that talks and wants to see.''

''I mean you no harm, fishwoman,'' Marcus said. ''I chose you deliberately to rescue me from the clothier's tent. For three days I lay there waiting for the right person to come along. I made myself ugly and uncomfortable for many a customer, as well as for Harad, before you entered his tent. I couldn't afford to be taken to some place where I might never escape.''

''Why did you choose me to carry you away?'' Eliana asked.

''Because of your smell,'' he said, then added quickly, ''Do not take offense, fishwoman. I am a man of the sea, and I hoped you would bring me, if not to one of my own ships, then at least to the docks, where chance might provide an avenue of escape. From your touch I knew you to be an honest person.'' The tip of his tongue darted out to lick a sparkle of salt from his lower lip. ''Though the feel of your man's clothing threw me a start.''

Eliana lifted the lid of a salt-fish barrel and removed a small menpachi. The fish's flesh was stiff, almost crisp, from the salting and drying process. She snapped a bit off the tail and nibbled on it as she listened to Marcus's tale.

''I had gone to Harad's tent,'' he said, ''because his goods had been used on one of the ill-fated voyages. There was no proof that he was responsible, but it seemed very likely. Like you, I have a way with magic at times. I can detect it by touch or by taste.'' He licked his lips again, and as Eliana crunched on another bite of menpachi, she wondered if the nobleman was hungry inside the cape.

He went on, "At first I sensed nothing amiss with Harad's wares, save that they were exceedingly shoddy, much too poor in quality to serve my crews' needs. I was in the back of the tent, near the mirror, when I saw Talmont approaching. I was immediately wary, for I knew Captain Sturming was personally overseeing the supply purchases for his upcoming voyage, and there was no other reason for Talmont to come to that place.

"Talmont entered the tent in the company of a second man, dressed in the clothes of a seaman but walking with the gait of one who's never known the sea. I turned away so he would not recognize me, and as soon as Harad's attention was turned, I slipped magically into my cape. I planned to listen to their conversation, and if they proved to be the evildoers, I would later change myself back and present my evidence to the priests.

"Talmont introduced his companion as Griswain, a crewman from the *Alakai*, but I think he must have been a priest of the evil powers wearing a seaman's disguise. Harad said nothing. He only pointed to several piles of clothing, including the one on which my cloak had fallen. Griswain pointed his finger and mumbled some charm, and an instant's mist of magic surrounded me. His spell altered the coats near me, changing them so subtly that it was difficult to tell anything had happened, except that they all looked better than before."

"What about you?" asked Eliana. "Are you really made of cheap cotton, faded and threadbare?" She hid a smile.

The lips turned down at the edges in a pout. "Only the poor merchandise was affected by the evil priest's spell. I was not changed at all, except that the priest's spell and my own interacted somehow, and I became trapped inside the cape. Harad had thought me just an ordinary customer, so he had not been upset when he found me gone. But later, when he found my cloak, he mixed it with the other garments and attempted to sell it as his own rather than set it aside as any honest merchant would.

"The magic being used there is evil, fishwoman, and thus far unknown to the Ithkar priests. I am sure of it, for it's that magic which prevents me from escaping this cape on my own."

Eliana considered. If the cape spoke the truth, then she must indeed set the nobleman free, and quickly, so that the evil magic and its practitioners could be reported and brought under control. But what if the cape lied? She might risk all of Ithkar by releasing Marcus, if by chance he himself was the source of the evil.

"I will give you your eyes," she said after a time. "But I will leave you in the cape until I can take you to a temple mage. You can tell your story to him."

"Good enough," Marcus agreed readily. "It is all I can ask. But let us hurry."

Eliana tore off another chunk of the menpachi's tough flesh and reached across the cape. She rubbed the salt-cured fish onto the place where the eyes should be. As she lifted her hand away, a line of dark lashes appeared. It was followed quickly by a second. The lashes fluttered, lifted, and Eliana found herself staring into the bluest eyes she had ever seen. They were like the sea when the water was deep and the sun high in the sky. The eyelids lowered, then blinked open again.

"Why," the mouth said, sounding very surprised, "you're quite beautiful!"

"Well, what did you expect?" Eliana replied tartly. "An old woman with the face of a fish?" She stood and lifted the cloak, swinging it to her shoulders so that the eyes could no longer peer into her own. "I will take you to the priests now," she snapped.

She thought perhaps her quick action had startled the nobleman, for he remained silent as she closed the shop and began walking quickly along the congested dock. Well, good enough, she decided. He had given her a start or two this day. She darted around a loaded pushcart, wrinkling her nose at the smell of day-old shellfish.

"I knew you were not old," the cape whispered into her ear.

She jumped, then adjusted the hood so that his lips were not so near her skin. She felt the cape chuckle.

Suddenly, it tensed. The woolen fabric stiffened, then pulled itself about Eliana. Marcus's voice at the back of her neck urged her to hurry.

"Talmont!" it whispered. "And Harad and the priest! They have seen us and are running to catch up. They must know who I am. But how can that be?"

"I saw Talmont look strangely at the cape after the fish fell," Eliana said. "Maybe he saw your hand as I did. If he spoke of it to Harad, they could easily guess that someone was inside the cape, and that you might have overheard their plans."

She glanced back just as Talmont thrust the shellfish wagon from his path. It overturned with a crash, splattering nearby merchants and dockworkers. One man reached out to stop Griswain but jerked his hand back before it made contact. Eliana knew it was magic that had forced the man away. She could sense it from as far away as she stood. The false priest would never have used his evil spells openly if they did not know Marcus was in the cape. They ran toward her like desperate men.

"Thief!" cried Harad. "Thief! She stole my cape!"

"Thief, is it?" Eliana growled. "We'll see about that. Tell me how they follow," she instructed Marcus. She leapt across a guide rope and raced for the far side of the pier. As she ran, she let out a great shout: *"Elianaaaaaaa!"* Instantly, the shout was picked up across the docks, workers and vendors and children of all ages sounding their unified support. A lad in cutoff trousers appeared at Eliana's side.

"Find Captain Sturming, off the *Alakai*," Eliana called to him as she ducked under a swinging beam. "Tell him Marcus is in danger. And there's magic afoot."

"Aye," snapped the boy, and he darted away as quickly as he had appeared.

Behind her, Eliana heard shouted curses and falling debris.

"They're gaining on us, fishwoman," Marcus called. Then, "But no, a wagon has just blocked their path. And a flock of geese just escaped its cage. . . . Good fortune favors us this day, fishwoman. The accidents of the docks protect us."

"It's friends who protect us, nobleman," she replied, "not accidents." The sound of her name still echoed along the pier. "We protect our own here on the wharfs. My cry alerted the others that outsiders were trying to cause harm. They won't interfere directly, but they will give us as much time as they can."

Marcus let out a whoop. "A basket of fishcakes just fell from its rod. Talmont's gone splat in the mess they made." Then, suddenly, his voice grew silent. Eliana glanced behind and saw a flash of fire and black smoke. A child screamed in terror.

The cape wrapped around Eliana's legs. "Stop," Marcus cried. "Take me off, fishwoman. I won't have your friends suffer from those evil men's magic when they do but protect my skin." Eliana ran on, fighting the entangling cape.

"Give me to them," he called. "They will but destroy the cape. I will feel nothing. They don't know I have spoken to you, so you can pretend ignorance of my presence and go to the priests secretly later on. Give me to them, fishwoman, that they will stop their spell-laying upon your friends." Another crash and more screams sounded from behind.

Eliana slipped into an alleyway between two storage stalls. "Stop trying to trip me," she called over her shoulder. "I'm taking you to the salt dealers, where I can throw you all at once into the cleaning vat. The brine will soak through the wool quickly and you will be released. Then at least you will be able to face your enemies as a man."

"You are a fool, fishwoman."

"Aye," she replied, fumbling with the cloak's neck clasp, still running full speed.

"And I thank you."

"Aye," she said.

There was a shout from behind, and Eliana knew their pursuers were close. She jumped over a stack of woven wrappers and entered the salt dealer's stall. Still pulling at the stubborn clasp, she ran to the side of a large vat used to rinse the grime from salt wheels as they were offloaded from the ships.

The vat was empty.

A splash of wetness across the planking, leading from the empty pot to the edge of the pier, showed that the vat had been dumped just moments before.

"Throw me in the river," Marcus cried. "The current's sluggish here. There should be enough brine left to negate the magic holding me captive."

"The clasp is caught," Eliana replied. "It will not open."

"Then jump!" he said. "Once the cloth is wet, I'll be free and can fight them off."

"But—"

"Jump!"

"I cannot swim," wailed Eliana.

The cape went limp; it immediately stopped urging her toward the water. Talmont's cry of triumph caused Eliana to turn back. The first mate and the priest were but yards from her, a gasping Harad close behind. Eliana could see other men running toward them, but they would never reach her in time to save Marcus.

"What do you want?" she cried as she continued pulling at the clasp.

Harad scowled. "Give me my cape, thief."

"I bought this cape. It was part of our bargain."

It was no use, the worn clasp would not open. There was only one way to wet the cape. She glanced behind her at the dark, deep river. The priest lifted a hand toward her, right forefinger outstretched. The evil intent of his movement slid like cold brine across Eliana's skin.

"No," she heard Marcus call. "Do not harm the woman." She squeezed her eyes shut.

And jumped.

The river was cold; Eliana immediately felt its sting. The water tasted of salt. It wrapped around her like a living thing, and she spluttered and fought, caught in a terror greater than the power of the river itself. Suddenly, a hand fastened on her arm.

"It's all right," she heard, or thought she heard. She kicked and scratched, trying to fight the river off. A second hand settled under her chin and pulled her to the surface.

"It's all right," came the voice again. "Stop fighting or you'll drown us both."

The cape! she thought suddenly. And Marcus! Suddenly she remembered what had brought her to this frigid, frightening place.

"Talmont!"

"We are safe," said the man holding her. There was laughter in his voice, and tremendous relief. "Look there, fishwoman, up on the pier. Your friends brought my captain, and he brought the fair priests. The evil magic has been controlled."

Clutching Marcus tightly, Eliana opened her eyes. She looked first into the sea-blue eyes of the nobleman, then stared up at the dock. Two black-robed priests flanked Talmont and his companions. All five were surrounded by the pale silver mist of a powerful binding spell. Directly above her, Captain Sturming knelt on the salt-limed planking.

"H-how did you g-get here so fast?" she stammered, coughing the last of the river from her lungs. "And how so w-well prepared?" She glanced again at the two priests.

"I knew Marcus had gone to the clothiers before he disappeared, and I recognized his cape when I met you at your stall," said the captain. "That's why I asked you to my ship.'' He reached down to her. ''When the lad came with your call, the priests and I were ready.''

Eliana grasped his hand and was pulled from the water. Shivering, she stood on the dock, hugging the sodden cloak around her shoulders.

''Why do I always look the fool when I meet this man?'' she muttered in misery. Marcus clambered up after her. He was far younger than she had expected, only a few years older than herself. His face formed a handsome frame for his sea-blue eyes.

The captain laughed. ''Madam, if I had a crew full of fools half so able as you, I'd open the western trade routes in no time.''

''Then perhaps you should hire her on,'' Marcus said. He shook his head so that water sprayed them all. ''I've heard it rumored this lady wishes to travel the traders' road. She's even bought a fine cape to keep her warm along the way.'' He met Eliana's startled look with a grin, then winked and added, ''I might even join this voyage myself.''

Slowly, Eliana began to laugh. She brushed salty water from her nose and her chin and glanced across the harbor toward the ship of her dreams.

''This is, indeed,'' she said, laughing, ''a day of strange fortune.''

CAT AND MUSE

Rose Wolf

> *"Weave a circle round her thrice*
> *And close your eyes with holy dread . . ."*

It's just my luck, thought Roswitha wryly and a little angrily too as she finished dusting the last of the shelves. It's just my bog-rotted, Lords-forsaken luck to be stuck behind this stand when the hue has just been raised for the greatest theft ever perpetrated at Ithkar Fair—and with *these* clay cats, of all things!

Setting aside the feather-frond duster, the girl squinted her nearsighted scholar's eyes up the street in the dawning dimness to where, in a cross lane, an excited crowd—mob, nearly—shoved and shouted, thronging in the wake of a dozen fair-wards who carried their formidable bronze-shod staves at port arms with grim intent. When the greater part of the mass had moved on past, Roswitha returned her attention to the business at hand. She continued to catch faint cries from the thief-taking expedition as she raised the stall's gaudy icon-painted awning, tugged out the fatly upholstered curule chair into which Merchant Shallocq was wont to lower his fatly upholstered bulk, and raked the dirt inside the square formed by the three waist-high wooden partitions backed by the ware-display wall; but by the time the first customer arrived, the uproar had died completely away. Nevertheless, Roswitha's thoughts were with the chase as she made the transaction, and when she had wrapped the cheap cat statuette in a square of threadbare felt and chinked the buyer's copper into a chain-draped cashbox, she paused for a moment's speculation.

Speculation? the little clerk thought to herself, and laughed softly. Say rather "peculation"!

Folding her arms in the front of her one good tunic, she turned to face the ranked rows of clay animals. To think that the original of one of you pottery putties is touring the fair right now in a thief's swag-bag! What an incredible deed that was: to steal the precious statuette of the sacred cat from the very lap of Lady Alimar Lords'-Friend! That thief must have been mad, desperate, or so pitifully eager for a place in men's memory that he would settle for ill fame as his monument.

Reaching out a browned but still sensitive hand, Roswitha stroked the stone-cool body of the nearest cat. The image, a stoneware object as large as her two fists together, was shaped and painted to resemble one of the exotic cats of the south so beloved of the Lady (although that goddess smiled upon all the furred kind): those with the colors of her harvest feast-days—white grain ears, rich loam, and an impossibly blue scrying-bowl of sky with no stain of cloud breath. True, the statue that the girl held, with its garish glaze and glass-pebble eyes, had more of the mudpie than the festival cake about it, but Roswitha supposed that any object that increased devotion to the powers of light was of worth, especially in these days with the worship of Thotharn growing ever more widespread and bold-faced. A thought occurred to her: was the thief of the sacred cat a devotee of that dark cult or the servant of such a person? Well, she would probably never find out, any more than she would claim the thousand coppers that the fair-wards had cried from the neighboring street to be the reward offered for the statue's return to the guardians of the temple. With a rueful shake of her head, the little clerk replaced the clay image on the shelf and pushed behind the worn tapestry dividing the private area of Shallocq's stall from the public, to examine the small piece of parchment that was all she might ever hope to own of that shrine of seekers and scholars.

For Roswitha was a scholar, and the child and namesake of scholars. Her calling (in every sense of the term) came from the legend of a holy woman who had written books and presented them to a great lord, who was so impressed by her work that he granted her his patronage. "If you are as diligent in your labors as that first Roswitha," the girl's mother had often assured her, "such a boon may well be yours." But in the three years that had passed since Roswitha had completed her studies, no minor landholder, much less lord, had sought her skills. Only shire-reeves and chapmen who wanted someone with sufficient *grammarye* (strange how that word meant both writing and witchery) had done so, to have her prepare husbandry tables and "balance" accounts to lessen the palm crossing levied by the priests! And this year at Ithkar Fair there had been even fewer of such commissions—so few, in fact, that Roswitha had been forced to take temporary service as a stall tender with Merchant Shallocq.

For this state of affairs the girl privately blamed the leaders of the Re-Epiphany—or, as the less reverent termed it, the "Three-Epiphany"—movement at the temple, who favored and fostered only scholarly efforts inspired by the hagiography of the Three Lordly Ones. Roswitha and her family, while they had always granted respect to those legendary leaders, had deemed them interlopers, maugre star birthing, and had given their devotion only to those deities sprung from the sky, soil, and stream of K'Ithholme-World. Such a one was Lady Alimar, for although she had dwelt during their planetfall with the alien trinity, she had been a true daughter of men. But oh, her tales had been star born! Reading them, the little clerk could well believe the apocryphal anecdote that the Three, having completed the Lady's initiation into the mysteries of word smithing, had touched her lips with a coal from the Undying Fire, stolen from the heart of a sun, which gave life and light to their skyfaring ship. And now her image sat in eternal conclave with the images of the Three and their other friends in the high hall *ecks*, or niches, in the apse of the temple, her scroll and stylus in her hands, and on her lap, in the classic pose of feline vigilance, the S'a-Muse cat, symbol of mystic wisdom and human/nonhuman fellowship. Until this morning. Again, *why, how, who?*

In the semigloom of the stall's back section, Roswitha fumbled with the rawhide thong that formed the latch of her broadside boards. She knew she must return, and quickly, to the selling area, for Merchant Shallocq would return at any moment, and if he found his wares unwatched, he might express his displeasure with a leathern tongue. But those ''S'a-Musings'' on Lady Alimar had aroused in her a sudden and powerful desire to examine the copy of the hymn to the goddess she had acquired from the temple scribe the previous evening. Strange, the clerk thought as the stubborn strands parted at last, and the parchment sheet slid, with a leaf-fall rustle, into her waiting hands. *I have never felt such a need to do anything in my life; this smacks of those Messages-of-Mind the wise-women whisper of. And to think that Brother Greggorie gave it to me! Could I be being somehow—led?* Lifting the parchment square to the narrow shaft of light that struck through an ill-patched place in the curtain, Roswitha joyed anew as the beam woke fire from the gold-leafed squares framing the fat uncials of the capital letters and jewel glow from the colored script of the text.

''You have a wonderful gift,'' the scholar had told the

monk, whom everyone jestingly called "the Short-Hand" by reason of his rounded and closely written style. Brother Greggorie had glanced up from the page whose illumination he was completing upon hearing Roswitha's words, and the polite reply he had had upon his lips had frozen, to be replaced by a look as of one confronting a fetch. Mechanically he had set his sigil to the sheet and thrust it across the trestle that served him as a workbench at the astonished girl.

"You likewise, lady-loved," he had replied in a low but carrying voice; and before Roswitha could ask a question or offer a payment, the temple scribe had turned his attention—deliberately—to another patron. The clerk had been left with mouth open and hands full of a copy of the anonymous hymn lyric "Hail to Thee, Bright Star" rendered with such craft and cost as to make it worthy of the richest merchant's book of hours.

Recalling this odd transaction as she perused her treasure once more, Roswitha considered the monk's cryptic pronouncement and was puzzled all over again. She had thought "You likewise" meant "I will give you a wonderful gift," and "lady-loved" indicated "one endowed with close female friends," but now—questions and questions! Where were the answers?

Questions were forgotten as Roswitha was drawn into the hymn itself. Gently but irresistibly its words insinuated themselves into her mind and its rhythm into her heart, so that by the time she had reached the chorus of the third and final stanza, she was chanting softly and swaying from side to side. Chant and sway? No—she should sing and dance! The girl had risen to her feet and begun to hum, thanking the Mother as she did that the sun was rising so swiftly today, permitting her to see the poem in the back-stall murk (for surely it was the light and not the letters that shone so brightly?)—

—when a shadow fell across the curtain, and not Shallocq's, either.

Moved still by that eerie compulsion from beyond herself, the clerk, with a speed and stealth she would not have believed possible, slid the parchment between its board covers, cinched the cord, and thrust the whole into the inner pocket of the alchemist's dross-colored robe, which she wore for travel and which she now pulled on. Stepping to the moth-eaten drape, she applied an eye to the sunbeam hole and saw a thin, shifty-eyed man of middle age swathed in the black mantle of a Niobean friar, one of that elusive and sinister brotherhood whose devotion to the Three Lordly Ones consisted of a perpetual funeral service. Silent and lithe as a slimpsel, he flowed toward the low shelf from which the clerk had removed her solitary customer's cat statuette, in the same motion drawing from beneath his voluminous robes a twin to that piece. Twin? Only as a peasant maid's wheat wreath twisted with ux-vine and Lady's tears for the Feast of Firstfruits was the double of the precious Wreath of Offering lying on the high altar of the Comforter's Shrine—*it was the temple cat!*

As Roswitha stared in dumb amazement, the thief placed the true statue on the shelf in the spot made vacant by the purchase of the terra-cotta piece. When he bent, a fold in his robe opened and a dead-black mask-shaped pendant on a skein of what looked like human hair was revealed. An instant later, the ornament was hidden once more as the man straightened, but not before the clerk had recognized the face of the mask, with its aristocratic features set in a poisonously beautiful smile, as that of the demon Thotharn. The watching girl bit back a gasp. So—not only was Shallocq involved with those who stole material goods from the temple, but also with those who would take from the gods the greatest and most unmaterial "good": worship. In the wake of shock came rage: how dared they so insult the Lady, she who had with her tales strewn the dreary path of life on K'Ithholme-World with the stuff of stars? Gods damn them to the hell of an existence without dreams!

As though he had divined Roswitha's thoughts, the renegade monk abruptly turned toward the curtain that concealed the girl and with a muttered exclamation grasped the fabric and tore it open.

But when the thief's eyes adjusted to the dimness of the storage space, he saw only a lumpy pallet, a stack of crates, and two barrels of refuse over which was thrown a beggarly cloak of anonymous hue. Seizing a prybar from atop the cases, he belabored the mattress a few vicious blows, then flipped it quickly over. With a grunt of exasperation, he turned his attention to the barrels; and what would have become of the hapless scholar stretched over them, none but Lady Alimar might have said, had not that one—or Ones greater—sent the fair-wards down the street at that moment, their weighted staves striking the cobbles of potters' slip like the machinery of the law. Spewing a curse so dreadful that it made Roswitha's short-cropped hair stand on end even beneath her hood, the bogus brother slid from the storeroom in a running crouch and poured himself into the alley behind the shop like a bucket of night soil.

Roswitha lost no time. Leaping from her improvised perch and hurrying to the shelf, she took up the precious figurine and returned with it to the back room. There— possessed once more, it seemed, by the strange compulsion— she swaddled it in rags, thrust it into the bottom of her vending basket, and arranged several imitation statues on top. Then, stripping off her cape, she laid it over the basket and, pulling the tapestry to, returned to her accustomed place behind the counter.

And here was Shallocq, sudden as a summoned friend.

"How goes business?" asked the merchant. He spoke with forced heartiness and grinned like such a lackwit that Roswitha was hard put to keep her own expression safely stupid, but the girl noticed that his plump, beringed hands kept clasping and unclasping and his broad brow beneath its gem-tasseled turban was twice filleted with natural diamonds of sweat.

"Poorly, alack," sighed the clerk, offering her employer the cashbox whose chains made more noise than its contents. "But one sale this whole morning—"

"To whom?" interrupted Shallocq, too eagerly. As Roswitha looked blank, he stammered, "I mean, to—to what manner o' man? Observations are vital—help you know your market—"

Black market, you mean, thought the scholar contemptuously. Aloud she said, carefully casual, "Why, to a young farmsteader who wants to 'mure it in the wall of the barn he's building as a vermin bane. I told him that a mouser was good, but a muser was better, and that if he wanted the thing to bless as well as curse, he should take it to the temple for a benison. Which reminds me"—here the girl paused to swing aside the curtain and draw forth the cloak-draped figurine basket, thankful for even so brief a chance to stem the tide of her false-sounding chatter and wipe her own sweating brow—"at the *orraree* this nooning the mystery play of Lady Alimar is to be given. Likely the country folk will gather there—in fact, our sole customer said he was bound to the place—so I thought it would be profitable to 'take the goods to the goodmen.' With your leave, Merchant Shallocq?" Roswitha finished by batting her eyes and smiling brightly, presenting the very picture of guileless youthful enthusiasm for a new enterprise. Inwardly she was quaking.

The chapman swiped distractedly at his bead-dewed face and shook his head. "No, girl, keep close for now. I—I might have an important customer, who knows"—giggle—"and I'd need you to tend the yokels. Put by your basket."

"But I *must* go!" blurted Roswitha, and then could scarcely keep from clapping a horrified hand over her mouth.

"Go?" The merchant was suddenly alert. "Go where?"

"To the—" Desperation and no holy compulsion supplied the answer. "To the drop seat!" And abandoning all pretense at propriety, Roswitha freed a hand from her burden and clutched her crotch.

Shallocq still looked suspicious, but after a moment he gave a mutter of exasperation and waved the girl off. Scarcely daring to believe her success, the little clerk swung out of the stall and was off down the cobbled and increasingly crowded street before the merchant could realize she was still carrying the basket.

Roswitha fought the impulse to look behind her until she reached the webster's stall at the head of the lane. There, ducking behind a rack of tabards, she peered through the neckhole of an outspread sample in the direction of the potter's stand.

Shallocq stood staring at the vacant spot left by the double "adoption." As the girl watched, a second figure joined him at his curious vigil—a small, limber man swaddled in a black monk's robe. The two conferred hastily, and then, with terrible inevitability, two heads came up, two arms flung out, and two mouths tore open in a single cry: "Thief! Thief! Wardens, ho!"

Resisting the urge to hurl herself down the street in a blind panic, Roswitha cut through the crowd before the webster's stand, pausing long enough to gawk convincingly— she hoped—back in the direction of the potter's stall with the rest of the fairgoers, then swung with only businesslike briskness into a side lane. North—she must proceed north, she knew, to reach the temple—and she was acquainted with all the public passages; but this tentways maze was known to few save merchants and less legal lighteners of purse. Bewildered, the girl had paused at a crosspath to consider her course when a gentle warmth began to radiate from the pocket in which she had placed the broadside case. Astounded but strangely unafraid, the scholar, following a hunch, turned to the right. Immediately the sensation ceased as though doused. A turn to the left, however, rekindled the viewless flame. Left it was, then. I certainly got a bargain yestereven with this gift, she thought almost cheerfully, moving as quickly as she dared. Learning and leading in one package! As though there were a difference . . .

Roswitha might have revolved this matter clear to the temple, had not yet another turn—and a guided one, at that—brought her to the mouth of a throughway and nearly into the arms of a squadron of fair-wards charging past. Dodging behind a knot of wrathgrape drinkers accepting tipples from a steinbeckoner, the girl hastened down the street. Above her heart, which was drumming beat to retreat, her head was chilly calm. Had she been meant to give herself over to the fair-wards—was that the meaning of her near collision? After all, what defense could Shallocq and sidekick bring to bear if questioned under truth spell? Roswitha had almost persuaded herself to turn back when a burst of cold welled from her breast "plate," so forceful it made her cry out and set hand to her bosom. Scrubbing a sleeve across her tearing eyes, she stumbled on. She had heard of the hounds of Thotharn, which harried men to Heldelving; but where would the cat of Lady Alimar chivy a woman? To the stars?

At the head of an alley, the beleaguered scholar ducked beneath a ward rope, fashioned of a length of hawser painted blue. In a dark alley of her own mind, a warning tocsin rang—disturbing such a barrier, magically charged as it was, was to summon not the fair-wards but the wizards, for the ropes guarded only sacred precincts—but so powerful this time was the compulsion that, literally, burned in her breast that the girl took little heed.

Arriving at the end of the way, she found it partially blocked by a great wagon-mounted tent bepainted with holy pictures even gaudier than those in Shallocq's stall, and she realized that she had come by a back lane into the *orraree*, and that before her stood the shake-scene stage of the mystery troupe.

The huge cart faced the circular court side on, its heavy plank panel dropped and propped slantwise to form a ramp for the ascent or descent of the players, its multilayered tent panels folded open to the backdrops that depicted Lady Alimar and the Three Lordly Ones.

With surprise and delight, Roswitha recognized the coach stage as the one that had come every year during her childhood to the village where her family lived and whose performances, crude and melodramatic as they were, had been the inspiration for the scholar's lifelong study of Lady lore. How she had thrilled to watch the enactment of the sacred stories, and what a dream beyond dream it had been to actually perform with them one season when the troupemistress's daughter had taken ill, playing the part of the country maid to whom the star-singer had told her tales! The little clerk longed to mount the ladder leading to the end of the wagon facing her, which served as the company's tiring room, and wish them well, but, hearing the hubbub of the thief takers approaching the *orraree*, she knew that she dared not take the time and turned regretfully away.

She had been about to mingle with the crowd already well come to the place of star-prayer when the whip-crack *smack!* of a hand connecting with a cheek sounded from the coach, followed by a spate of furious words in the strident voice of a woman: Dame Alyson. Curious, Roswitha paused. The troupemistress seldom played the termagant in life, no matter what her role on stage—what was amiss?

"*Phaw*, Coll, to smell you a body'd know what you did with your share o' the take, if they hadn't eyes to see! Drunk as a maggot in a rum cake, you are, and it's curtain up at the nooning bell! Who's to do the priest, then, with your wife in childbed and your brother lame from that ox kick! Belike not even the Dark One'd have you in your condition, but he can try for all I care! Get out—*now*!"

With these words the door in the end of the show wagon was flung open, and a disheveled young man in peasant dress was ejected forcibly therefrom. He landed in a pile of fodder laid for the wagon beasts and promptly either fainted or fell asleep. Dame Alyson, appearing at the door, glared down at her inebriated son-in-law; then, looking up, she shook a hammy fist at the sky. "Faith," she muttered, "it's small wonder the Lady is figured as a cat—she bares her claws today, and no mistake!''

All at once Roswitha had an idea. Rounding the wagon wheel that had hidden her, she scrambled up the ladder to the tiring room and braced herself, panting, in the door frame, just as the nooning bell began to toll from the bell tower of the temple. A comforting pulse of warmth from the broadside in her bosom lent her courage as she dropped a curtsy to the thunder-browed thespian. ''Dame Alyson, it's I, the bookworm, and I've come to help you set the Lady apurring.''

The temple bell had tolled twice more, and such of the inhabitants of K'Ithholme-World as were gathered in the *orraree* of the fairgrounds had witnessed the arrival, visitation, and departure of the Three Lordly Ones once again. Now a small figure in a blue priestess's robe, its face hidden in the shadows of a deep-cowled hood, stepped forth from the curtain. Approaching the statue of Lady Alimar (as presented by the good Dame Alyson, seated stock still in trumpery crown and gown and holding stylus, book, and—between these—a remarkably authentic-looking figurine of a cat), the stage religious made a deep obeisance; then, turning to the audience, she opened a parchment pressboard and prepared to speak. The onlookers shifted restively—with the Three Lordly Ones gone, the magic, for many, was already beginning to fade—so the general thought was, Let her speak the moral and we'll to dinner! Merchant Shallocq and the false friar, watching from the fore of the crowd, felt the weird compulsion that had held them there begin to ease, and they, too, were of their fellow audience members' inclination. So, even, were the fair-wards and the wizards who had been summoned to the *orraree* by the triggering of the ward-rope alarm.

Until the ''priestess'' began to sing.

Beneath its borrowed habit, Roswitha's body was cold

with terror, in stark contrast to the illuminated sheet of verse she held, which throbbed with such a potent secret fire that the scholar feared the very gold would run molten from its letters. What must I do, she shouted silently, and what will happen when I've done it? What if *nothing* happens? What if—?

But as she framed her fears, the heartlike pulse of the parchment slowed, steadying and deepening into a drumbeat rhythm. The girl lifted one foot, then the other, and stepped forward, to stand between the crowd and the "Lady," a moon eclipsing—but only momentarily—a star. Then her steps found the beat and her voice a tune, and the spell took her.

> West by light
>   Would we fare—
> East by night
>   Should we dare—
> Otherwhen, Otherwhere,
>   Morn- or even-tiding,
>   We shall find thy biding.

> All that lives
>   Dwells thy slave:
> That which strives
>   Manly brave;
> Cleaves the air, carves the wave;
>   Fur, fin, flesh, we own thee,
>   In our hearts enthrone thee.

> High and low
>   Have thee prayed:
> Hearing, know—
>   Knowing, aid!
> For this ruth, mystic maid,
>   Shall thy praise be spoken,
>   Raised in song unbroken.

CHORUS: Hail to thee, bright Star,
          Lady Alimar:
          Hail to thee, fair and free,
          We thy servants are.

Three verses Roswitha sang, dancing one circle round the
Lady for each, and pausing on the chorus to stand facing
outward to north, to south, to east, and, as the final notes
swelled in her throat to a triumphant cry and she raised the
parchment into the air and flung back her head, to west, her
starting place—before the thief and his fence. As she lowered her arms and raised her head, her hood fell back, and
she met Shallocq's stare eye to eye. For a moment he stood
dumbfounded; then, recovering his wits, he bellowed, "There
she is—that's the thief—and there's the temple cat!" In the
friar's hand a dirk of dead-black metal, pommeled by a
mask of dead black that smiled and smiled, materialized,
and in one fluid motion he threw it, straight at Roswitha's
heart.

Instinctively the girl raised the broadside board to shield
her breast, but the dagger never reached its mark. As soon
as it passed over the circle she had described in her dance, a
wall of blue radiance shot up from the ground around the
circle's entire perimeter. The blade was swallowed like the
swamp-taken city of Eld, and Roswitha and the heroic
Alyson were enclosed in a breastwork of azurine light—the
hue of S'a-Muse eyes.

Desperate but undaunted, the merchant and the demon
worshiper launched themselves at the barrier, Thotharn's
devotee shrieking wildly to the Dark Lord for aid. Answered he was, but by the Lady, not the Lord. A starfire
nimbus enveloped the figurine of the cat, and forth from the
jewel-bright eyes leaped twin beams of blinding blue force.
The lances struck Shallocq and his cohort, transfixing them.
Their bodies blazed up in a soundless holocaust, and an
instant later they were gone as though they had never been.

For the first—and last—time in her life, Roswitha fainted.

• • •

The little clerk returned to consciousness under the brusque ministrations of Lady Alyson. She found herself lying on a pile of costumes in the show wagon, a quintain beneath her head and a wet and exceedingly unfragrant sock draped over her brow. Bending above her were three men: a priest of the temple, a fair-ward, and a wizard. She struggled to sit up, and Alyson moved in, twitching away the compress and rearranging the priestess's costume about the girl's shoulders. The troupemistress's face was triumphant, and as she placed the precious cat statuette in the hands of her stage protégée, she gave that individual a resounding smack. Curtsying boldly to the trio of officials, the quondam goddess hefted her never-heavier cashbox and, to its golden-tongued gabble, jigged from the room, loudly humming "How Pleasant It Is to Have Money, Heigh-Ho!"

Roswitha could not suppress a smile at this impromptu performance, but her laughter died on her lips as she met the solemn gazes of the rest of the audience. Her friend's fortune was assured, yes—but what of her own?

Feeling small and vulnerable, but determined not to reveal her fear, the girl straightened her shoulders and met the eyes of the officials squarely. She tightened her fingers around the figurine and felt its plump coolness solid and comforting as a well-filled waterskin to a traveler daring the Sere.

"I'm for the dungeon now, sirs, and well I know it— you'd hale me in for murder if not for magic—but the Lady be my witness I did none of these things o'purpose. I was led by some power—though I doubt one can be led far where he does not inwardly wish to go, and I'm sure you'll say the same. Ah, well." Here the girl sighed, looking less like a victorious wise-woman wielding a mighty artifact than an erring child sent to bed with a comforting plaything. "As long as I can take my book."

The three officials exchanged glances; then the fair wizard (who looked so much like a *fairy* wizard with his curling gray beard that Roswitha felt a little heartened in spite of herself) smiled and chuckled.

"Spoken like a true scholar!" he said, nodding approvingly. "Be easy, girl, you'd not be sent to any torture chamber even if we had one. But it's just as certain"—his expression grew grave once more—"that we cannot have you roaming about the fair, much less the country, using so much power unchanneled and unchecked. So I believe a period of confinement is called for—in the temple, where you may learn the proper use of your psychic talent and employ your scholastic one to codify the works in the archives which deal with the Lady. What do you say?"

Truly this was a fairy godfather! *"When?"* Roswitha gasped out almost before the *magestreet* had finished.

Now all the men laughed aloud. "At once," replied the wizard, "or as soon as we can summon a carry chair for you, Lady's lady. Rest here until we return." The trio arose and passed down the ramp of the show wagon, to disappear into the still considerable crowd at its base.

Left alone, the little clerk laughed, too. On a whimsical impulse, she swung the figurine above her head and, holding it face toward her, gave it an enormous wink. A moment later she was frowning. Why did the statuette's one eye suddenly seem obscured? A smudge of Dame Alyson's greasepaint, perhaps—Lords knew she'd been wearing enough—that was it, surely. Roswitha set the cat on the floor in a sunbeam and groped for her sock compress to use as a cleaning rag. When she turned back, however, both the creature's eyes shone as vividly as before. An uncanny suspicion crossed her mind, but she dismissed it roughly. No, now really—

But even as the girl watched, the entire process was repeated, unmistakably and undeniably, in the middle of the spotlight.

Roswitha began to laugh. She was still laughing when the

fair officials returned a short time later to escort her to the temple. After all, unknown scholars simply were not given coveted appointments to the finest archive of learning in the land—

—any more than stone cats winked.

THE TALISMAN

Timothy Zahn

Ithkar Fair had been in full voice for three days by the time Arnis arrived, and as he made his way gingerly through the jostling crowds it occurred to him that right here was the most hazardous part of his whole journey. One careless elbow—one midafternoon drunkard stumbling into him—and he could lose an entire year's work. A year's work, and Torren's life, all gone like dew. Clutching his pack gently to his chest, his elbows spread to give it what protection he could, Arnis wended his way through the gauntlet.

It was a long way to the fair's inner court, but the Three Lordly Ones were kind, and he made it without incident. Senta, as expected, was already set up in their booth; and from the looks of the men studying her display of bone carvings, she was indeed attracting the right kind of customer. Two nobles and a priest, by their garb: the kind of customers who paid in gold. And with enough gold, nearly anything was possible . . . even the healing of a small boy.

"Arnis!" Senta smiled in greeting as he rounded one final clump of passersby and set his pack down on a corner of the display table with a quiet sigh of relief. "I was beginning to wonder if you wouldn't be coming this year."

"I was delayed," he told her. "Torren was . . . ill."

"Oh." Her mouth twisted slightly. "The Death Swamp again?"

One of the nobles studying the display spoke up before Arnis could answer. "Ah—you're *that* Arnis? The one with strange bone carvings?"

"I am, my lord," Arnis said, and bowed. Undoing his pack, he began pulling out his own wares and setting them out beside Senta's.

They were not the finest carvings in the world—Arnis would be the first to admit that. His hands lacked the delicacy, the gift for exquisite detail, that marked the difference between the adequate and the truly masterful. Senta's carvings were the latter: animals and flowers that looked as if they'd once been alive; miniature castles and statuettes that might easily have been the actual items shrunk by magic. Next to those, Arnis's work appeared almost like the lessons of an apprentice.

But appearance was not everything . . . and it was for things unseen that people valued Arnis's simpler work.

The noble leaned over for a closer look, gestured to a carving of a drala fruit. "What does this one do?"

Arnis picked it up, feeling the familiar tingle as he did so, and handed it to the noble. "Place it in your cupped palm, my lord," he instructed, "and think of a melody."

The other pursed his lips . . . and suddenly music could be heard, delicate tones sounding as if played on tuned bells. The carving played for nearly a minute, as all three customers and Senta looked on in fascination. Then it stopped, its final note lingering like perfume for the ears before fading into silence.

Senta was the first to speak. "Beautiful," she whispered.

"Indeed," agreed the second noble. "Highly practical as well. With this, one could dispense almost entirely with bards and musicians."

"Only if one would be content with tunes already known," the first said doubtfully. "How much, craftsman Arnis?"

"Ten gold pieces, my lord," Arnis said, daring to quote an almost unreasonable price.

The noble didn't flinch. "You ask a great deal for what is minor magic."

"True, my lord; but the power is fixed within the carving and will not fade with time. The bone came from the Death Swamp, where many strange magics exist."

"Yes, I had heard." Carefully, the noble returned the drala to its place on the table. "I shall consider it," he said, and with a final look at the entire display moved on.

The second noble and the priest also left a minute later. "Don't worry—that one will sell for the full ten golds," Senta said. "I'd buy it myself if I had the money. You were telling me about Torren. What's happened to him?"

Arnis shrugged as casually as possible. No sense in Senta worrying, too. "Oh, you know him—he thinks journeying into the Death Swamp twice a year is weighing too heavily on me."

"He's right," she put in. "Each year when you come to Ithkar your face is lined evermore deeply. So Torren took it upon himself to bring you new bones?"

Arnis closed his eyes briefly, covering the sudden moisture there. "Yes. Against my wishes and command."

Senta smiled sadly. "He's a good son."

"But he's only ten. The Death Swamp is no place for him, even on the safe routes I know."

She was silent a long moment, and Arnis resumed his unpacking. He had just twelve items in all: eleven carvings, plus—

"A carving of an *egg*?" Senta asked in astonishment.

"It's not a carving," he said, handing it to her. "No, don't worry—it won't break. In fact, I ruined two knives trying to mark its surface."

She turned it over in her hands. "Just like a large goose's egg, except heavier. Is it stone?"

"I don't know. It feels more like metal, but I don't

know.'' He hesitated. ''Torren found it on his last trip into
the swamp.''

''Then it must have magic in it.''

''Perhaps. I brought it in hopes of finding a wizard who
could unlock any secrets it might have.''

A richly dressed couple paused at the booth, and Senta
turned her attention to them. *To unlock its secrets,* Arnis
added silently to himself, *and perhaps purchase it at a high
enough price to buy healing for my son.*

And if there is indeed nothing of value to it? Sternly, he
pushed that thought from his mind. *If not, then Torren
would probably not survive another month.*

Heart aching with his private pain, Arnis began arranging
his precious carvings on the table as attractively as possible.

It was four days later, and three of the carvings had been
sold, when someone finally took an interest in the egg.

''Craftsman; craftslady . . .'' He nodded to Arnis and
Senta in turn. ''I understand you have enchanted articles for
sale here.''

''That is true, my lord,'' Arnis said, giving the other's
garb the benefit of the doubt. A minor noble at best; more
likely a well-off merchant. Still, someone with money to
spare. ''These carvings before me have been made from
bone from the Death Swamp—''

''Yes, I've heard,'' the other interrupted. ''What do they
do?''

''This one plays any tune you can think of; this one
appears to frighten off wild animals . . .'' Arnis went through
the short list, throwing surreptitious glances at the customer's face as he did so. Something about the man seemed
oddly familiar . . . disturbingly familiar, in fact. Should he
know his name? He hoped not—the last thing he could
afford was to offend a potential buyer.

He finished his recitation, and the other nodded. ''I see.
Not exactly the sort of thing I was looking for, though. Can
you carve pieces to order?''

"I can carve any shape you wish, my lord, but the magical qualities are affected only slightly by my work." Arnis shrugged. "As it is, each bone's magical power is different, and I must discover it through trial and error."

"Hmm." The man pointed at the egg. "You didn't include this in your listing."

"That one is no work of mine, my lord. It is just as it was found in the swamp. I had hoped later for the time to find a wizard and ask his opinion of it."

The other picked up the egg, hefted it once, then peered closely at its surface. "Perhaps I can help you," he said slowly. "I have some small knowledge of magic myself." He looked at Arnis, then Senta, as if measuring them. "There are spells to read such enchanted items."

"I've heard of such spells," Arnis said carefully. "But I have little money to spare."

"What, with the prices you are surely charging for these baubles?" The other snorted.

"My son is gravely ill." Arnis sighed. "None of the healers near us can help him. I need gold—a great deal of gold—if I am to hire a master wizard who can save him. I don't suppose you might be such a one? . . ."

"My skills lie in other areas." The wizard regarded Arnis thoughtfully, fingering the egg all the while. "But I'll strike a deal with you, craftsman. I'll attempt to draw out its secrets for you. If its powers are small or worthless, there will be no fee for my services. Otherwise, I will take a tenth of the price you are able to sell it for. Agreed?"

"Agreed," Arnis said promptly. A tenth was a reasonable price; and as matters stood now, the egg was worth nothing at all.

"Good. Tonight, then, outside the fairgrounds by the river." He replaced the egg on the table and turned to go.

"Wait! *Out*side the fairgrounds?"

The wizard half turned back. "Spells of such power are forbidden inside the enclosure. Tonight, an hour past sundown."

And he was gone. Senta took a long hissing breath, her eyes following to where he had disappeared into the crowd. "I don't like it, Arnis," she said. "Outside the protection of the fair, what's to keep him from just stealing it from you?"

"Come on—he doesn't even know whether it's worth stealing yet," Arnis scoffed . . . but the same thought had occurred to him.

"I don't trust him," she continued as if he hadn't spoken. "You notice he never gave his name—and yet, he looked like someone I should know."

"Maybe he passed the booth once five years ago or something," Arnis said impatiently. "What does it matter?"

Senta turned to face him. "You didn't tell me Torren was that ill," she said in a gentler tone, her face softening. "Perhaps one of the temple heal-alls—"

"It will take a master wizard healer," Arnis told her shortly. "I *know* where to find one; the problem is payment. If wizard whoever-he-is can help me sell the egg at a good price, then he can dictate his own terms. Including where and when we meet."

Senta clamped her teeth together and turned back to her part of the table without a word.

The wizard was waiting just a little way beyond the watch fires at the enclosure entrance when Arnis arrived. "It occurred to me my instructions to you had been somewhat vague," he explained, taking Arnis's arm and leading him away from the enclosure. "I thought it would be simplest to meet you here."

And easier to see if I had brought friends or fair-wards along for protection? Arnis swallowed, suddenly aware of the hopeless inadequacy of the small engraving knife in his tunic should the wizard have something deadly or devious in mind. They passed a group of fair-wards, and he thought once of calling to them, of breaking off this foolishness before it was too late. But Torren's gaunt face floated before his eyes, and he passed the fair-wards without a word. Whatever the risk, his son was worth it.

The wizard led him past the handful of tents that had been set up outside the enclosure and near the river, bearing toward the dark stretches away from dock and canal. At last, when the noise of the fair was barely audible above the rustle of the wavelets and the buzz of night insects, he stopped. "Let me have it," he said, holding out his hand.

Arnis reached into his tunic, fingers brushing against the knife hilt as he did so, and drew out the egg. The wizard took it, and by the faint light from upriver Arnis could see his lips moving. Abruptly there was a faint clink, as of two pieces of metal tapping one another. The wizard muttered something and again studied the egg's surface. Then, cupping one end in his left hand, he squeezed down on the other end with his right; lifted the hand quickly—

The egg split open into two halves, snapping nearly an inch apart yet remaining in some way connected together . . . and Arnis gasped at what he saw in that newly opened gap.

At first appearance it was like a tangle of fine silk threads, but silk that glowed with ghostly purple light. A closer look showed the threads, far from tangled, were arranged in a definite pattern . . . but as his eyes endeavored to trace the design, Arnis found an inexplicable chill seize his being. Squeezing his eyes shut, he took an involuntary step backward. "What *is* it?" he asked with a shiver.

"My vengeance," said the wizard. His voice was almost a purr.

Arnis snapped his eyes open. The face had seemed only vaguely familiar earlier . . . but that voice as he'd said "vengeance"— "You're Dukker!" he blurted. "The outlaw wizard!"

Dukker's bright eyes—*how had he failed to notice those eyes?*—pinned Arnis like an insect against a wall. "Yes," he acknowledged at length. "And you, craftsman Arnis, have given me the tool of my revenge against that thrice-accursed snake-spawned Klon.''

''Klon was only doing his duty,'' Arnis objected as the memory of that incident flooded back. Dukker, a spell of destruction winding like a mad wraith through a glassblower's booth for some imagined insult on the artisan's part. A half-dozen fair-wards writhing on the ground in Dukker's agony spell, while the wizard laughed and sneered. Klon, alone of all of them, rising above the pain to bring Dukker to the ground with a blow of his quarterstaff at the knees and then to slam his fist behind the wizard's ear before he himself swooned. Dukker, declared outlaw by the high priest, carried bound and gagged outside the fairgrounds, only his bright eyes free to show his hatred of all present. Ten years ago . . . and yet the hatred in Dukker's face as if it had been yesterday.

''His duty, was it?'' the wizard snorted. ''Was it his duty to loudly insult my lineage in language even the gutterfolk don't use?'' He pressed the egg closed, cutting off the purple light. ''For that alone he deserves to die.''

''He was trying to distract you, to keep you from killing the glassbl—''

Abruptly, Dukker's hand made a short gesture, and Arnis's tongue seemed to turn to lead. ''You talk too much,'' the wizard said quietly. ''I must still determine if this object is truly what I suspect it to be.''

Yet for several heartbeats he did nothing but stand and watch. Slowly, sensation returned to Arnis's tongue and mouth until he was able to lick his lips. ''Excellent.'' Dukker nodded. ''No more than half a minute—it *is* a short-lived spell, after all. *Now*—'' He squeezed the egg open and repeated his earlier gesture.

Again Arnis's tongue was frozen . . . but as the minutes passed the spell showed no sign of wearing off. Dukker gazed at him impassively as he tried with an ever-increasing feeling of panic to force his tongue to move. But to no avail. Standing there in the faint light, the sounds of the riverside all about him, he fought the rising terror and tried to come up with a way to escape. But there was no way out. None. With a defensive spell around him he might have been able to flee without danger; without one, the wizard could drop him before he'd taken two steps. There was nothing he could do but wait, and so he did.

Finally—finally—the wisps of feeling began to return, and at last he was able to gasp moisture back into a mouth that felt as parched as a desert. "Wh-why?" he managed to croak.

Dukker ignored the question. Glancing up at the stars overhead, he nodded in evident satisfaction. "Half an hour, at the least. I was right." Carefully, he closed the egg. "And now, craftsman, I must decide how to silence you."

A cold hand clutched at Arnis's heart; but the terror of the past half hour had left him too drained to feel aught but a dull ache. "Will you at least tell me what it is my son found?" he asked. "Surely I deserve that much."

Dukker shrugged. "It is of no consequence one way or the other. In the language of the Three Lordly Ones, it is an *ampli-fire*—a talisman which increases many times over the effect of magic spells. Possibly lost in the Death Swamp by one of the Three themselves."

A talisman of such power—? "But the wizard-of-the-gate allowed it into the fairgrounds—"

"Of course he did, the fool. He had no idea what it was. I suspect all of the Three's weapons were equally harmless in appearance."

"Weapons?" Arnis felt his mouth fall open. "The Three were not in any way warlike—"

"Fool! Do you think they constructed this *ampli-fire* simply to create music and halo-butterflies for the amusement of their children?" He held up a hand as Arnis started to speak. "Enough. I have granted your last request, and I will not debate theology with you. Perhaps you will meet the Three soon; if so, you may ask them yourself how they used their *ampli-fire* in their wars." The egg snapped open

. . . and, belatedly, Arnis filled his lungs for a final scream for help.

The sound never came. Dukker's gesture silenced him for a third time . . . and then, at a longer series of gestures and words, the remainder of his body was taken from him as well. Slowly, his legs began walking him toward the river.

Where he would die.

Arnis had no doubt of that. Dukker would walk him straight into the water, in over his head, where he would drown. By the time his body was found, all traces of the spell would surely have vanished, and he would be merely one more anonymous death on the fair's records.

His feet slapped mud now. Two steps later he was ankle deep in water; then, all at once, it was up to his waist, climbing his chest. For a moment his bewitched feet fought for purchase, and Arnis thought he would slip beneath the wavelets right there. But he recovered his balance, gaining another few heartbeats of life. The water reached his neck . . . his chin . . . He took one last breath and closed his eyes. . . .

The water surged up over his head, and his feet finally ceased their march as the river bed fell away beneath them. *A few more heartbeats and it'll be done,* he thought almost distantly. *I'll be dead, and Torren will follow soon, and Dukker will be free to plot his vengeance with no one the wiser—*

Senta!

A horrible surge flooded into his mind and body. Dukker was *not* yet free—he would have to kill Senta to finally cover all traces of his theft and remove any suspicion of involvement in Arnis's own death. Senta—

His ebbing will to live reversed its flow, and with it came a mental strength the like of which he had never before known. Senta could not die—*would* not die—for his own foolishness in trusting Dukker. Summoning every ounce of his strength, he hurled it against the spell binding his body.

To no avail.

Again he strove, and again, and again. But each time it was the same. He had failed . . . and as his lungs began to ache, he knew there would be no time to try anything else. Once, he'd hoped to someday make enough money from his work that he could ask Senta to marry him. Now, instead, he had assured her an early death. Perhaps her eternal hatred would be his punishment in the next world—

And without warning his head broke through the water.

He gasped, gulping in great lungfuls of cool night air. A hand shifted from a hitherto unnoticed grip on his arm to cup his chin; a body, barely felt through cold-numbed skin, pressed against his back. A mermaid? he thought, dazed mind afraid to believe it. "Rgh?" he growled, the only sound he could make.

"Shh!" a voice whispered tautly in his ear. "He might yet hear you."

Not a mermaid. Merely an angel.

Senta.

"I didn't trust him, so when you left I followed you." A breeze wound its way along the river bank, and she shivered violently.

Arnis nodded, holding her closer to him. They'd been in the water together for a long time, until she'd judged it safe enough to emerge. Even then, it had been over half an hour before he could move his body, and she'd had to drag him out of the river without any help from him.

"You're lucky he didn't see you," Arnis told her, shivering a bit himself. That was good—it meant his body was sufficiently awake to react to cold. Soon he'd give walking another try.

"Not him." Senta shook her head. "He's far too arrogant to think simple people like us might be able to interfere with his plans. It *was* lucky I was using the river reeds for cover, though, or I wouldn't have been able to get into the water fast enough."

Arnis found her cheek, stroked it. "I'm glad *you,* at

least, were too smart for him. I just hope you can keep it up.''

''What do you mean?'' she asked, twisting in his arms to look at him. ''Surely it's over now. We denounce him to the fair-wards and—''

''And the priests order him captured.'' Arnis sighed. ''And with the *ampli-fire* he brushes away every defensive spell they create and kills them all.''

She was silent a long moment. ''Oh, gods,'' she whispered at last. ''He could do it, couldn't he? And destroy all of Ithkar Fair if he chose.''

''I see no way of stopping him,'' Arnis admitted. ''Surely the temple boasts more powerful wizards than Dukker—they bound him once, after all. But with the *ampli-fire* . . .'' He shook his head.

''Then we must at least warn this Klon,'' she persisted.

He grimaced. ''You don't know Klon, do you?'' He felt the shake of her head. ''I do, a little. He acts good-natured enough, but underneath it he's as hard and high-minded as they come. If we told him Dukker was back, he'd set off to capture him; if we convinced him the fair would be put in danger, he'd simply make sure to confront Dukker outside the barricade.''

''And would go to his death either way,'' Senta murmured. ''Drawing Dukker's anger onto himself alone.''

''Though he'd never admit that was his purpose.'' Arnis shivered violently. ''Help me up, please. I think I'll be able to walk now.''

He was. Not very steadily, but at least his knees stayed firm beneath him. ''So what are we going to do?'' Senta asked as they stumbled toward the bright watch fires at the fair's entrance.

''I don't know,'' Arnis admitted through chattering teeth. ''One of us needs to keep an eye on Dukker—that much is certain.''

She nodded. ''My job.''

"No, mine. *You* are going into hiding where he can't find you. As far as he knows, you're the only other person alive who knows he has the *ampli-fire*. You can clean out the booth and leave a message at one of the nearby ones that you were suddenly needed at home."

"There *are* locater spells."

"Which would probably bring every wizard at the fair down on him before he'd finished casting it. If that doesn't bother him . . . well, we can get someone to work a concealment on you, perhaps, and hope Dukker doesn't care enough about you to do his locater spell with the *ampli-fire*. It's the best we can do."

"And then you walk around in his wake, waiting for him to notice you?" Senta scoffed. "I might as well have let you drown."

"Wizards aren't all-seeing godlets," he reminded her. "As long as I'm careful and wear a disguise, he shouldn't recognize he's being followed. Besides, I'd wager the thought will never even enter his pride-swollen mind."

"Arnis—"

"There's no other way, Senta. Not without causing a panic and maybe a disaster. If we can figure out how Dukker plans to get his revenge before he actually finds Klon, we may be able to figure out how to stop him. Or maybe the temple priests can." He shrugged helplessly. "Or maybe we should just turn around now and get out of here while we can."

Senta squeezed his arm. "Come on—I know a group of hawk trainers who will give us shelter for the night. In the morning things may be clearer."

Dukker passed the sweetmeat booth at the end of the row with a lingering glance at its display and turned the corner in the direction of the armorers' section. Twenty yards behind him, Arnis paused just long enough to stuff his hat inside his tunic and replace it with a new one before following. Senta's hawk trainer friends, with the bare bones of the story, had advised him to change tunics every hour and hats more frequently still. Arnis had wondered where they'd learned such tricks; but the advice had so far stood him in good stead. In two days of cautious tailing, Dukker had given no sign of noticing the man he'd tried to kill.

And in that time he'd learned a great deal about the outlaw wizard.

Dukker's arrogance he'd already been made aware of; what he hadn't before realized was that the wizard didn't reserve his contempt for low born craftsmen. Everyone, whether beggar or noble, left Dukker's presence with either hunched shoulders or else the pressed lips of anger. Arnis wondered for a long time that the wizard risked drawing so much unfriendly attention to himself; only gradually did he realize Dukker was likely doing it on purpose. With the power of the *ampli-fire* in his grasp, he had no need to be subtle in his leisurely search for Klon. He could allow his true feelings toward others to show without fear of censure or punishment.

With the *ampli-fire* Dukker was invincible.

A pair of religious beggars stepped into Arnis's path. Pushing past them, he hurried toward the corner. He couldn't afford to lose Dukker now.

The clear solution was to somehow relieve Dukker of his talisman—even Arnis could see that far. But finding *how* to do that was another problem entirely. Dukker appreciated fine wines but so far had shown no tendency to indulge overmuch. He also seemed fond of cream-filled pastries, meat pies, and the attentions of pretty, dark-haired wenches.

Fill a pastry with sleeping potion? Or hire a whore from the enclosure's outer fringes to steal the *ampli-fire*? Arnis ground his teeth in frustration as each plan crumbled like old ox horn before the awareness that, for all his arrogance, Dukker was too clever to be taken in by such a simple ruse.

Arnis rounded the corner booth—and skidded to a halt.

No more than ten yards ahead, Dukker's green cloak

rippled in the breeze as the wizard glowered at a trembling but stubborn-looking armorer journeyman who stood before him. The usual flow of buyers had halted, and already the two men were at the center of a small circle.

"Repeat that, churl." Dukker's quiet voice carried easily over the noise.

The armorer flinched, but his own voice was steady enough. "I said you had no appreciation for true ironsmithing skill, my lord."

To Arnis it hardly sounded like an insult . . . but Dukker apparently saw it differently. "I'll show you what I think of ironsmithing skill," he snarled. Gesturing to a heavy breastplate on display, he began speaking in another language.

Arnis shifted his attention to the breastplate. Beads of molten metal were beginning to form on its etched surface—to form, and to run off onto the table, each sizzling and smoking where it struck the wood. But the armor was well forged, and it held . . . and as the words ended and the spell began to fade, Arnis noticed a small smile on the armorer's lips. A smile Dukker would surely not endure. Holding his breath, Arnis waited for the wizard's reaction.

It came swiftly and without a single word on Dukker's part. Reaching beneath his cloak, he withdrew the *amplifire* and opened it . . . and with a roar of tortured metal the breastplate melted before its owner's horrified eyes, setting the table alight as it burned through to become a foul-steaming puddle on the ground.

Somewhere in the circle a woman shrieked; and as if that were the release for a spell, the entire crowd exploded into pandemonium. The armorer's table was burning brightly now, and a score of men leaped to save the other articles there and to move the table itself safely away from the booth behind it. Where molten metal lay stray grasses were smoldering, and water was fetched for both that and the table. Those trying to escape the fire or Dukker or both scurried about like mad insects, adding to the confusion and the noise.

And in the midst of it all, Dukker vanished.

Arnis pushed his way back through the crowd, the sharp taste of defeat in his mouth. For certain, now, it was all over. He had lost Dukker. Worse still, with such a blatant use of unauthorized magic to spur them, the fair-wards would now be moving in on the wizard, playing directly into his plan. Within a day, perhaps sooner, Klon would be dead . . . and many others likely with him.

An unoccupied chair sat at the end of a toolmaker's table, three booths back from the armorer's. Sinking into it, Arnis buried his face in his hands and wondered what he was going to do.

The edges of the chaos swirled about him . . . and gradually he became aware that someone was shouting at him from behind the table. Raising his head, he looked up into the furious eyes of a bear-sized man. "Here, you, wha've you done t' m' stock?" the man bellowed over the noise.

"What do you mean?" Arnis called back. "I haven't done anything—"

"Don' gi' m' that! Jus' *look* at this." The toolmaker held up a thick piece of wood and a heavy knife, the edge of which glowed visibly even in broad daylight. Gripping the haft loosely between thumb and forefinger, he let the blade swing down into the end of the wood—

Slicing a piece cleanly off without the blade even slowing.

Arnis jerked back as the end clunked onto the table near him. "How'm I s'posed t' sell someti'n like this?" the toolmaker shouted, waving the knife at Arnis. "Ay? How's th' buyer s'posed t' use it—how's he even t' get it home? Ay?"

"Believe me, I had nothing to do with this," Arnis protested. "Maybe the wizard who sharpened your blades made a mista—"

"You're tryin' t' get me thrown out, aren't you? For usin' unallowed magic. Who hired you—that swine Grezel? Well, he's not gon' get away with it." He waved suddenly with the knife. "Ay! Fair-ward!"

Arnis turned to see a smoke-smudged fair-ward pushing his way through the dispersing knot of people around what was left of the fire. "Ay! Fair-ward!" the toolmaker called again.

"What is it?" the fair-ward growled as he reached the table.

"This wizard's bewitched m' stock." He demonstrated with the knife.

The fair-ward turned baleful eyes on Arnis. "Well?" he challenged.

"I've done nothing," Arnis told him. "I just sat down here—"

"And I suppose you had naught to do with *that*?" the other interrupted, jerking a thumb toward the charred table.

"Of course not." Though it *was* his talisman Dukker had used, Arnis realized uncomfortably. Without permission, certainly . . . but might that still make him an accomplice under fair-law? He had no idea. Best not to mention it at all.

Perhaps the fair-ward caught a reflection of that thought in Arnis's face, or perhaps the trouble at the armorer's booth had left him in a foul mood. Whichever, the words were hardly out of Arnis's mouth before he was hauled bodily to his feet, the bronze tip of the fair-ward's staff coming to rest against his throat in emphasis. "Pure as the Three Lordly Ones' sheep, are you?" the fair-ward snarled. "Well, you can tell your story at the temple. You—give me that knife for evidence."

And a moment later Arnis found himself being pulled toward the temple. The temple, and prison.

The red skies of early dawn were just beginning to give way to clearer light, but already several of the cookshops were open for business, their customers the early risers of neighboring booths and a handful of those hardier souls who had not yet sought their bedrolls from the night before. Gazing at the nearly empty aisles, Klon the fair-ward leaned on his staff and inhaled the good aromas. His stomach rumbled, reminding him it had been a long night and that he hadn't eaten since sundown. He was just deciding which of the cookshops smelled the best when a man in a green cloak stepped around the corner ahead and walked purposefully toward him.

Klon straightened up and watched the other come. His face—unknown, but an echo of times long past. Picking up his staff, Klon held it in ready position and waited.

The other stopped five yards before him. "Greetings, Klon," he said coolly. "You should know that you are even now seeing your last sunrise."

Klon pursed his lips. "I've been told that many times before."

"But not by me. Else it would have come true."

"Perhaps. Is this where your promise to return for vengeance comes true?"

Dukker smiled, a snakelike expression. "You remember me. Excellent. I wouldn't have you die in such agony without knowing why."

Klon swallowed the lump that had suddenly appeared in his throat. "I would have expected you to choose a time when more would witness your triumph," he said.

Dukker snorted. "And allow you a panic-stricken mob of cattle to escape into? I showed the rabble my power yesterday; I need not repeat that. They will have opportunity enough to see me when I am ruler of Ithkar and all the lands around it."

"You?" Klon scoffed. "There are more powerful wizards than you right here in the temple, let alone in the courts of the nobles."

"So they believe as well. They will soon learn differently."

There was a moment of silence. "What do you intend?" Klon asked at last.

"Oh, I had planned a scheme of remarkable subtlety." Dukker shrugged. "One which would have left you dead with fair-law unable to touch me. But all that is unnecessary now." Reaching into his tunic, the wizard produced an egg-shaped object. He squeezed on both ends, and it opened to emit a strange light—

And abruptly music filled the air. Music like the ringing of tuned bells, filling the aisles and booths, causing the cooks and buyers to turn in wonderment.

And at that signal eight more fair-wards stepped quietly from their concealment within and between the booths to form a circle about the wizard.

Dukker's startled expression changed quickly to one of contempt. "So—the woman bone carver recalled my name and went to you, did she?" he called over the tinkling music. "It means merely that in your death you shall have company."

"You are a fool, Dukker," Klon said flatly. "You claim to be wise, yet you cannot see beyond your own nose." Reaching to a pocket, he carefully removed the source of the music still filling the air: a small carving of a drala fruit Arnis had lent him. A carving whose magic depended on it being held in a hand . . . usually.

Dukker stared at the carving . . . and suddenly his eyes blazed with understanding. Without warning he snapped his hands outward to send a roiling stream of flame at Klon's chest—

The ward spell placed upon him by the priests in the temple absorbed the fire without effort. Another death spell flashed through the air, and another, and another . . . and each time the ward spell, strengthened by the *ampli-fire* in Dukker's hand, held fast. "A fool, wizard," Klon repeated, "and a blasphemer of the Three as well. Not even a god makes war with a talisman that adds to his enemy's spells at the same time it strengthens his own." Raising his staff, he gave the signal.

Dukker shrieked, whether in fury or fear Klon didn't know. Staves held ready before them, their own ward spells glittering against the wizard's attacks, the fair-wards moved in.

• • •

Senta watched the party wend its way through the crowds until they were lost to sight. Then, with a tired sigh, she walked back down the short aisle to her booth.

The old priest who'd volunteered to watch it for her looked up as she approached. His eyes searched her face, perhaps mistaking her tiredness for worry. "He'll be all right," he told her, patting her hand. "With a wizard, a heal-all, and three fair-wards along, no bandits would dare accost him."

"I know." She nodded. "*You'll* have more to fear in that regard once the *ampli-fire* is returned to the temple."

The priest shrugged. "It will be safer here than Arnis could possibly keep it. And its powers more fruitfully used, as well."

Again she nodded. It *was* fitting, after all, for the talisman of the Three to reside in their temple. And while the price for its use would be high, the poor who needed its power for healing would be cured without charge. It had been the only part of the arrangement Arnis would not barter with, despite opposition from the greedier of the temple's bargainers.

The priest cleared his throat. "I take it you'll be joining him once the fair is ended?"

"No," she said, thoughts elsewhere.

"No?" He frowned. "But I thought—surely the yearly fee for the *ampli-fire* is adequate for him to take—" He broke off abruptly.

Senta's mind came back. "To take a wife? Why, certainly, my lord. But at my home, not his. We've already decided the region of the Death Swamp is no place to raise a family. When the fair is over, *he* and his son will be joining *me*."

"Ah." The priest looked relieved, embarrassed, and pleased, all at the same time. "For a moment I was worried . . . well. Good day, craftslady Senta."

"Good day, my lord."

She watched as he strode off and then pulled from her

pocket the betrothal gift Arnis had given her before leaving with the *ampli-fire* to go and heal his son. As the story of all this spread throughout the fair, curiosity alone would be bound to bring new customers by. Cradling the drala carving in her palm, she listened contentedly to its tunes and waited for the crowds to arrive.

BIOGRAPHICAL NOTES

André Norton

Ann R. Brown and her British husband, David, run Incahoots Decorative Rubber Stamp in Tucson. But their real chosen home is in the fantasy world Ann devises in her stories, and very rich that home is. From that realm comes their Gaelic Prayer—"Beannachd do T'anamis Duaidh''—A blessing to thy soul and victory.

Georgia-born **Mildred Downey Broxon** has lived over most of the North and South American continents. She has worked as an industrial painter, special teacher, and psychiatric nurse, having degrees in both psychology and nursing. After her first story was published in 1972, she served two terms as vice president of the Science Fiction Writers of America. She is also a member of the Society for Creative Anachronism and the Mystery Story Writers of America. Her many interests reach from Irish mythology and history to gourmet cooking and world travel. The widow of Dr. William Broxon, she lives in the Ballard area of Seattle surrounded by books, cats, and seven typewriters.

Esther M. Friesner has a Ph.D. in Spanish from Yale and taught there for several years. Now she is the author of seven fantasy novels, three of which constitute the beginning of a series—the Chronicles of the Twelve Kingdoms. A member of the Society for Creative Anachronism, she finds that her "medieval plays" gain warm reception. In 1985, a Victorian melodrama of hers played in a Colorado dinner theater.

Craig Shaw Gardner's short stories have appeared in a number of anthologies such as *Dragons of Dark, Year's Best Fantasy No. Five*, and others. His first novel, *A Melody of Magic*, was recently published by Ace Books.

Sharon Green states that she has been reading fantasy and science fiction from the age of twelve and writing even before then. Having heard a speech of Robert Heinlein's, which incorporated the advice "Don't write about it, do it!" she has been doing it ever since.

Caralyn Inks is a longtime fantasy reader who is a graduate of the 1984 Clarion Workshop. At present she is designing fantasy books and games for children. She lives in California with three children and three cats.

Out of the wide plains of Texas to misty forelands of her own devising, **Ardath Mayhar** makes a remarkable transition. Her words sing, which is not remarkable in an author who was first a poet. She is able to re-create skillfully other writers' dreams, also, as in her justly acclaimed addition to H. Beam Piper's legends of the Fuzzies—*Golden Dream*. Then there are the worlds of her own in which one can lose oneself from the first sentence onward—*Soul Singer of Tyros, How the Gods Wove in Kyrannon*, and all the rest.

Shirley Meier lives in an old but renovated house in lower Cabbagetown with a household of six—three being feline. A member of The Band of Seven, a special writers' group, she has produced a first novel. Along with her interest in

Tao Zen Chuan karate and philosophy, she says that she has done a stint as a classical DJ and also worked in travel agencies, dry-cleaning stores, and both a law firm and an electronics firm. Her studies are in the field of psychology and anthropology.

Sandra Miesel holds master's degrees in biochemistry and medieval history and has identified medieval manuscripts for fun and profit. As a widely published author with three Hugo nominations, she specializes in the use of myth, religion, history, and art. A leading authority on the works of Gordon Dickson and Poul Anderson, she has edited a collection of both writers' stories. Her first novel, *Dreamrider*, was nominated for the John W. Campbell Award. When not attending her husband, three children, and a cat, she collects art and stitches original needlework.

Writing about and working with animals has heretofore been the life work of **Kathleen O'Malley.** She has managed show-dog kennels, Arabian horse farms, dairy and beef cattle, and assorted pigs, sheep, and ponies. A manager for the D.C. Animal Control for two years, she has a strong background in animal medicine. At present she is working for the U.S. Fish and Wildlife Service to help with the breeding and reintroduction of endangered species such as the Sandhill Crane and the Masked Bobwhite Quail.

Claudia Peck is a graduate student and teaching assistant in the Creative Writing Program at the University of Colorado in Boulder. She has had several short stories in print, including material in Eldritch Tales, Forms, and Owlflight, and has recently sold a novel to Doubleday.

A former member of the Peace Corps, **Carol Severance** is also a Clarion West graduate. She has three degrees in art and journalism and has worked as a writer and editor of many kinds of nonfiction. At present she lives in Hawaii with one patient anthropologist husband, two lively teenagers, and a houseful of geckos.

Since a child, **Rose Wolf** has been interested in fantasy, learning in the elementary school library that she could actually write the stories she told herself. And she has been doing that ever since. Presently she is completing a Ph.D. with a dissertation in the form of a fantasy novel.

Timothy Zahn took the plunge into full-time writing in 1980, after the death of his thesis adviser effectively canceled his plans for a career in physics. Though his work normally falls under the heading of science fiction, he enjoys these occasional dips into the realm of fantasy, the most recent of which was the novel *Triplet* (Baen Books, July 1987), which contains a mixture of sf and fantasy elements. Living in a newly purchased house with his wife and five-year-old son in central Illinois, his hobbies include home maintenance and sneezing during corn pollination season.

ANDRÉ NORTON

THE BEST IN FANTASY